Lord Ravenscroft is Not a Gentleman

BARBARA RUSSELL

OLIVER-HEBER BOOKS

one

Rosherville Pleasure Gardens, 1878

EDITH HAD ALWAYS wanted to visit the famous Rosherville Pleasure Gardens—until she did.

The place wasn't different from Hyde Park, really. Lots of trees, bushes, and green grass. So she didn't understand why Rosherville was all the rage at the moment. To make things worse, the breeze kept turning over the pages of her *Anatomy, Descriptive, and Surgical* handbook— the abridged edition because the original one was too heavy to carry around, but it was better than nothing.

Focusing on the development of the human skeleton and memorising the names of all the bones was a chore, what with the children playing cricket, ladies chatting, and birds singing. Honestly, she should have stayed home and studied.

She groaned inwardly when another gust of wind deposited a buttercup in the middle of the illustration of a skull. She brushed the flower off with a huff.

Preparing for her upcoming admission test at the London School of Medicine for Women was her priority. The incredibly difficult test was only a week away and would decide her future, but instead, she was promenading in a crowded, loud, glorified park, getting behind on her work.

A laughing child jolted her. Another child running on the gravel distracted her, and the chatter confused her.

"Can't we find a quieter place?" she asked her mother and sister.

No answer.

"I said—" She lifted her gaze from the book and searched around. Mother and Marianne were nowhere to be seen.

"Mother? Marianne?"

Many ladies strolled under the shade of their parasols along the gravel path. Other people rested under the weeping willows on picnic blankets, and birch trees swayed in the wind. But there was no trace of her mother or sister.

She snapped the book closed. *Bother.* She'd lost them. They must have taken a turn when she hadn't paid attention, likely on that particularly crowded path where they'd slogged forwards through pressing bodies.

Her current situation was worse than the last time when she'd lost Mother and Marianne at the British Museum during that exhibition about...she didn't remember. She'd been studying the pathways of the main arteries back then, and the museum's corridors had confused her. Rosherville Pleasure Gardens were ten times bigger than the museum. It'd take ages to find her family.

Standing in the middle of the path, she craned her neck right and left, trying to choose a direction. She didn't have the slightest idea where to go. The last place she remembered having been with Mother and Marianne was... the swan pond. Maybe. Marianne had made a remark on how fashionable a certain viscount was, and Mother had told Edith, '*You never listen to me.*' Or something like that.

The problem was Edith didn't know if the swan pond was right or left. Holding the book against her chest, she turned around and started to walk. Surely, Mother and Marianne were searching for her, and if she walked along the main path, she was bound to meet them.

She was striding past a gigantic oak tree when something large and black dropped in front of her. A scream tore out of her as a groan of pain came from the crouched figure at her feet.

"Ouch!" Not a creature but a young man.

He clamped a hand on his arm, staggering to his feet.

"What are you doing?" She clenched her book more tightly. "You gave me such a fright."

He raked a hand through his black hair that touched broad shoulders. "I fell."

"So have I noticed, too."

He angled towards her, showing a pair of sharp blue eyes that could have been cut from a sapphire. "I wanted to reach the top branches of the tree."

She gazed up. The tree was a tall one. Several feet, for sure. "For what possible reason?"

He lifted a shoulder. "The view? It's beautiful up there. Peaceful. And climbing a tree is a good exercise." He tried to brush a few leaves from his dark-green waistcoat but winced. "Bugger. I think I broke my wrist."

The shock due to his vulgar language couldn't push aside her medical interest in his injury. Broken bones. That was a great coincidence.

"Let me see. I might help."

He opened and closed his hand. "Are you a nurse?"

"I'm studying to become a surgeon like my father." She showed him the book.

His eyebrows knit together. "A woman surgeon? Really? Isn't that odd? I've never heard of a woman surgeon."

Oh, that was the wrong thing to say, to the wrong girl, at the wrong time. She studied too hard to hear that being a woman was some sort of defect.

"What do you mean by that? Women are perfectly capable of

understanding anatomy and medical procedures, and if you are one of those people who believe that women shouldn't be admitted to a medical school, well, I'm afraid I don't have anything else to say to you. Good day, sir. Or on second thought, I don't care if your day is good or not."

"There's no need to get angry." He held up a hand. "I'm not one of those people. I was merely surprised, and I don't make the rules. Society doesn't approve of women who take up a traditionally male career. I really don't care about what career a woman chooses, and I agree with everything you said. Is that better?"

Softened by his reply, she reminded herself she would face many conversations like this one when she became a surgeon. "It's 1878. Society has changed."

"I'm not sure about that." He showed a lopsided smile that, she had to admit, had a certain charm. "Name one woman who's making a career as a surgeon."

Ha! "Sophia Jex-Black, Elizabeth Blackwell, Elizabeth Garrett Anderson, Rebecca Lee Crumpler—"

"All right. You win." He bowed. "I had no idea so many ladies were doctors. Shall we start over?"

She hesitated before answering. "Let's start over."

"Good. Would you mind?" He stretched out his arm towards her. "My wrist hurts."

She paused again, not sure if touching this stranger was appropriate or not. Perhaps she should find Mother first and examine him later.

He inched his hand closer. "What is it? Do you already think it's something terrible?"

She chewed a corner of her mouth. "I need to touch your arm."

"I gathered that much."

"I'm not sure it's appropriate."

"It's 1878. Society has changed," he said.

The cheek of him.

"Fine. Hold this and please don't drop it." She handed him the precious book and tugged his sleeve up. Nothing was red or swollen. She touched his wrist. "Does it hurt here?"

He gritted his teeth. "Bloody hell."

"Would you stop swearing, please?"

"It hurts," he said, barely moving his lips.

She touched the sore area. "Tell me if you feel intense pain or numbness."

"No numbness, and the pain is bearable as long as you don't press too much."

"I don't think it's broken, just sprained, perhaps." She took her book back.

"Thank you for your help, miss."

"Excellent. You're welcome. I wish you a good day, sir, and this time, I mean it." She resumed walking, but he followed her.

"Wait. I was thinking—oh no." He stopped.

"What is it?"

"That's Mr. Montague, my tutor." He pointed to a short man with round glasses, stopping and questioning everyone on the path. The young man put a finger on his lips before hiding behind a bush.

"What—"

"Good afternoon, miss." Mr. Montague stopped in front of her and took off his hat.

"Sir."

"Apologies for the intrusion, but I'm looking for my charge, a tall boy with dark hair and blue eyes in a dark suit with a green waistcoat. Have you seen him?"

"I..." She glanced at the bush. "No, sir. Sorry."

Mr. Montague sighed. "Thank you, miss." He left, muttering under his breath.

"Thank you." The boy came out of his hiding place when Mr. Montague was out of sight.

Edith frowned. "I never lie. You made me lie."

"Everyone lies." The wind ruffled his unfashionably mussed hair, but the style suited him. "Anyway, I should escort you wherever you're going."

"Not necessary." Besides, her destination was debatable.

"A gentleman is supposed to escort a lady, I think."

"Yes, but I'm not sure gentlemen are supposed to climb trees or lie to their tutors."

He put a hand on his chest. "Ouch. You hurt me, miss. I'm a sensible soul."

"You mean sensitive. I don't believe you're very sensible."

"I won't get offended." He stepped in front of her, blocking her path. "We started off with the wrong foot. May I introduce myself?"

She rose on her tiptoes to see past him if Marianne and Mother were in sight, but he was a tall one. "I have the feeling that, no matter what I answer, you're going to introduce yourself."

"I am Peregrine St. George, at your service." He bowed from the waist, causing his black curls to form a curtain over his face.

St. George. She stopped searching around. "Are you related to the Earl of Ravenscroft?"

"Hell... I mean, yes! Albert, the earl, is my brother." He offered her his arm. "May I have the honour of escorting you, miss... ?"

Dash it. If Mother learnt Edith had been rude to an earl's brother, she would never hear the end of it. Also, admittedly, Lord Peregrine was being nice to her.

She slid her arm through his. "I'm Miss Edith Winkworth, my lord."

"Please, call me Perry. Everyone does." He smiled as they resumed walking. "Where are you heading?"

"Actually, I lost my mother and sister. I was looking for them."

He eyed the book. "A wild guess, but did you lose them because you were reading?"

"Yes, I did." She stopped at a crossing.

These paths looked all the same. Bushes and gravel everywhere.

"Why did you come here if you wanted to read rather than take a walk? People come to the pleasure gardens to promenade."

"And climb trees?"

He nodded. "Climbing trees puts us in contact with nature."

"Tell me the truth. What were you doing up there?"

He exhaled. "You lost your mother and sister by accident. I lost my tutor on purpose. I was hiding through the branches, waiting for him to pass."

"Why did you want to lose him?"

"The man didn't stop talking about which plant was what, spouting Latin names without breathing. I mean, I don't look like an ancient Roman, do I? I had no idea what the hell he was talking about, so I got rid of him."

She let out a small gasp. "I'm not sure I approve."

"I'm not sure I care." He gazed around. "Which way?"

Shocked by the young man's behaviour, she took a moment to answer. The right path showed a green gallery of tall trees; the left one seemed to lead to an orangery, and the straight one bent to the left and vanished from view. None of them were familiar.

"I don't know."

"We should go to the main entrance. Your mother and sister might be there, waiting for you."

"Which path then? This one?" She pointed to the right.

He shook his head. "Left."

"Are you sure?"

"Absolutely. I come here often with my tutor. Hence my eagerness to get rid of him," he said as if being rude to his own tutor were perfectly normal. "Anyway, enough about me. I want to know more about you. You want to become a surgeon. That's admirable."

"I find the human body fascinating."

"What a coincidence. So do I." Again his cheeky smile. He even winked.

"Goodness." She rubbed her forehead. Better to change the subject. "What do you want to do?"

He shrugged. "My brother is an earl. I won't need to work. I don't need to learn a trade. That's it. The end."

She opened her mouth in a stunned, silent shock. "You should cultivate an interest. Keeping the brain active and engaged is the key to a happy, healthy life."

"Maybe when I'm older. I don't want to spend my best years bent over books, obeying my tutor, or restricted by rules I don't approve of. You should try, letting yourself go, I mean."

"You're a hedonist."

"A fancy way to say a rake. But you must admit, I do have charm." He puffed out his chest and gave her a mischievous smile.

With his midnight hair, fine features, and sapphire eyes, no one could deny he was good-looking, and his smile was charming. But a man without a purpose, who chased nothing but pleasure, didn't hold her interest for long.

He clicked his tongue. "Your silence speaks louder than your words. You don't find me charming. I'll show you." He came to a stop and turned his head around. "See that lady over there, the one in the white dress?"

She brought a hand up to her brow to shield her eyes from the sunlight. "Yes."

He released her arm. "I'm so fantastically charming that people do whatever I ask."

"I seriously doubt that."

He leant closer, scandalously so. He was so close she smelled his fresh cologne and the soap on his skin. For a crazy, wild moment, she thought he was going to kiss her. How absurd. She wasn't sure why the thought sent her heart into a frenzy. Maybe it was dread.

To her disappointment... no, no, she meant to her relief, he stopped his lips an inch from her ear to whisper, "That woman is going to dance for me, lift her skirts, and show me her petticoats and bloomers."

She clamped a hand over her mouth, utterly stunned. A gentleman should never, ever mention feminine undergarments in front of a lady.

"I don't believe you," she said through her fingers.

"Challenge accepted. Watch me." He grimaced when he opened his injured hand, but aside from that, he seemed rather confident.

She watched him stride across the grass to the lady, half-fascinated, half-horrified. In fact, she felt sorry for him because surely the lady was going to slap him for his impudence, hit him with her parasol, or even cry out for help. Poor Peregrine. He was about to face the biggest embarrassment of his life.

He bowed to the lady who bowed her head. Edith couldn't hear what they were saying, but he leant closer, scrubbing the back of his neck. The lady dropped her parasol and let out a squeal before lifting her skirts. She twirled around, kicking her legs and showing her bloomers to the whole wide world. Incoherent sounds came out of her, and jumbled movements took hold of her. There was no mistaking the fact she did show him her undergarments.

"Heavens." Edith put a fluttering hand on her chest, waiting for the lady to slap him. But no, the lady seemed absurdly grateful.

Perry talked to her, and the lady covered herself before bowing her head again. How was that possible?

He strutted towards Edith with the swagger of a cricket player who had just won the World Cup.

"Well?" He took her arm again. "Who's the charming one now? Am I not the prince of charm itself?"

"I can't believe it. How did you do it?"

He wiggled his finger to sign 'no.' "You don't want to know how sausages are made. It ruins the magic."

"There's no magic in a sausage."

"I beg to differ."

Oh, the patience she needed to deal with Lord Peregrine. "Seriously. How did you do it? What did you tell her?"

"No. One secret for another." He turned around a corner between two tall hedgerows. "You tell me something about you first, and I'll reveal my secret."

"What do you want to know?"

"Tell me about your most embarrassing moment. Spare no detail. The more scandalous, the better."

Hmm. She pondered her answer, not because she wasn't spoilt for choice among embarrassing moments, but because she couldn't think of anything scandalous. At the embroidery club, she'd won the award for the most commendable member three years in a row.

"Well? There must be something," he said. "It's taking you too long."

"All right. My most embarrassing moment happened quite recently." Goodness, just thinking about it warmed her cheeks. "It happened with my anatomy tutor."

He brightened. "Interesting. An anatomy tutor. It sounds promising."

"Oh, shush. So I was taking a test, and question number ten asked which cranial nerve is the longest one..." She put a hand on her cheek; the memory still haunted her. "I wrote *'vague'* nerve instead of *'vagus'* nerve." She chuckled.

He remained deadpan, staring at her as if she'd told him she wanted to remove his appendix without anaesthesia. "Is that it? Nothing else happened?"

"My tutor laughed. A lot. So embarrassing."

He gave her an assessing glance. "Goodness, girl. You must have the most boring life in London, for crying out loud."

"It was a truly embarrassing moment, and I told you that I don't lie."

"Blimey." He pinched the bridge of his nose. "I have no words."

She wasn't boring. Absolutely not. She had plenty of fun. "I told you about my embarrassing moment. It's your turn now. What did you say to the lady?"

His lopsided smile caused a dimple to appear on his cheek. "I told her that I'd seen a snake slithering under her skirt."

She skidded to a stop, crunching the gravel. "Lord Peregrine, you are not a gentleman."

He looked affronted. "She thanked me for having saved her life. She said I was a hero."

She shot her gaze skywards. Talking to him was an exercise in patience. Thank goodness, they arrived at the main entrance to the gardens.

"Do you see your family close by?" he asked, still holding her arm.

She gazed around, but dusk was creeping over the gardens, and even though many gas lamp posts were lit, she couldn't see the path clearly.

"No. They wouldn't leave without me. They must be around."

He checked his pocket watch. "They'd better hurry. *Princess Alice* sails in less than twenty minutes for the Moonlight Trip back to London."

"Are you going to take it?"

"Yes, that was my tutor's plan."

She moved closer to him as a chill seeped into her. "Mother won't be pleased. It's not the first time I've got lost."

"May I give you a piece of advice?"

"Do I get to choose?"

"Spend less time studying. Instead, try to enjoy life a little bit more. You won't regret it. You're too young to do nothing but study. Live a little. Try different things. Tell lies. Steal something. Kiss a stranger. There's plenty of time to become a serious adult."

She waved a hand between them. "You should do the opposite. Read more and spend less time playing pranks on unaware ladies. You won't regret it, either."

He lifted a shoulder. "One day. Maybe."

"Edith." A familiar voice came from behind Edith.

She turned around to see Mother running towards her with Marianne.

"Mother." Edith waved in relief.

"Where have you been?" Mother crushed Edith in a hug. "I was frantic with worry."

"You ninny." Marianne hugged her, too. "We didn't see anything of the gardens because we were too busy searching for you."

"I'm so sorry. I got distracted reading and lost you." Edith could bet her mother would give her a piece of her mind later when they were alone.

"May I ask who this gentleman is?" Mother angled her head towards Perry.

He bowed from the waist. "*Enchanté*, madam."

Enchanté?

"I'm Lord Peregrine St. George."

Marianne blushed. Mother looked stunned.

"Lord Peregrine, are you the brother of the Earl of Ravenscroft?" Marianne asked.

"I am he, Miss Winkworth."

"Lord Peregrine was kind enough to escort me here," Edith said. *And shock me.*

Mother and Marianne curtsied.

"Thank you for taking care of my daughter, Lord Peregrine," Mother said.

"It was my pleasure, madam," Perry said. "Shall we head for the port? I have to board *Princess Alice*."

"So do we." Mother took Edith's arm. "We'll sail together."

Perry smiled again, and Edith didn't mind.

two

EDITH, MOTHER, MARIANNE, and Perry walked to the inland port in awkward silence.

Mother stared at Edith as if asking what had happened with the brother of an earl. Marianne shot furtive glances at him, who, oblivious to the tense atmosphere, hummed a tune under his breath. Life had to be cheerful for Lord Peregrine.

The Rosherville Pleasure Gardens were emptying themselves of the crowd of tourists and promenading people, and soon the inland port was full.

"How is His Lordship, my lord?" Mother asked as they waited to embark on *Princess Alice*.

"Albert is incredibly busy. He spends more time reading documents in his study than sleeping." He gave Edith a pointed look. "Surely, too much time spent reading and working can't be good for the soul."

"I agree with you, my lord," Mother said. "I always say the same thing to Edith. It's good to have a dream and work hard to realise it, but everyone needs a respite. Work and leisure time should both be present in the life of a young woman or man."

Edith would have plenty of time to enjoy herself once she

passed the admission test. Well, not likely. If she was admitted to medical school, she'd face years of hard, intense studying, and she wouldn't complain. She was looking forward to studying hard.

The steamship was so crowded that she had to squeeze herself between Marianne and Perry, and she was scandalously pressed against him. He didn't seem to mind the closeness, though.

The thick, oily smell of the burnt coal mingled with the putrid one from the Thames. Her stomach churned. If she didn't find a spot where the breeze blew some fresh air, she'd faint. The Thames was indeed an open sewer, as some physicians claimed.

She made her way through the crowd, wincing as anonymous elbows sank into her stomach or back. Finally, they reached a less crowded spot on the back of the ship, right next to the handrail.

"So many people," she said, standing next to Perry. His clean pine tree scent was literally a breath of fresh air.

"If we hadn't wasted an hour searching for Edith, we would have taken the previous and less crowded steamship," Marianne said.

"I said I was sorry." Edith jolted as *Princess Alice* let out a loud whistle before sailing along the river.

"It's not the first time you've vanished," Marianne said.

"Girls, please." Mother's expression turned stern.

Darkness fell quickly, and only the lamps on the ship shed some light around Edith. Not that there was much to see aside from the passengers' faces and Perry's elegant profile.

He cleared his throat. "I was wondering if you ladies would enjoy an afternoon stroll to the park next week. Albert and I often promenade in the park in autumn, or used to before he became overwhelmed with work. The colours of the trees are beautiful."

"Next week I have my admission exam for the London School of Medicine for Women." Edith patted her precious book.

"When is the test?" he asked.

"On Friday."

"We'll take a walk on Saturday. Would you come?"

"Of course she would," Mother said, touching her arm.

"Edith needs to go outside more and be in contact with nature as I do," Marianne added unhelpfully. "That was the whole point of today's trip."

Edith raised her eyebrows at her sister. "Contact with nature? Your idea of contact with nature is to open the window of the carriage as you go shopping on Oxford Street."

"To each their own." Marianne tugged at the velvet ribbon of her hat. "You, on the other hand, spend so much time at home that you don't even know what Hyde Park looks like in autumn. Besides, you should get ready for your Season."

The Season. If she passed the test, she wouldn't have time for a Season.

Perry leant over the rail. A deep frown marred his brow. "We've changed course."

"What?" Edith asked, glad to change the subject.

"I've taken *Princess Alice* a few times, but this is the first time she's changed course. She should sail on the other side of the river. This is a busy time on the Thames. Changing routes is dangerous." He bent further over the rail. "Another steamship is coming. I can see her lights. She's going to hit us."

Edith wasn't familiar enough with Perry to understand if he was pulling a prank or not. "Are you sure?"

"Yes, it's *Bywell Castle*. She always sails down the river at this time. She's going to ram into us." He raised his voice, his chest heaving. "People, everyone, you must abandon ship."

No one paid him the slightest bit of attention.

"Abandon ship!" he yelled, trying to weave through the crowd, but he didn't move an inch.

"Stop pushing, lad!" a man complained, shoving Perry in turn.

"You might be mistaken," Edith said.

Although someone else shouted '*abandon ship*' from somewhere.

He breathed harder. "Too many people, and too little time.

Edith, Mrs. Winkworth, Miss Winkworth, listen to me. You must untie your petticoats."

Edith gasped, Mother touched her neck, and Marianne covered her mouth with a hand.

"Lord Peregrine," Edith said, her face burning, "please, I beg you, don't play silly tricks on us."

He took her shoulders. In the dim light, his sapphire eyes glowed with a maniacal glint.

"I swear on my soul. It's not a joke. *Princess Alice* is going to be speared by *Bywell Castle* in a matter of minutes. We'll sink faster than you can realise what's happening, and your heavy petticoats will drag you down into the water. You must get lighter and jump now."

"My lord," Mother said. "This is absurd."

"Trust me, please. Your lives depend on that." He sounded honest, but that wasn't the point. He genuinely believed *Princess Alice* would sink, but he might be wrong. "Look for yourself."

Without preamble, he took Edith by the waist and moved her closer to the rail.

After the initial shock of being grabbed and dragged, she stared ahead. A large, tall ship with a pointed hull aimed straight at them. The ship's lights were getting closer. Edith wasn't an expert in sailing, but even she could tell there was no chance either of the ships could swerve in time.

"Good lord. Perry is right." She panted. "We're going to sink."

"Edith, please," Mother said.

"He's right." Edith unfastened her petticoats or tried to. The book impeded her movements. Dropping it pained her, but she had to. "We're about to sink," she yelled. "Abandon ship!"

Her hysterical scream had no effect on the crowd. Someone laughed; the vast majority ignored her.

"The water is a problem." Perry helped her untie her petticoats with efficiency. "The river has strong currents, and the water is filthy with the streams from the sewers. But we'll have a chance of surviving. If we stay here, we'll die." He yanked her petticoats off.

"What are you doing?" Mother said.

"Mother, please." Edith's plea was covered by the shouts and the piercing peal of the sirens, either from *Princess Alice* or *Bywell Castle*.

The ship rocked, likely trying to change course at the last moment.

"Jump, jump." Perry ignored Mother and Marianne's protests and yanked their petticoats down none too gently, ripping the fabric.

The sirens rang louder. *Princess Alice* swung hard, causing her passengers to be tossed and jolted.

"Mother, listen to him." Edith squeezed her mother's hand and climbed over the rail.

The inky water was a dark abyss, ready to swallow her. She wasn't sure she could jump. Marianne shook her head, muttering something Edith didn't understand.

"Go!" Perry shoved Marianne towards the rail right when a thundering, splintering noise boomed.

The ship swayed right and left like a giant crib. Screams filled the night as Edith was pulled and pushed from every side. Marianne cried out next to her. Mother screamed. They jumped, holding each other's hands. Edith hit the water, and its rotting smell nearly made her pass out.

Then it was chaos.

three

AGONY. SHEER AGONY was the only thing Perry could feel, smell, taste, and hear.

Surely, someone was battering his skull with a sledgehammer and a lot of passion because that was the only possible explanation for the ridiculously intense pain in his head.

"Perry..." someone whispered his name, but he couldn't tell who the person was and couldn't open his eyes.

He was so tired. He wanted to sleep and forget the pain. Whoever called him could wait.

A pungent smell woke him up. Perhaps an hour, a day, or a month had passed since he'd last opened his eyes. The headache that threatened to break his skull in two was barely bearable. He fluttered his eyes open, which required an outrageous amount of energy; it was also pointless. The only thing he saw was a giant, blurry grey-and-white halo.

"Lord Peregrine," a woman said.

Hell, the smell. It was a combination of carbolic acid and strong lye scullery soap. Other sounds reached his ears, but using them to simply listen to his surroundings hurt. So he closed his eyes and ran his tongue over his parched lips. He wanted to sleep some more.

Once again, someone woke him up by shaking his arm. They should leave him bloody alone. He needed to sleep.

"Perry." That was Albert, scared to death if the tremor in his voice was any indication. "Can you hear me?"

Bugger. Perry forced himself to open his eyes again. Great. Now the giant blur had changed colour. Instead of grey and white, it was brown. He tried to talk, but only a strangled noise came out.

"He opened his eyes," Albert said with the tone of someone who gave extraordinary news. "I'm here, Perry. You aren't alone."

Yes, he'd gathered that much. But he'd like to know where 'here' was. The brown thingamabob around him could be anything.

"Perry." The second voice belonged to a girl. He'd heard that voice... somewhere.

Oh, right. Miss Edith Winkworth, the girl who never stopped reading and who had spectacular forest-green eyes. Eyes that had captured him. He'd met her at the Rosherville Pleasure Gardens right before he'd boarded the steamship.

A shock of stillness went through him. Now he remembered. *Princess Alice* had been hit. He'd jumped into the river with Edith, her mother, and her sister a moment before the steamship had been sliced in two. The water had been pure, undiluted slime from the sewers. Awful.

The stink had made him gag. The slime had coated his nose and mouth. Then large pieces of broken wood and even larger pieces of scorching metal had rained all around him as the steamship had been shattered into smithereens. Something had hit his head. Hard. At least now the headache and the previous lack of memories had a cause.

Soft fingers touched his hand. "Perry, it's me, Edith."

He blinked furiously to clear his vision until something

vaguely resembling a human silhouette appeared. Her strawberry-blonde hair formed an indistinct golden halo.

"You're at St. Bartholomew's Hospital," she said.

That made sense.

"You've been unconscious for almost two months."

That didn't make sense.

"Can you hear me? Blink once if you can."

He did as told since his throat didn't work.

Relief flooded her voice. "He said yes."

"It might be a coincidence. Ask him something else." That was Albert, always the optimist.

Her delicate fingers brushed his knuckles. The sensation was nice. "Do you remember me? We were on board *Princess Alice* when it sank."

He blinked once.

"Good lord, Perry, you're awake." Albert must have taken his hand because the sensation felt different. "I was so worried. The doctors had no idea if you would ever wake up."

"He must be thirsty," Edith said. "He keeps licking his lips."

A gentle hand lifted his head, and a cool glass was pressed to his lips. He swallowed the deliciously fresh water. His throat burned, but his sight improved a little. After that, he was too tired to blink. Edith's sweet voice saying his name was the last thing he heard before drifting to sleep.

Finally, Perry's headache was a dull throb. When he woke up—he had no idea if another two months had passed—his ears didn't buzz anymore, and he could see properly. Although the walls were far too bright for his liking, and whoever had washed the bedsheets had used starch enthusiastically since they were slabs of marble that chafed his sensitive skin.

The only window let the pale sunlight in. The weather and the frost on the glass made him think he hadn't been unconscious through the winter.

He meant to call Albert, but what came out of his mouth was

a chilling sound like that of a growling beast, ready to pounce. Footsteps approached. A nurse he'd never seen peered at him.

"Your Lordship is awake." She hurried out of the room.

Voices. Footsteps.

"Perry?" Edith's face swept into view.

Except it wasn't the face he remembered. Not exactly. Her face was gaunt. Her eyes were clouded, and her hair was a dull colour, not the glossy strawberry-blonde he liked so much.

"Can you see me?" she asked.

He opened his mouth to talk, but only an odd whimper came out. That wasn't possible. He'd clearly meant to say 'yes,' but somehow, his tongue refused to obey. He tried again and winced at the shrieking sound of his own voice. He'd heard dogs with better, more dulcet tones.

She put a hand on his forehead. "Don't force yourself to speak. You received a serious blow to the head. The physicians, even my father, said that a brain injury was likely."

Brain injury. He stared down at his body and did a quick check. His toes moved at his command, and his fingers seemed all right. His arms and legs were still attached to his body, and he controlled them. Yet he couldn't speak.

He touched his throat, meaning to ask her if the incident had hurt his vocal cords.

She brushed a curl of her hair with a bony hand. "Your throat is fine. We think the problem is only your brain. The blow impeded your speech ability. But don't despair." She squeezed his hand. "You woke up, and you're conscious and understand me. That's an excellent start. Give yourself time. Father said that speech impairment was a possibility after a head trauma. But your ability to speak will return."

He tried again to speak. Bad idea. What came out wasn't simply gibberish but awful noises. He gave himself goosebumps. The glass would shatter if he kept trying.

He lay down on the pillow, exhausted.

She sat on the chair next to him. "Are you thirsty?"

He nodded.

As she helped him drink an entire pitcher, her neckline lowered a few inches. He didn't like how her collarbone protruded from her shirt. His chest tightened for her. He probably looked the same or worse, but she'd suffered, too.

"Hungry?" she asked.

He shook his head and pointed at her.

"Do you want to know what happened to me?"

He nodded.

"The sinking of *Princess Alice* was such a tragedy. It's a miracle we are alive. More than seven hundred people are dead."

Seven hundred. He ran his tongue over his dry lips again. The steamship shouldn't have been so crowded; she shouldn't have changed course.

"Your tutor, Mr. Montague, is fine, by the way. He didn't board the ship because he was searching for you." Edith lowered her long eyelashes. "In my case, the problem was the water. It was so rotten and polluted that I caught an infection. I lay in a bed in this hospital, with a high fever for days on end, between life and death. I was delirious and in pain, casting up my accounts. I felt my body burn from the inside out. My mother and sister were sick, too. Well, all the passengers, who didn't die on *Princess Alice* and swam in the water, fell sick. Many of them died. The doctors said that some people got cholera. Others had typhoid fever. Others got obscure, haemorrhagic diseases or dysentery."

Haemorrhagic diseases. He frowned and gave a light shrug, mouthing he wanted to know what type of disease causes a haemorrhage.

"People bled from their internal organs because the infection damaged them."

Sometimes ignorance was bliss.

She held his hand, and her touch had a soothing quality he liked. "The fever took a toll on my family and me. We've barely recovered. But we're alive. Thank you for warning us. Those moments before the tragedy were precious. So many people drowned because their clothes pushed them down. We would have died if we hadn't removed our petticoats or jumped when you told us to. Thank you." Tears glistened in her eyes.

He closed his fingers around her, wishing he could tell her she didn't need to thank him, and that he was sorry for how much she'd suffered.

She wiped her cheeks quickly. "My father visited you as well, and we all took turns to watch over you, including your brother. You were never alone during your sleeping months. Day or night, someone was always here with you."

Somehow, he'd been aware of that.

"Speaking of your brother, I'll send word to him. He wanted to know if you woke up again." She went to stand, but he didn't let her go.

A moment of panic lashed out at him like a snake snapping at his throat. He didn't want to be alone in that bright, smelly room.

"It'll take but a moment," she said, seemingly reading his mind. "I'll be right back."

He shook his head.

She caressed his cheek with such tenderness, his pulse slowed. "I know the feeling, the fear that takes you out of nowhere. I believe this fear comes from the knowledge that death was very close. You're alive, Perry, and you'll get better. I promise."

He blinked tears away. They burned more than they should.

"Let me warn your brother."

He slowly released her hand. The moment she left the room, he wheezed. Panicking was silly of him, but he closed his eyes and waited until she returned.

"I'm here." She held his hand, and he gripped it with desperation for no reason. "Don't be ashamed of crying. Not with me."

He didn't want to, though, but he needed a hug. As if reading his mind, she sat on the bed and held him, wrapping her arms around him, and he sagged against her for who knew how long. She rubbed his back and gave him the strength he needed.

"Better?" She released him.

He nodded. Much better. He wanted to tell her how grateful he was. Another day, if and when he spoke again.

She smiled, and although her face carried the signs of her ordeal, the smile brightened her.

Albert barged into the room, dishevelled, pale, and generally looking terrible.

Edith rose from the bed and curtsied. "My lord."

"Miss Edith. Perry." Albert too had lost weight, and deep purple shadows circled his eyes. "Perry." He touched Perry's face, chest, and arms as if wanting to make sure everything was real.

"I'll leave you." Edith picked up a book that lay on the table and left.

Of course, she had a book. She must have read the entire encyclopaedia of medical science while watching over him. She gave him a timid smile before closing the door.

A lump swelled in Perry's throat as Albert hugged him, crying. Perry hugged his brother back, and they remained like that without saying a word.

"I was so worried." Albert wiped his face with a wrinkled handkerchief. "I have to thank Dr. Winkworth for his help. He visited you every day, gave you water and soups, and moved your limbs regularly. I'm in his debt."

Now that Perry paid attention to his own movements, there was a certain resistance and lack of coordination in them. He couldn't quite lift his arm as high as he wanted.

Albert sat down on the chair. His tie was askew, and a stubble covered his jaw. "Do not worry. I'll employ the best physicians to help you recover fully. I found a clinic in Switzerland specialised in cases like yours."

Switzerland? He frowned and made the mistake of trying to

voice his questions. Albert looked horrified at the odd sounds coming out of him. Real gibberish.

"Don't fret. I promise the trip will be good for you. Even Dr. Winkworth agrees. The clinic is in a beautiful town surrounded by the Alps. It's equipped with the latest medical devices. I'll come with you, and together, we'll get through this moment."

Perry rubbed his sore neck. He wasn't sure he had the energy to leave, but Albert was right. If Perry wanted to recover, he ought to do everything the physicians said.

Albert hugged him again. "We'll leave as soon as you can travel."

Fantastic. He so looked forward to spending days on end on a train, ship, and carriage to go to a foreign country he didn't speak the language of.

Oh, right. The last one didn't matter.

four

THE 'AS SOON as you can travel' statement turned into six weeks thanks to Perry's weak health.

He couldn't complain though since he'd left the bright white hospital to stay at home. Everyone, from the servants to his brother, pampered and spoiled him. Edith and her father visited him almost every day to keep him company. He was never alone.

Since Christmas was coming, Perry and Albert would leave in March when the nice weather would allow for a more pleasant trip. Perry's condition hadn't improved much. He couldn't talk, his movements were jerky at best, and sometimes a buzzing noise would ring into his ears for no reason. On a positive note, his headaches had almost disappeared, and he was, well, alive.

Sitting on an armchair in the drawing room with Edith and her father, Perry focused on one of the many physical exercises he had to practise every day. Doctor's order.

"Hold my hand as hard as you can," Dr. Winkworth said, taking Perry's left hand. "Use all the strength you can muster, my lord."

Bugger. He wanted to tell Dr. Winkworth to stop calling him

'my lord.' He'd written down his request many times, but the older man refused to call him Perry.

Since his ability to speak had been impaired, he'd taken the habit of having a piece of paper and a pencil at hand at all times. Not that writing was simpler than speaking. He had to focus on controlling his hand and forming the letters. Sometimes he'd sweat so difficult writing was.

He put all his effort into contracting his fingers and squeezing Dr. Winkworth's big hand as much as he could. But the result was disappointing, to say the least. He wouldn't be able to snap a dry twig with his weak fingers.

"It's all right, my lord." Dr. Winkworth released him and took notes on his notepad. "You're making progress. Your right hand is definitely stronger than the left one."

Really? He didn't feel any difference.

"Now try to push against my palms." Dr. Winkworth opened his hands.

Perry took a deep breath. The good doctor was broad, tall, and strong, a stark contrast with Edith who was short. But they shared the same green eyes and steely determination.

She watched him practise with an anxious expression that was becoming her perpetual one.

He pushed with all his strength, confident that a vein was about to explode in his neck from the exertion, but the resulting movement never matched the energy he poured into it.

"That's all right." Dr. Winkworth released him.

"You're doing great, Perry," Edith said.

He smiled. Her encouraging words never failed to make him feel better. Her health had improved as well. In fact, aside from her constantly worried expression, she was the same lovely girl he'd met at Rosherville Gardens.

"When a head trauma is involved," Dr. Winkworth said, taking notes, "the aftermaths are unpredictable. The strength of the blow being equal, each person reacts in a different way, and we don't know why. Some patients recover very quickly. Others take longer." He shook his head. "Your ordeal was a senseless tragedy. The only good thing about the sinking of *Princess Alice* is that the government decided to clean up the Thames. No more polluted water." He turned to his daughter, smiling fondly. "Would you like to specialise in head traumas, darling? You've become quite knowledgeable in the past months."

Edith lowered her gaze. "I don't know, Father. I think for now I'll focus on getting stronger."

Dr. Winkworth's brow furrowed. "I have to go to the hospital, my lord. I'll see you tomorrow for more practice." He stuffed his notepad into his leather bag. "Darling." He kissed his daughter's cheek. "Don't tire His Lordship."

"I won't, Father." She sat on the chair her father had vacated. "Are you tired?"

He showed her the page of his notepad where he'd written 'no.' He scribbled on an empty page, "Troubles you?" hoping she'd understand.

"I've been thinking about the future and about you." Her cheeks blushed.

He pointed a questioning finger at himself.

"Remember what we talked about during our walk through Rosherville Gardens? I came to the conclusion that your words were wiser than I thought."

He shrugged before writing again. "I no wise." Awful grammar, but that was the best he could do with his uncoordinated movements.

She laughed. "Yes, you're very wise."

When she laughed, her eyes sparkled like the sunlight flickering through the emerald leaves of a forest.

He shrugged again and drew a question mark.

"You told me I should enjoy myself more, find a balance between studying and living a normal life. I agree. Being so close to death made me realise how quickly we could go."

It was only then he realised something. The tip of the pencil broke so fast he wrote.

"Your test?" he asked.

He blamed the blow to his head for having forgotten about her admission test at medical school.

Her smile vanished. "I lost my opportunity. I'll try next year. It doesn't matter."

He took her hand and rubbed her knuckles, hoping she understood how sorry he was.

"It's all right, really. You're getting better. My family and I are alive. That's all that matters." Yet a tear slid down her cheek.

He caught it before it wet her lips, perhaps pressing his fingers too harshly against her silky skin.

He wanted to mouth, "Don't be sad," but his lips didn't move as smoothly as he wanted. He hoped he hadn't said anything ridiculous.

She drew her eyebrows together. "You want a cat?"

There. He wrote down simply, "No sad."

She burst out laughing. "See? I'm not. You made me laugh."

He cupped her cheek because he didn't want to write he cared about her. He wanted her to feel it.

She put her hand over his and leant into his palm. "Despite everything, I'm glad we met, and I'm not saying that because we shared a terrifying moment. You're a wonderful person, Perry."

He shook his head. Wonderful. Not even his mother had called him wonderful, never mind wise.

"The way you so bravely face your problems is admirable." She kissed his palm, and a shot of sensation went through him.

It was the first time in weeks that he'd felt an emotion so strong. His body had been numb most of the days, or in pain, but Edith's kiss woke up every inch of him.

"I wish I were like you," she whispered.

He stroked the curve of her cheek with his thumb. Even if he were able to speak, he wouldn't find the words to express his gratitude and affection for her.

"When you come back from Switzerland, I'll be here for you." She hugged him gently, and he leant against her.

He promised he'd change himself as well, and he wasn't talking only about his health. If she was going to be less strict about her studies, he would become more diligent.

For her. For himself. For what he'd learnt in the murky water of the Thames.

IF PERRY COULD JUMP in happiness, he would.

He had to be content with dragging his feet around the dining room. A room that was decorated with colourful wreaths, branches of mistletoe, and the tallest Christmas tree he'd ever seen. Albert had spared no expense and had also invited Edith and her family for the Christmas dinner. During the months Perry had been unconscious, Albert had grown close to the Winkworth family, and Perry couldn't be happier.

Using a pair of crutches, he staggered to the window to check the street again. He smiled when a carriage stopped in front of his house. Dr. Winkworth climbed out of the carriage to help his wife and daughters. Edith tilted her head up towards the window and waved, holding her hat in place.

He didn't usually notice what girls wore, but her pretty dark-red dress brightened her face and exalted her eyes.

Albert touched his shoulder. "Are they here? Good. If you get tired, let me know, and I'll send everyone home."

Perry smiled and mouthed, "Thank you." He wanted to say more, that he appreciated everything Albert did for him, but his body wasn't ready.

Even though his facial muscles didn't completely obey him, his brother had learnt to understand what Perry meant to say.

Albert's eyes became suspiciously shiny. "I don't tell you often enough how much I love you, brother. We had our disagreements" —especially since Perry had behaved with a shocking lack of respect for the rules—"but we're a family. I'm happy you're alive and recovering. This Christmas could have been very different." His voice cracked.

Perry released a crutch to pat Albert's shoulder. "I love you too, brother," he mouthed, not sure Alber would understand.

The butler opened the door and bowed, breaking the moment. "My lord, Dr. Winkworth, Mrs. Winkworth, Miss Winkworth, and Miss Edith."

Albert wiped his eyes and composed himself quickly. "Show them in, Mason."

The family entered, wearing their finest, and Edith was the finest of all. Her eyes were so bright they would attract moths from every corner of London. Her cheeks had regained their fullness, and her hair shone with a lovely glossy hue, exactly as he remembered it.

"Thank you for coming." Albert shook hands with Dr. Winkworth and bowed to the ladies.

Perry did his best to bow without tripping over.

Edith rushed to greet him in a flutter of skirts and velvet ribbons. "How are you?"

He gave her a slow blink, a sign that he was all right.

After a round of bows, greetings, and comments on the weather, they sat at dinner. The long table was adorned with red napkins, red silk flowers, and tall candles, brightening the room.

Albert had to help him sit down in a manoeuvre that wasn't exactly agile or dignified, but Perry had stopped getting bothered about his lack of autonomy a while ago. He worked hard to recover his mobility, but not asking for help wouldn't improve his situation. Besides, he was happy to sit and listen to the chatter, even though he couldn't join the conversations.

"I'd love to have a Season this year," Marianne said, glancing at her parents.

"We'll see," her mother said.

"There are excellent alienists in Switzerland," Dr. Winkworth said to Albert. "Their medical techniques are incredibly advanced."

Perry raised his eyebrows in a silent question to Edith next to him. After all the time they'd spent together, he was convinced she could read his mind.

"Alienists study the diseases of the soul, of people who are alienated from their minds. Fascinating." She smiled at him when their gazes met.

He focused on holding the spoon correctly, lest the white soup end up everywhere, but it required more effort than it should. Sweat damped the back of his neck. He couldn't even follow the conversation so concentrated he was. Without saying a word, Edith helped lift the spoon to his mouth.

He bowed his head in gratitude.

"You're welcome," she said.

He should feel embarrassed or ashamed for his clumsiness, for needing help to change his clothes or tie his shoes. Even washing his hands required the help of a servant. But if there was one thing he'd realised in the past months, it was that he was surrounded by love and care. Everyone did their level best to help him, and he couldn't be more grateful.

Besides, he firmly believed he'd learn to walk and talk again. He'd put all his efforts into recovering and finding a way to show his gratitude to those who had helped him.

After dinner, he sat on the sofa as Marianne played the piano, and the others drank their old-fashioned neguses at the low table. The scent of the mulled wine teased his senses while the sweet music eased the tension never leaving his muscles.

He'd never cared for the piano. In fact, he'd never cared about a great many things that involved hard work or studying, but months spent learning again simple tasks like washing his hands had taught him to appreciate hard work more.

Edith sat next to him in a froth of skirts. "Your brother told us you're leaving in spring. Are you happy?"

He nodded. He looked forward to meeting these Swiss specialists. The sooner he started his therapy, the better.

The red velvet ribbon tying her hair matched her lips. They distracted him as of late, especially when she smiled.

"You've made such great progress. When you're back, you'll be as good as new."

He doubted that. Whatever was going to happen in Switzerland, the incident would mark him forever.

"I'm going to miss you," she whispered, maybe because she didn't want her parents to hear.

He reached for the notepad and pencil on the low table. It took him a few long moments to write the word 'books.'

She waited patiently before craning her neck to read it. "Books. Do you mean why I don't have a book with me?"

He nodded.

She averted her gaze. "I've been so poorly as of late that I don't have the energy to read or study properly, not as I used to. I tried to start studying again, but I'm having problems staying focused. I get tired easily and have to read a passage a few times before I understand it. I guess my brain needs a respite from what happened."

"You're sitting under the mistletoe, Edith," Marianne said, playing a Christmas song. "And Perry is right next to you."

An instant flicker began in his chest, spreading warmth to his neck and face.

Edith flushed to the roots of her hair, glancing at him. "It wouldn't be appropriate."

Marianne leant forwards from the piano stool. "They aren't paying attention, and Mother can't see you from where she sits."

Perry craned his neck. Marianne was right. The sofa where he and Edith sat faced the hearth while Dr. Winkworth, his wife, and Albert were in a corner on the opposite side of the room. But concern about privacy might not be the reason Edith didn't want to kiss him.

"I'll turn away as well." Winking, Marianne faced the piano again, pressing the keys with more energy.

Edith trapped her bottom lip between her teeth. "Do you want to kiss me?"

Hell, yes. He nodded.

"You know, mistletoe is actually a parasitic plant. It steals water and minerals from the host."

He laughed, but the sound was croaky and spooky, so he shut his mouth. Only Edith could say something like that.

He took the pencil again; just holding it caused his fingers to stiffen. He meant to ask her if she wanted a kiss, considering it would be a sloppy one, when a strong tingle started to bother the tips of his fingers as if needles pierced his skin. A flash of white light filled his vision, and the pencil and notepad slipped out of his grip.

The next thing he was aware of was that he was lying on the carpet between the sofa and the piano, surrounded by everyone. Edith, Marianne, Dr. Winkworth, Mrs. Winkworth, and Albert stared at him in shock.

He had no idea what had happened to him.

"Perry." Too much worry filled Edith's voice.

He propped himself up on his elbows, but Dr. Winkworth stopped him.

"Stay down, my lord. You had a seizure." Dr. Winkworth touched Perry's wrist, taking his pulse. "Do you remember anything?"

He shook his head. A seizure. His muscles were indeed sore.

Edith put a cushion underneath his head. "You dropped on the floor. Your limbs went completely stiff at first."

"Then you were twitching and kicking, and your eyes rolled back," Marianne added. "Goodness, you scared us all."

"What is it?" Fear carved deep lines on Albert's forehead. "What kind of new malady is this?"

Perry breathed hard. Not even the seizures on top of everything else.

Dr. Winkworth checked Perry's eyes. "A strong head trauma might cause seizures. Sometimes, the seizure is an isolated event, and it won't repeat itself. Other times, the seizures persist. My lord, if I may suggest something."

"Yes?" Albert sounded desperate and horrified.

Dr. Winkworth squeezed Perry's hand in a gesture that seemed to say, 'I'm sorry, lad.' "You should leave for Geneva tomorrow. Don't wait for the spring. The sooner your brother starts his therapy, the better."

Edith blinked watery eyes at him, and at that moment, Perry realised he didn't have a say or a choice.

WATCHING Perry twitching on the floor had been one of the most shocking sights Edith had ever seen.

She'd read about people who endured fits and seizures since they were born and were afflicted by the little-understood disease for all their lives. Those who suffered from seizures were often considered lunatics and either shunned or locked up in an institution, never to be mentioned again. She had no idea a blow in the head could start them.

Standing on the pavement in front of Perry's house the day after the Christmas dinner, she wondered if she'd ever see him again. His condition required a difficult, long treatment. He wouldn't return any time soon.

Perry went down the short flight of stairs from the front door with the help of the butler and the footman. The attack from last night had left him pale and visibly shaken, likely worried, and her chest tightened for him. Even Mother, Marianne, and Father stared at him with worry.

The earl waited next to the carriage that would take them to the train station. His black great coat gave him a solemn air, and with the grey sky and freezing air, the atmosphere looked like that of a funeral.

She had yet to decide which one of the two brothers was paler.

Perry climbed into the carriage, helped again by the butler. He slanted her a sad glance that broke her heart.

"My lord," she said to the earl. "I hope you'll send us news on Perry's progress. I'd like to write to him as often as I can."

"I will, Miss Edith, but I must ask something from you."

"Anything."

He inched closer. "Discretion. My family's name depends on keeping Perry's... condition a secret."

"Alas," Father said, "seizures are still stigmatised today as they were centuries ago. We won't gossip about Lord Peregrine, my lord."

The earl gave a nervous nod.

A flare of anger bothered her. She had no intention of blabbering about Perry's health, and he shouldn't be locked up in an asylum for his seizures. That was barbaric.

"I won't say anything, my lord," she said without looking at the earl.

Father stuck his head inside the carriage and talked to Perry in hushed tones.

"Miss Winkworth, Mrs. Winkworth, Miss Edith." The earl touched the rim of his hat. "Thank you for everything you did for my brother."

"We all love Lord Peregrine, my lord," Mother said, almost sobbing.

"Have a safe trip," Marianne said.

Edith stuck her head inside the carriage as well. "Get well soon, Perry," she whispered. "I'm still waiting for that kiss."

He flashed his pirate-like smile, and for a moment, he looked the same wild boy she'd met months ago. She squeezed his hand and laced her fingers through his.

"I'll write even if you can't write back."

He gave her hand a last squeeze before releasing it.

"Goodbye, Miss Edith." The earl climbed into the carriage.

Emotion thickened her throat as she said goodbye to Perry. "Have a safe trip. I hope to see you soon, well recovered."

He gave her a nod that lacked confidence. Then the footman shut the door of the carriage, and she remained on the pavement, watching Perry leave under the grey sky.

five

Five years later

AFTER FIVE BLOODY years in a small town in the middle of the Alps, where even the birds never chirped too loudly and the thunder apologised for its booms, Perry wasn't used anymore to the loud chaos and crowds of London.

He'd returned to London a few days ago after a tortuous, painful trip through the Continent that made him question how people could travel for enjoyment.

Nothing in London seemed familiar. Not even his house. The city had turned into a vast, chaotic metropolis with too many carriages and people who were always in a hurry.

He wondered if he'd recognise Edith. She was a Doctor of Medicine now, and he looked forward to congratulating her in person.

Drinking his tea, he watched Belgrave Square from the window and winced at the crowded pavement. People nearly jostled each other so packed the streets were. He would shout if someone bumped into him. How he'd managed to be around so many people and even find it pleasurable, he couldn't fathom.

"Good morning, Perry." Oliver, his best friend and personal physician, strolled inside the dining room.

"Have you recovered from the trip?"

His speech was nearly flawless now, only a little hesitant. Lots of practice, determination, and patience worked miracles. Especially since he took the opportunity to learn German to exercise his speech. Just pronouncing the name of the town where the clinic was—*Eichhörnchenstadt*, literally, Town of the Squirrels—had been his main speech exercise for weeks.

Oliver arched his back, his hand on his hips. "I still feel sore. We took literally every type of transport humans have created since the dawn of time. All that up and down those bloody mountains. Now I understand why nobody wants to invade Switzerland."

"Have some excellent English tea, the cure-all."

"How are you today?" Oliver took out a notepad and a pencil from his pocket and waited for Perry's reply before writing.

Always the same question. "I'm tired of London already. I didn't remember the air being so thick with smoke."

"Yes, that's all fascinating, but you know what I mean. I need data, data, and more data. I can't make bricks without clay. Nausea, headache, anxiety, tingling?" Oliver stuffed a piece of buttered scone in his mouth.

"Trouble sleeping."

"Interesting." Oliver scribbled that piece of information on his notepad. "Anything else?"

"No, I'm quite all right. Just annoyed by the noise."

"Irritability," Oliver muttered while writing. "Mobility?"

"My left leg becomes a little numb sometimes."

"Hmm." Oliver took note of that as well. He'd been diligently recording Perry's life for the past four years. Everything from what Perry ate to how many hours he slept and how his mood changed. "Great. If the horrible trip didn't break you, you have an excellent chance of being able to do everything you want. I think you're ready for your debut in polite society as the new Earl of Ravenscroft."

Perry nearly spilt his tea. "Not bloody likely. Too soon."

"Nonsense. You can't escape your duties."

"The fact I'm the earl now doesn't change anything. I don't have to change my habits."

Oliver pointed the pencil at him. "It changes everything. You must accept your new reality and embrace it. Think about me as well. Me, Dr. York, the official physician of the Earl of Ravenscroft. It has a nice ring to it."

"No. It's too early. I still hope Albert will change his mind. Hell, I'm sure he'll change his mind and come to his senses. His decision was a fleeting affair."

"Really?" Oliver sorted through the pile of letters and messages resting on a silver tray. "Did you take a look at the correspondence arrived yesterday?"

"Only to check if Miss Winkworth sent a message."

But she hadn't. Likely, she was busy being a doctor. He was so proud of her. Dr. Edith Winkworth. *That* had a nice ring to it.

He'd buy a plaque with her new title for her to hang on her study door. In fact, celebrating her success was one of the reasons that convinced him to return to London now.

"Did you read all the other letters?" Oliver asked.

"I believe I pay a secretary to do that for me." He turned his back to the window.

Enough people for today, and Edith wasn't in sight. He hoped she'd surprise him and come to see him.

"Well, sometimes you should do it yourself." Oliver handed him a postcard from Bahia, Brazil.

Perry hadn't read the message yet, but annoyance already soured his mouth. Yes, the postcard was from Albert. His writing had acquired a flourishing quality since he'd moved to the other side of the pond.

Dear Perry, Salvador is the most beautiful, vibrant city in the

world. Gabriela and I are happier than ever. Thank you for under-
standing. Wish you were here.

"Does his decision to renounce the title look like a fleeting affair?" Oliver said.

Fantastic. Really bloody fantastic. He tossed the postcard on the table. Frustration caused his vision to darken.

"Your brother isn't going to change his mind." Oliver put the postcard back on the tray. "And even if he did, unfortunately, his wife, no matter how famous she is, will never be accepted as the Countess of Ravenscroft. A Brazilian singer with no connection to British nobility? I wouldn't wish on her the type of reception she would receive in London."

Perry took deep breaths lest his body start to quiver. The quivering was sometimes the prelude to a seizure, but not always. Still, controlling his emotions was a good idea.

He also bit down a comment about Albert being selfish, regretting his bitterness. Albert had sacrificed years to follow Perry's recovery, and those years had taught him to enjoy life more. Hence his renunciation of the title.

A part of Perry understood Albert's choice. Albert had always worked hard to take care of the estate and family business, and Perry's incident had vexed him more than Perry could probably comprehend.

Then one night, Albert had gone to a theatre in Geneva to watch the *Aida*, met the *prima donna*, Gabriela, and hey presto! They'd fallen madly in love and got married. Goodbye title and responsibilities. Never mind that Albert's brother was learning to speak and walk again. Perry was perfectly able to be the next Earl of Ravenscroft—Albert's words, not Perry's.

"There must be a cousin who wants the title," Perry said. "I can certainly ask my uncle, Neville. He's my age, born quite late in my grandfather's marriage. He's young and fit."

"What else do you know about him? I remember him writing to you a few times, but he never visited you."

Perry shrugged. "He's a quiet man for all I know. He likes to gamble sometimes, but he doesn't squander his money, and his name never appears on the scandal sheets. Although we had a row years ago."

"See?" Oliver said. "He isn't fit to be the earl."

"We were lads. He meant to court a lady who at first was pleased by his attention, but then she changed her mind. He believed I'd influenced her decision."

Oliver's eyes grew wide. "Tell me the truth. Did you seduce the lady?"

"Don't be ridiculous. My uncle looked for someone to blame and chose me. Father intervened and settled the matter. But it's all water under the bridge. I shall write to him."

"You don't really mean to renounce your title."

"I do." He sat on a chair, suddenly tired. "Look at me. I can't be the earl, not when I can have a seizure in the House of Lords or during a ball. People will say I'm unhinged and that I should be locked up in an asylum. Not to mention that my speech is a little hesitant on a good day, terrible when I'm anxious. Public speeches are out of the question."

Oliver waved dismissively. "Every member of the House of Lords has fits caused by rage when in Parliament, and I don't understand half of them when they speak, anyway. You'll blend in without problems."

"I'm serious." Perry tapped the table with a finger.

Oliver took more notes. "Think about your father and your mother, bless them. They would have wanted you to be the earl."

"No, they were more than happy Albert inherited the title. My father didn't have any faith in my skills, and Mother said I was a rascal and a good-for-nothing."

"Then think about me!" Oliver stopped writing, outraged. "I can't be the personal physician of the third cousin, twice removed, of the Earl of Ravenscroft. Nobody cares about that."

"Neville is my uncle."

"You're missing my point."

"Your salary will remain the same," Perry said. Money was often a good argument with Oliver.

"Exactly! This is your family legacy, and you shouldn't let your condition limit your possibilities. Your condition doesn't define who you are. Embrace your title, become famous, and...give me a raise."

Perry sighed. "There are things I can't do."

"Like what?" Oliver gave him a smug look.

"Like mingling with normal people. Enjoying a party without the constant worry of having a seizure in front of everyone. I can't even have a simple conversation without wondering what people are thinking of me, if there's something wrong with me, or why I trip on words when I speak."

"Tosh." Oliver scribbled on his notepad, muttering, "*The patient shows a lack of confidence, vision, and pride.*"

"I don't lack confidence, and would you please stop referring to me as *the patient*?"

"I'm a professional." Oliver clicked his tongue. "You do lack confidence. But I have a remedy for you."

Perry held up his hands. "Absolutely no. No more experiments with supposedly magical herbs from distant lands or calming techniques from the far east that involve sharp needles."

Oliver shook his head. "This remedy is here in London, and it's called the Scarlet Room."

"Oh, sod off. What is it?" Perry rubbed his brow. "Not another spa."

Oliver scraped a chair closer to him. "It's a club, an exclusive and expensive one, but you can afford it, and well, so can I since I'm your physician."

"Oh, really? I guess your sudden interest in a seedy club has to do with the medical treatise on human behaviour you're writing for your specialisation in alienism."

"More or less," Oliver said. "That quiet town in Switzerland didn't offer many opportunities for collecting data. And the Scarlet Room isn't seedy. It's underneath London. Everything is possible in the Scarlet Room because there are no rules. You can do whatever you want, be whoever you want. What happens in the Scarlet Room stays in the Scarlet Room. No etiquette either."

Perry stared at the overexcited face of his friend. "How do you know about this place?"

"Because I, unlike you, enjoy talking with people, and Geneva was filled with Londoners."

"How can an indecent club help me?"

"You'll have the chance to be around people without any obligation of being polite, introducing yourself, smiling, and talking about the latest cricket match. You can ignore or be ignored, mingle or be on your own, observe or participate. You can do what pleases you while getting familiar again with being around people. Also, the other people will leave you alone if you want to. Perfect."

Not the word Perry would use. "I'm not sure."

"Don't say no immediately, as usual. Before throwing your life, money, and title out of the window, start by reintroducing yourself to people. After that, I'm sure you'll feel better."

Perry absolutely, utterly doubted that.

six

E DITH'S HEAD FELT light after last night's debaucheries and a morning spent cataloguing bottles of drugs in the hospital's dispensary.

She'd been up all night, dancing, drinking champagne, and singing out of tune with other people. Then they'd played cricket at midnight in someone's garden while wearing only their undergarments until a couple of police constables arrived, and she and her companions had to flee, barely escaping capture. What a shame...the fact that they had to flee, not the narrowly accomplished escape; that had been exhilarating. For a brief second. Her work at the dispensary instead sucked all the excitement out of her.

That was why she was out again with her friend, Daphne. She needed a new thrill.

That afternoon, the rocking of the carriage didn't help her stomach still upset from the champagne, or her headache throbbing from the lack of sleep.

There was another reason for her to be upset. Perry had returned to London and had sent her a message inviting her to his home. She hadn't answered yet. She didn't have the courage to.

Just thinking about seeing him again made her want to cast up her accounts.

"Where are we going?" she asked, hoping her friend wasn't dragging her to another party.

"Bloomsbury. An atelier. I'm so excited to introduce you to Mr. Carter," Daphne said, applying a generous layer of rouge to her full lips.

"The famous painter?" That caught her interest.

"The very same. We became friends recently, but we grew close in a short time. He's the most delightfully intriguing man you'll ever know."

No, Edith doubted that. Perry was the most intriguing man she'd ever known, so intriguing that she didn't have the courage to disappoint him and confess she'd told him a huge, stinking pile of lies in her letters. She wasn't a doctor nor had she studied at the London School of Medicine for Women.

She hadn't touched an anatomy book in years, or any other book. The only activity remotely close to medicine was her voluntary job at the dispensary. Far from being a surgeon. She was a fraud, and lying in a letter was too easy.

Perhaps the only reason she was so restless that day was because a meeting with Perry was unavoidable. Sooner or later, he'd learn the truth, and she'd face the consequences of her lies.

Daphne leant closer and whispered, "Valentine wants you to pose for him, for a painting."

"What?"

Despite the headache, that news got Edith's attention. One of the most acclaimed painters of the moment wanted to paint her. For what possible reason?

"You probably don't remember him, but Valentine saw you last night when we were playing cricket. He was so impressed by your fierce character that he wants you for his next painting."

If by 'fierce character' Valentine meant running away from the police in her undergarments, then she had plenty. "Is that why we're going to see him now?"

"It is. Please, say yes. He's such a wonderful gentleman and a great painter."

"Oh." Posing for the most admired painter of the moment. Being painted into an immortal masterpiece.

The painting could be the change and the new beginning she needed. Something that marked her turning over a new leaf, and she would have a beautiful painting to remind her of that. How powerful and extraordinary that would be.

Ten minutes later, they were in Bloomsbury, and Edith's focus was all on the paintings. She had to admit that Mr. Valentine Carter's face was a piece of art itself. His perfect features defined the face of an angel. His piercing eyes changed colour every time he moved, catching the light. The wicked smile ruined the heavenly illusion, but in a good way; it made him more human.

His atelier in Bloomsbury was a chaos of half-finished canvases, cloths stained with a dozen different types of paint, and mismatched sofas and armchairs. Discarded shirts were scattered everywhere. The smell of turpentine teased her nostrils and her sensibility, shocking her back to reality.

Perhaps this whole idea was a mistake. The more she chased pleasure, the more difficult it became for her to understand what was right and what was wrong. The more lost she became.

She shouldn't be in a painter's atelier. Daphne was with her, but having a companion wasn't the point. The point was that she couldn't stop thinking about Perry's invitation.

"Edith, my new muse." Valentine kissed her hands with just enough passion to be polite. "I was desperate to see you again. That quick, fleeting encounter wasn't enough."

"I'm sorry, but I don't remember it."

"Never mind." He kissed her hands again and tilted his head right and left while staring at her. "The colour of your eyes is extraordinary in the sunlight. It'll be a challenge to get it exactly right."

"Actually, I'm not sure I want to pose," Edith said, but Daphne nudged her with her elbow.

"Wait before making a decision," Daphne said. "He truly wants you to pose for him."

"Edith, I think you're lovely." He cupped her face gently, but she wasn't sure she enjoyed the contact or the fact he addressed her in such a familiar manner. Although since he'd seen her playing cricket half-naked, he'd feel allowed to use her Christian name. "Your face is exquisite, and your lips..." He pressed a thumb against her bottom lip, and she jolted, stepping away from his reach.

Daphne laughed. "Heavens, stay calm. No need to be so jittery." She strolled around the messy room with ease, avoiding the scattered items without looking. "Valentine is an artist and a professional. Everything he does has a purely artistic reason."

"Will you pose for me?" Valentine studied her face with an intensity that made her uncomfortable. "Please say yes. I can't pay you a proper salary, but I'll give you two sovereigns for the trouble."

"What sort of painting do you have in mind?" she asked, intrigued despite herself.

"Please, Valentine, paint Edith as one of your goddesses." Daphne winked at her. "You won't regret it."

"I'll show you." Valentine took Edith's hand and led her to the next room.

A series of paintings lined a wall. Nude paintings. Well, not exactly nude. The models wore very flimsy, transparent tunics that added an ethereal touch to their well-portrayed curves.

She swallowed past the knot in her throat. Goodness.

Scandalous poses aside, the paintings were extraordinary. The combination of beautiful lines, colours, shadows, and light created a dramatic effect, enhancing the beauty of the models. Even their expressions held an otherworldly quality that mesmerised her.

There were Hera, holding a sceptre, Artemis, surrounded by moonlight, and Calypso, sitting by the sea. The sea... not her favourite view. Just the sight of the sea, lakes, rivers, and streams turned her belly cold.

She paused at Athena's painting. In the painting, the woman was standing with her hand wrapped around a long spear. The veil of fine muslin that covered her body—or rather, uncovered it—truly made her look like a goddess, powerful and striking. Her hair flowed down to her waist in luscious curls, and her expression was a daring one. A true goddess of war.

"What do you think?" Daphne said.

"They're stunning but revealing." She hoped she didn't sound like a prude.

The paintings were undeniably pieces of art, not at all vulgar or brash. They depicted the human body as the ultimate work of art, exalted by Valentine's expert hand. But to be one of Valentine's goddesses was another matter. They were still nude paintings.

"This is about expressing yourself," Valentine said, turning her towards another painting. "About finding who you really are. These paintings are the mirrors of the models' souls. Look. This is Aphrodite."

Edith's face flamed. Heavens. Surrounded by red petals and the colours of dawn, Aphrodite reclined on a red Chesterfield sofa, her auburn hair reaching past her waist. One hand was squeezed between her thighs, and her droopy eyes didn't leave doubt on what she was doing, unashamedly so. Still, it was likely one of the most beautiful paintings Edith had ever seen.

"Which goddess would I be?" she asked.

"Astrea." Valentine showed her a drawing of a beautiful blue-haired goddess shining with starlight. "She was known as the Star Maiden or the Star Goddess. Your delicate lines and wide eyes inspire me to paint you as my Astrea."

"You'd be perfect," Daphne said.

Edith was tempted. Of course she was. Being portrayed in one of these extraordinary paintings would be an honour.

"But I'm not sure I want to get undressed."

Daphne smiled. "I posed for him as well. Not for one of his goddesses, but it was a nude painting. You can't imagine the freedom and confidence the experience gave me."

"These paintings never leave my atelier." Valentine gestured around. "I don't sell them. They're for me only. I show them to a very restricted number of friends, but the goddesses never, ever leave this room. You won't be seen by anyone but me."

"This isn't about propriety." Daphne put a hand on her shoulder. "This is about freedom, happiness, about expressing yourself, about fighting your fears."

"Fears?" That piqued her interest.

"Yes. Posing for a painting so daring is liberating, empowering. All your fears will be gone forever."

Well, that was intriguing. She glanced at the confident Aphrodite again. The goddess stared at the viewer as if to say, '*I don't give a toss about what you think of me. I don't think of you at all.*'

"I'll do it."

seven

DUSK CREPT ALONG the streets by the time Edith had finished posing for Valentine.

The tunic she'd worn to pose as the Star Maiden had been more covering than she'd imagined, but the hours spent sitting and doing nothing had made her restless. That was why she went out for a walk with Daphne, then to buy jacket potatoes from a street vendor, and now she was again in a carriage with Daphne, heading to a club. Valentine himself would join them as soon as he finished coating the painting.

She reclined her head, wishing for the nagging whisper in her head to stay quiet. Doubts often tormented her and begged her to go home whenever she wanted to have fun.

Admittedly, after last night, she should probably spend a quiet night at home, drink tea, and go to bed early. But she could drink tea and sleep any night. Life was short.

She'd spent too many years worrying about her future, her studies, and her manners. The *Princess Alice* disaster had opened her eyes. Perry had been right. She should enjoy herself while she could before her life was snatched from her in a moment.

"Is this Scarlet Room an opium den?" she asked.

Enjoying herself didn't mean turning her brain into a bleeding pulp. She'd studied enough medical books to know what opium, snuff, and cocaine did to the body, no matter what some physicians said. An early grave wasn't her idea of enjoying life.

"Well, if you want it to be an opium den, yes," Daphne said. "The point of the Scarlet Room is that you can do whatever you want there, from smoking opium to drinking yourself to a stupor, to dancing and having tumbles in quiet corners, or in front of everyone. There's something for everyone and every taste."

Boring. The thought came unbidden to her mind.

For someone who wanted to enjoy herself, she found that almost every activity was boring or became boring after five minutes. Oddly enough, she'd never been bored when she'd spent her days bent over books of anatomy.

"The only rule is not to talk about the Scarlet Room with anyone," Daphne said.

"How did you learn about it then?"

Daphne waved a hand. "Well, I guess you *can* talk about it, but only with people who would enjoy it without judging it. Anyway, it'd be better if you'd keep your mouth shut."

That wouldn't be a problem. Aside from Daphne, Edith didn't have anyone to talk to. The people she went to parties with weren't really friends. Just acquaintances to have fun with, never to talk to or confide about the turmoil that made her sad sometimes.

But sadness had no place in her life; it reminded her of how close to death she'd been. She was young and deserved something different, something more exciting than worrying about studying.

She would never confide in her parents, and since Marianne had married that viscount, she spent more time with her new friends than with her sister.

The carriage stopped in front of the entrance to a narrow alleyway on the border with Whitechapel. A dense fog lingered, thick and motionless, as if London were holding its breath. The glow from the gas streetlamps created a sinister halo against the backdrop of the dark brick walls. Overall, the view was an echo of how she felt inside.

"We'll have to walk a little." Daphne jumped out of her seat with the same enthusiasm as someone hopping into a colourful party.

Instead, Edith inched out of the carriage, ready to get back inside. The air was thick with humidity and the smell of cheap ale.

"No need to worry." Daphne waved her closer. "Trust me. It's going to be wonderful."

Edith doubted that, but the alternative was to return home and think about the best way to tell the truth to Perry. No, a foggy, damp alleyway where a felon might lurk was better; it promised to keep her mind busy.

They took the dimly lit, dirty alleyway. It was so narrow they couldn't walk side by side, and Edith's skirt skimmed the walls.

She nearly slipped on the wet cobbles as a rat rushed past her. "Where are we going?"

"Patience." Daphne marched on, seemingly oblivious to the darkness and gloominess of the alleyway.

"Someone might attack us. Don't you read the newspapers?"

"No, I don't. They're depressing." Daphne paused, a hand on her hip. "Where's your sense of adventure? You're complaining a lot as of late."

"That's not true."

"Last week, you left Neville's party early."

"I was bored." Also, the fact Lord Neville was Perry's young uncle never failed to upset her. "And he always hugs me, touches me, and kisses me even when I ask him to stop."

Daphne rolled her eyes. "Goodness, you're becoming so prudish. He's just being affectionate. Since you got that news about... what's his name?"

Edith pursed her lips, not wanting to comment on her relationship with Perry.

"Oh, right," Daphne said, "Peregrine. Since he wrote to you

that he'd return here, you're all fidgety and forlorn. Isn't he Neville's nephew and the new Earl of Ravenscroft?"

"He has nothing to do with my mood."

Daphne inched closer, which brought her almost face-to-face with Edith since the space was limited. "Is there some juicy story between you and him aside from that dreadful incident? Something you didn't tell me? A dirty tumble?"

"No, Perry and I have never been *affectionate.*"

"Oh, Perry." Daphne chuckled. "Fine. Keep your secrets."

"Besides, I thought Neville was interested in courting you."

"He is, but we're happy to pursue other interests at the same time. He needs to marry. I need to get married. We liked each other, but I don't want to stop having fun just because I'm going to be a wife. Neville and I have a clear understanding."

Edith widened her eyes in silent shock. To each their own, but she wanted to find someone who deeply cared for her and with whom she'd share her life with love and respect.

Daphne pointed a finger at her. "That stunned expression again. You truly are becoming a prude. Neville and I only think about a smart match. I have a sizable dowry. He's fairly wealthy. We enjoy each other's company. That's all."

"If you two are happy, then it's all right," Edith said.

"Just follow me. Whatever afflicts you, the Scarlet Room will cure it."

There was some truth in Daphne's words. Perry's return troubled Edith although the whole affair was her fault. She'd chosen to lie to him, and now she had no choice but to face him and confess. She hoped the Scarlet Room lived up to its expectations and made her forget about everything for a few hours.

Daphne stopped in front of a flight of stairs heading down. The view was a far cry from inviting. Edith almost expected a man wielding a bloody axe to jump out of the shadows and attack them.

"Nearly there," Daphne said.

Their footsteps echoed off the brick walls. The cobblestones were as slippery as soap, and the ominous sound of water dripping from somewhere gave her goosebumps.

She paused at the bottom of the stairs. "I'm not sure I want to keep going."

"My goodness!" Daphne's voice thundered in the confined space. "What is wrong with you tonight? You do nothing but whine. Trust me. Have I ever disappointed you?"

In terms of entertainment, no. Daphne had always found the craziest things to do and the wildest people to spend time with.

Daphne took Edith's arm. "We need to hurry because the gate-keepers of the Scarlet Room open the doors only at certain hours through the night. If we miss this opportunity, we'll have to wait two hours until the doors open again, and I don't want to spend two hours in a cold alley."

She almost wished they missed their opportunity to have an excuse to return home. Goodness, her emotions were all over the place. Her head was going to burst.

The passage widened and opened onto a landing where other people waited in silence in front of a set of double doors. The ornate doors with their golden knobs and corners were a stark contrast with the dark alleyway.

Edith and Daphne's arrival caused a quick stir through the small crowd, but no one said anything. She shifted her weight from one foot to another, asking herself once again if she really, really wanted to go on.

Why she was so upset, she wouldn't know. Perry wouldn't see her tonight. She had plenty of time to prepare a speech to explain to him why she'd lied. Her relentlessness started to annoy even herself, and the constant water dripping grated on her nerves.

The doors inched inwards, revealing a rather normal and cosy sitting room. The view was nothing exciting. She'd imagined something more Gothic or outrageous.

"Finally." Daphne took her hand in excitement.

"Welcome." A man in a dark suit similar to that of a butler bowed to the small group.

The others filed inside, whispering in thrilled tones. Edith instead dragged herself forwards.

When the butler locked the doors behind them, she tugged her capelet more tightly around her shoulders as a sudden chill slithered down her back.

The others chatted, raising their voices. A sofa and a few armchairs were scattered around, and a warm log fire burned in the hearth. The butler placed a stack of papers on a polished table. The lights from the gas lamps glinted off its shiny surface, bothering her eyes after the darkness. Light after darkness always hurt.

"Ladies and gentlemen, before you proceed into the Scarlet Room, you need to sign this contract and pay the sum of seven pounds each. If you find yourself unable to sign the contract or to pay the fee for any reason, I must ask you to leave."

"You have the money, don't you?" Daphne asked.

"Of course. Marianne gave it to me."

Because Edith couldn't ask her parents for money, and because she'd exhausted the money she'd set aside. And her parents... they didn't know how she spent her nights.

She read her copy of the contract, forcing herself to focus.

The customers had to pledge not to reveal anything that happened in the Scarlet Room, not to use what they saw or heard as leverage against other customers, not to gossip about other customers' choices of entertainment... and many other things Edith wasn't supposed to do under the pain of receiving a ridiculously high fine or even imprisonment.

There were other rules, terms, and conditions written in fine print; something about verbal contracts stipulated between two customers. When a customer proposed a deal or a dare to another customer, and both parties agreed to the deal, then both parties were considered—

"Just sign," Daphne said, flipping through the pages to the last one. "It's all legal jargon we wouldn't understand anyway."

That was true, and Edith's head hurt. She didn't plan to talk to any stranger anyway, so she wrote her name and address and signed the contract.

Daphne didn't even read it. She quickly wrote her name and handed the contract back to the butler with her money. After everyone had signed, the butler led them to a cloakroom.

Edith reluctantly removed her capelet. It provided a sort of comfort.

"You won't regret this." Daphne shrugged off her cloak and handed it to another dark-suited man.

A little frisson of excitement went through Edith when finally the butler opened a second heavy-looking set of double doors. Loud music, laughter, and happy voices ricocheted off the walls. Dark-red was the predominant colour, from the curtains to the carpet and wainscoting. Even the candles were red. It was like entering the gaping maw of a monster.

Daphne grabbed Edith's hand and dragged her inside. "Let the fun begin."

The smell of opium mingled with that of different perfumes, flowers—all red, of course—and something else spicy. Scantily dressed people played at a pool table. There were ladies sitting on gentlemen's laps, kissing couples, and in general, people with not many clothes on.

Others drank, danced, or sang seemingly without rhyme or reason. In the dark corners, she caught glimpses of couples doing more than kissing. In another corner, other couples did... something she couldn't fully understand with ropes and scarves; if it was a style of tumble, she wouldn't know which one.

The whole atmosphere was exciting, and above all, it obliterated any other thought in her mind. Exactly what she wanted.

Her smile faltered as she swept her gaze through the room. The sight of a swimming pool filled with water dampened her enthusiasm. Just looking at the quivering surface made her want to throw up. Her breathing sped up as the phantom chill of the Thames's water froze her.

Confused visions of herself swimming in the river flashed through her mind. Most of the time, the desperation and fear of that moment threatened to overwhelm her. She'd calculated that she'd stayed in the water for no more than fifteen minutes among flaming pieces of wood and shards of metal. A rather short time. Her daily lunch took twice that time. Yet those fifteen minutes had seemed a year and tortured her to this day. How odd.

She'd do her level best to avoid and ignore that pool.

"Come. What happened to you?" Daphne tugged at her hand. "Valentine is over there at the card table. I'm in a mood for a card game." She led Edith to a side room that looked like a whist club.

Edith averted her gaze from the pool, but she came to a grinding halt when she spotted Neville sitting next to Valentine. "That's Neville."

Daphne exhaled noisily. "Well spotted."

"I'm not sure I want to spend the evening in his company."

"Ignore Neville if you want. Tell him to leave you alone again. But don't let him ruin your evening and don't ruin mine."

Ignoring Neville wasn't easy, especially since he looked like Perry. Same midnight hair and blue eyes. Even their straight noses and strong jaws were the same. But since she could do whatever she wanted in the Scarlet Room without any consequences, she would deal with him however she pleased.

Whatever card game some people were playing, it didn't involve money since no gaming token lay on the table.

"How does that game work?" she asked, pointing to a table.

"You lose, you remove a garment." Daphne wiggled her eyebrows. "Isn't that thrilling? And remember, anything that happens here stays here. No consequences."

Edith's pulse spiked. Finally, excitement. "Good evening."

Neville and Valentine stood up, habits she guessed since they weren't obliged to.

"Hello, gentlemen." Daphne clamped a hand on Neville's neck and pulled him down for a passionate kiss.

Edith couldn't completely stifle a gasp as they kissed rather ardently.

"Edith is becoming a prude," Daphne said, once she disentangled her tongue from Neville's. "But she did pose for one of Valentine's paintings today."

Neville chuckled. "He's lucky to have beautiful models who pose for him."

"Who wouldn't pose for him?" Daphne said, taking a chair.

Neville shuffled the cards, staring at Edith with an intensity she didn't like. "Is something the matter? You look upset."

"It's because of that nephew of yours," Daphne said with a dismissive hand. "Since Edith learnt he was back, she's very uptight."

"Daphne!"

Neville stopped shuffling the cards. "Why would that be?"

Maybe it was Edith's imagination, but she heard a strained note in his voice. "I haven't seen Perry in years. I'm nervous."

"Are you two close?" Neville asked, leaning forth.

"We're friends."

Daphne poked her with an elbow. "More than friends, I'm sure."

Neville narrowed his glacial eyes, resuming the shuffling.

"The way Edith blushes said it all," Valentine said.

Edith ignored them. "What's the game?"

"Whist." Neville dealt the cards. "Our clothes are the tokens. Let's place a bet. The winner can choose to have a tumble with one of the losers, or more than one."

Edith closed her fists. "Absolutely not."

"Spoilsport. Just play. Why do you care?" Daphne said,

handing her a glass of champagne she'd taken from somewhere. "It's just for fun. No consequences, remember?"

"Well?" Neville prompted. "I'm game."

Absolutely not. She would never, ever have a tumble with either Neville or Valentine.

She took the glass of champagne. "I don't make these types of bets."

She was a liar and a fraud, but she still had some dignity.

And that was it.

eight

NOT FOR THE first time that night, Perry wondered why he'd agreed to come to the chaotic, noisy, and crowded Scarlet Room.

One thing had to be said about the place—no one bothered him. He'd sat in a relatively quiet corner of the club, watching people do all sorts of depravities—some more interesting than others—and not one person had tried to drag him out of his corner or asked him why he didn't join the fun.

Oliver was playing pool with a group of rowdy gentlemen, laughing and singing so loudly Perry was sure his friend would have a sore throat the next day. Aside from playing pool and making silly jokes about the balls, Oliver's companions didn't do anything outrageous; they were also fully clothed. There was really something for everyone in the Scarlet Room.

He twirled his glass of whiskey. The ice had melted half an hour ago. He hadn't drunk a single drop because alcohol and seizures weren't a good combination. But not holding a glass at a party was usually frowned upon, although Oliver had assured him no one would care. Anyway. The glass gave him something to toy with.

He needed to keep his hands busy because staying here was a pointless exercise. And he'd signed a contract and paid seven quid for this rubbish.

If he had to be honest, years ago, when he'd sought only pleasure, he would have lost himself in a place like that, doing everything, talking with everyone, or trying that intriguing sensual game with the ropes. Now he preferred a piano concert or a gripping book. The only good thing was that, if he had a seizure here, no one would mind or say anything. There was some comfort in that.

He took a walk around the wide room; it was as wide as a cricket field. He couldn't see the other end, so tightly it was crowded. He strolled, not caring about what people did. Half-naked people, drunk people, people stunned by the opium. Usual things. This type of excitement was overrated and had stopped exciting him a long time ago.

His wandering came to an abrupt halt upon seeing someone he hadn't expected to see.

Not here. Not now. Not like that.

Dr. Edith Winkworth was drinking champagne and playing cards at a table, wearing only her chemise, corset, bloomers, and stockings. The dark-haired woman next to her was equally undressed. Of the two gentlemen with her, he could see only a blond one who seemed in the buff. The other was half hidden by a Grecian column.

But he didn't give a damn about the card players. His attention focused exclusively on Edith. Sweet, beautiful, bookish Edith. The woman who had called him a hedonist and wanted her Christmas kiss.

She climbed on the chair, waving her cards as if they were a fan. Her companions beat their hands on the table, inciting her to dance. She obliged, shaking her hips while unfastening her garter. Her hair was down, reaching her waist in a golden cascade.

A cold shock went through him. The half-naked woman dancing on that table couldn't be Edith—the quiet, serious scholar who had sent him long letters about her efforts to become a doctor. Or maybe he was a damn prude.

She improvised a can-can dance, raising her leg up. The woman at the table clapped and whistled before whispering into her companion's ear. The blond man grabbed Edith and carried her across the room, singing with her. She tossed her cards around with a flourishing gesture, seemingly not caring about the man holding her in a rather intimate manner.

Perry followed them in a trance. Edith hadn't replied to his invitation for tea. He'd thought she was too busy to see him. She was busy indeed.

He mentally scolded himself for judging her. He'd done the same things she was doing, and perhaps tonight was only a temporary diversion from the stressful life of a doctor. Anyway, how Edith passed her evenings was none of his business. He didn't deny being curious and a little worried, though.

The man headed for the swimming pool in the middle of the room, followed by the dark-haired lady.

"A dive!" the lady yelled, raising a fist.

Oh, no. Perry hitched a breath. As far as he knew, Edith hadn't overcome her utter fear of the water, although she might be all right in a small pool.

Edith's laughter ceased. She gripped the man tightly, her face paling and her hands like claws.

No, maybe not.

"No, not the pool," she screamed.

"It's shallow," the woman said. "Not deep at all."

"No, no, no!" Edith's piercing scream of fear rent the air.

She struggled against the man, but he kept laughing and carrying her. Her fear took Perry out of his stupor.

He marched towards them. "The lady said no."

The man ignored him and threw Edith into the water. Her shout of pain and fear chilled Perry's blood. He rushed past the man and the lady as Edith sank into the water with a big splash, sinking out of view. He didn't bother removing his clothes and dived into the pool.

It wasn't as shallow as the woman had said. His feet barely touched the bottom, and Edith was fully submerged. He groaned when Edith stopped moving, her limbs growing stiff. She didn't even shiver. The pool might not be deep, but in the panicked, paralysed state Edith was, she could drown.

His heart pounding in fear, he pulled her up. She was frozen in shock and so pale even her lips had lost colour.

"Edith." He cupped her face, searching her beautiful green eyes, but if she recognised him, she didn't give any signs. "It's me. Please say something."

Her companions were nowhere to be seen, and he couldn't care less. He gathered her in his arms and climbed out of the pool, dripping water from his suit. Climbing out wasn't an easy procedure given his lack of coordination and the slippery tiles. His heavy, wet clothes didn't help.

The indifference of the people he'd been so grateful for minutes ago now irked him. No one came forth to help him, likely thinking he was only playing some wicked game with a half-naked, half-unconscious woman.

Holding Edith, he made his way through the crowd of people who were dancing, drinking, and kissing until he found an empty spot.

"Edith." He laid her down on a sofa and patted her cold cheeks. Her eyes wide open but unblinking worried him. "Please say something."

She wheezed. Each breath sounded raspy. Her pupils were so dilated they turned the whole irises black. He unhooked her corset and shrugged off his wet jacket to cover her. Her wet chemise was plastered to her skin, hiding nothing.

Spewing out water, she took a big breath that brought some colour to her cheeks, but fear clouded her eyes.

"It's all right." He rubbed her back, holding her. "You're out of the water. You're safe."

She shivered, resting her cheek on his chest. His heartbeat pounded faster out of sheer fear for her.

Even though he didn't remember anything of the night of the incident after the blow to his head, holding her, drenched and shivering, brought him back to the inky water of the Thames.

She could have drowned in the pool, paralysed by shock. She could have died under the indifferent gazes of the people thinking only about their own pleasure.

"Edith." He caressed the top of her head. "You're safe."

She didn't seem to hear him. She could collapse if she didn't breathe deeply. He had no idea if she'd been underwater for too long. His breath sped up with all the horrible possibilities. He'd been slow and clumsy. She might have been without oxygen for too long.

She blinked, finally gazing at him. "Perry?" Her lips quivered.

A little, involuntary spasm started in his arm, and it was his turn to freeze.

Not now.

A bitter taste filled his mouth. The spasms made him release her none too gently as the seizure took hold of him. He tried to fight it, tried to force his muscles to loosen, but he blacked out.

EDITH STILL REMEMBERED a few things about seizures—the patient's head needed to be kept still and slightly up to prevent suffocation, and even the legs needed to be held down if they started kicking to avoid injuries or straining the muscles.

The shock of seeing Perry drop to the floor had woken her up from her freezing panic. After she held his head still on her lap, she didn't have time to think about what Perry was doing in the Scarlet Room of all places.

Edith swept her gaze through the room, but the people around her didn't pay her the slightest bit of attention. Those who did looked away disgusted. Daphne, Valentine, and Neville had vanished.

"What's happening to him?" a man asked, stepping away.

"Help me," she said.

The man ignored her.

"It's all right, Perry." She stroked his cheek.

He convulsed, heels kicking against the tiles, but she didn't let him go.

As the seizure died down, he sagged against her, his arms becoming limp. His eyes rolled back into the skull, and his mouth twitched. Edith's heart clenched for him. He'd written to her the seizures weren't common, but they still plagued him. The uncertainty of not knowing when he might have a fit had to be exhausting for him.

"You're safe," she whispered, sweeping his wet hair from his cheek.

"That's the most disgusting thing I've ever seen." A woman stared at them in shock. "Sick people shouldn't be here. I don't want to catch a disease."

"It's not contagious," she yelled. Wasted breath.

The woman marched away, followed by her friends who showed matching frowns.

Perry stirred and groaned, catching her attention.

Perry. She couldn't believe it was really him.

The scandal of the Earl of Ravenscroft marrying an opera singer from the Americas and renouncing the title had filled the newspapers for weeks on end, but not a drop of ink had been spared about Perry. No newspaper had mentioned his return to London or his newly acquired title. In fact, if it hadn't been for their correspondence, she wouldn't know anything about him.

"Perry," she whispered, which likely meant he couldn't hear her since everyone around them was shouting or singing.

He fluttered his eyes open, and once again, the clear blue of his eyes struck her. Why had she thought his eyes were similar to Neville's? They were nothing alike. Neville's eyes had a constant, hard glint that chilled her. Perry's eyes were warm and had a naughty twinkle that cheered her up.

"Edith." He tried to move his head off her lap, but she stopped him.

"Don't. You need a moment to recover. How do you feel?"

"Sore." He opened and closed his hands slowly. "How are you?"

Cold, shocked, worried, ashamed. At least the water had got her sober.

"I'm fine. You took me out of the pool, didn't you?" she asked.

"Yes. You were petrified." His speech was a little hesitant, but nevertheless, it was a miracle he talked.

Goodness, she'd missed his deep voice so much. After all, she'd heard it for only a few hours during their careless stroll through the Rosherville Gardens before the incident.

He grimaced again. "I was horribly scared when I saw you sinking. Then the seizure hit me. Thank you for your help."

She took advantage of his position to check the pulse in his neck. It beat steadily. During the seizure, it'd spiked to a frenzy.

He watched her with a solemn gaze that seemed to see right through her lies. Certainly, he had questions about her behaviour. What he knew about her was a fairy tale of her own making. A recently graduated doctor should be in a hospital, training and working with the patients, not in an infamous club.

"I'm all right. I can stand up." He slowly propped himself up on his elbows before sitting next to her on the floor.

He didn't say anything but stared at her. His wet eyelashes were spiked together, and his white shirt was plastered over his chest muscles.

She tugged at the jacket covering her; it had to belong to him. "I'm sorry I didn't reply to your invitation."

"I guessed you were busy."

There was a note of sarcasm in his tone, or maybe she simply felt guilty.

"Goodness, you can talk." She couldn't stop a smile. "Hearing your voice again is wonderful. You wrote that you didn't speak well. You were too hard on yourself."

"I have some bad days." He ran a hand through his wet hair. It fell nicely over his strong jaw. "I'm glad to see you despite what happened." He waved towards the pool and between them.

"I'm glad, too."

She was about to ask him what he was doing in a place like the Scarlet Room when a blond man stopped in front of them. He had to be one of the few gentlemen still fully clothed or dry. His brown suit was pristine. Not a crease on it.

"I say!" The man grinned from eye to eye. "A completely drenched lady, wearing your jacket, and you're drenched as well on the floor with her. That's the reason I took you here."

"Excuse me?" She pulled the lapels of Perry's jacket closer, shivering. After the scare had passed, her wet clothes chilled her.

Perry exhaled. "Dr. Edith Winkworth, may I introduce you to Dr. Oliver York? I wrote about him in my letters."

Dr. York thrust his chest out as if proud.

Dr. Winkworth. Dash it. Edith stopped herself from correcting him. It wasn't the right moment.

"I'm not simply a doctor," Dr. York said, hooking his thumbs into his waistcoat. "I'm Lord Ravenscroft's best friend, personal physician, and future alienist as soon as I finish my treatises." He winked at Perry. "Not everyone can say that. In fact, only I can."

Edith gave the doctor a bow of her head. It was odd to have such a polite, formal introduction while being half-naked and drenched. But to his credit, the doctor's stare didn't linger on her legs. He seemed happy for whatever reason.

"Fantastic. Fantastic." Dr. York bowed. "Dr. Winkworth, I'm

happy to make your acquaintance, and I'm pleased we're colleagues."

Not really.

"Please carry on doing whatever you were doing with Perry before my interruption."

"Actually, I want to go home," Perry said. "I've just had a seizure."

Dr. York's face changed instantly, becoming serious. "A seizure? How long did it last? Was there stiffness involved or spasms? What triggered it?" He patted his jacket and trousers.

"I don't know." Perry nodded at the pool. "I jumped into the water, and after I came out, I had the seizure."

"Why did you jump into the pool?" Dr. York fished out a notepad and a pencil from his pocket.

"My friends tossed me into the pool as a jest," Edith said. "Perry helped me get out. I'm not fond of water. He was very kind."

"*Very kind*," Dr. York repeated under his breath, writing on the notepad.

"May I escort you home?" Perry asked.

Home? Now? Absolutely not. She needed to get dry, dressed, and composed before returning home. Or rather, sneaking into her bedroom without waking up her parents.

"I don't want to go home. My friend, Daphne, is here."

His dark eyebrows formed a deep V. "Your *friend* did nothing to help you. She encouraged that man to toss you in the water."

Yes, that was something she'd discuss with Daphne. "I know, but we came together."

"You could have died," he insisted.

"I'll give her a piece of my mind, but I should seek her." Her voice trembled. Lying in a letter was one thing, but lying to his face was quite another. "I don't want to go home in this state." That was likely the first true thing she'd told him in years.

Perry opened his mouth, but Dr. York cut him off.

"I have a fantastic idea as usual. Why doesn't Dr. Winkworth come to Perry's house? As a physician, miss, you should know you might catch a cold unless you change into dry clothes. Perry will be more than happy to provide assistance, won't you, Perry?"

"Of course." Perry kept frowning. "Where are your clothes?"

"Over there at the card table." She made her way across the room with Perry protecting her from the crowd like a gargoyle and Dr. York muttering something she didn't catch.

The table where she'd played cards with Neville, Valentine, and Daphne was empty, and her shoes and clothes had disappeared as well.

She shivered, trying to cover more of her legs. "I don't have any idea where my clothes or friends could be."

"I should have offered you my jacket earlier." Dr. York handed her his jacket. "Perry's is wet as well. So, will you come with us, miss? We promise to be gentlemen."

Perry's frown was so deep she wondered if it'd leave a permanent crease on his brow.

Well, she needed to get dry and change, and going to Perry's house was better than going home half naked and dishevelled. Not to mention she was angry with Daphne for how she'd behaved.

Also, she had no doubt Perry would be a gentleman.

nine

PERRY TOWELLED HIS hair dry, standing in front of the blazing log fire in the hearth in his sitting room.

His warm and dry clothes chafed his skin still sensitive after the seizure. He hadn't had a seizure in months, almost a year, and tonight's fit concerned him. The timing didn't make sense. The previous months had been rich with exciting and anxious moments, stressful days, and a few sleepless nights, but no health problems.

Edith's presence could be the cause of the seizure. Aside from seeing her again, what had happened tonight wasn't anything new in terms of emotions. He couldn't deny she was a source of concern.

Oliver entered the room, carrying a tray with a steaming teapot and a few cups. "Your butler brewed it, but after that, I dismissed him. He was rather agitated seeing you drenched."

"Mason gets easily worried. Did you manage to take Edith upstairs without too much fuss?"

"Of course, I did. She's changing in the guest room after I handed her some of your clothes. How are you? Any specific feelings?" Oliver placed the tray on the low table and immediately took out his notepad.

Perry stared at the dancing flames for a moment, trying to collect his thoughts. "I'm sore, but I'm all right. I experienced some tingling before the attack. What triggered it?"

Oliver raised his gaze from the page. "Difficult to say. It can't be the water. You've swum in a pool regularly in the past years. You also exercise every day, so it can't be physical exertion, and you were doing well despite all the people around you, weren't you?"

"Yes. Being surrounded by people was less annoying than I'd thought, and I didn't drink anything."

Oliver took more notes. "I need to think about this. There must be a trigger. Perhaps seeing Dr. Winkworth again had shocked you so much to start the seizure."

"Maybe, but the last time I experienced a strong emotion, nothing happened."

"True. The trigger must be something more specific than surprise, shock, or excitement."

The door inched inwards, and Edith poked her head inside. "May I?"

"Please." Perry poured a cup of tea for her.

A thousand questions twirled in his mind, but the most important thing at that moment was that Edith was safe and well.

She wore a thick blanket over one of his dressing gowns. Despite the attire making her shapeless, she looked beautiful to him, from her strawberry-blonde hair to her rosy cheeks that matched her plush lips.

"Dr. Winkworth." Oliver bowed. "I wish to reassure you that your reputation won't suffer from tonight's incident. We're discretion itself. Perry and I won't utter a word to anybody, and even if we blabbered about what happened tonight, I don't think anyone would believe us. I have doubts myself."

"Oliver," Perry warned.

Edith shrugged, clenching the blanket. "Thank you."

Oliver bowed again. "I'll retire then. Perry, I'll be in my room if you need anything."

The moment he shut the door behind him, Perry couldn't take his gaze off her. He knew her well. They'd spent months together when he'd been recovering and had exchanged letters for the past five years. But somehow, he had the feeling she was a different person.

She sat in the armchair close to the blazing fire, holding her cup of tea. "You're most kind."

Taking her to his home was the least he could do.

"I was worried about you. When that man carried you to the pool, at first I thought you'd overcome your fear of water. But when you shouted no, I had to intervene."

She tucked a long curl of hair behind her ear. "Yes, fear of water still afflicts me."

"As seizures afflict me. Curious, isn't it? Certain things don't go away, no matter how hard we want them to."

She gave him a small smile that didn't reach her eyes.

He cleared his throat, meaning to talk to her about something that had tormented him from the moment he'd seen her again.

"I was surprised to see you in the Scarlet Room."

A tremor went through her hands. "What do you mean? Why would you?" Her voice shook.

"You've never found that type of entertainment enjoyable, and from your letters, I didn't get the impression you changed your mind about that. For the past years, you did nothing but study hard. You never mentioned nightclubs."

"I just wanted to enjoy myself for a night." She knit her eyebrows. Her tone was defensive but lacked confidence at the same time.

"I understand, but..." He rubbed his temple as a mild headache started to throb. "What I mean is that I'm surprised, and you will excuse me if I don't consider the people who were with you as your friends. Friends don't put their friends in danger or humiliate them."

She blushed up to the roots of her hair. "Daphne is wild, but I don't think she consciously wanted to hurt me. We've been to many parties together, and nothing like that has ever happened."

"Many parties. So a night like tonight is a regular occurrence."

"You've been away for years," she said, staring into her cup. "Not that it's your fault, but things have changed. I've changed."

The aftermath of the seizure soured his mood, making him grumpier than usual. Also, he wasn't used anymore to dealing with people aside from Oliver and other medics.

He tossed the towel on the sofa. "So I've seen. The Edith I know, the Edith who wrote me letters for years would never, ever put herself in danger with people who don't give a toss about her before abandoning her."

"You were there, too." Emotion flamed red in her cheeks.

"Yes, but I wasn't about to drown, was I?"

She didn't answer, but another shiver shook her.

"I'm worried about you. Anything could have happened to you with those people you call friends. Anyone could have taken advantage of you while you were frozen in shock." He sat next to her. "What would have happened to you if I hadn't pulled you out of the pool?"

"You're right, really. What I did was reckless." She pressed a finger between her eyebrows. "I'm very grateful for your help, but the situation isn't as dramatic as you picture it."

"Which part of risking to drown isn't dramatic?"

She put her cup down. "I'm so sorry."

"What for?"

She turned towards him, her eyes shining and her lips parting.

He couldn't understand if she was about to burst out crying or to slap him.

"What troubles you?" he asked.

"You don't know everything about me," she whispered.

He inched closer, so close he could see the golden specks in her irises. "Then tell me everything."

She drew in a deep breath, and he smelled the scent of his clothes from her.

"Perry..." His name sounded like a plea. "I don't..." She swallowed hard a few times. "You wouldn't be so kind to me if you knew everything about me."

"I would," he said without hesitation. "What does knowing everything have to do with taking you to my home in the middle of the night when you need help?"

She chose silence, but the fact she kept shivering worried him.

"Are you worried about me judging you?" he said when she didn't talk.

She nodded without looking at him.

"We're friends." He rubbed an aching spot on his forehead. "I'm not going to judge you just because you attend a few wild parties. I'm surprised, yes. Also, I'm concerned about what might happen to you, especially when you panic and freeze, and I don't understand why you never mentioned Daphne or rowdy parties in your letters. That's all."

She drew in a deep breath and paused before speaking. "I...I should go home."

That wasn't what she meant to say. He was sure of that. But pressing her for answers wouldn't help her feel comfortable with him.

"I understand," he said.

"Would you be so kind as to give me a few coins for a cab, and may I get a different set of clothes, please?" she said. "I'll send someone to return you the money and the clothes."

"Of course. I'll take you home personally."

She closed her eyes for a moment before answering. "Thank you."

The words came out strangled as if her throat were swollen. She opened her mouth, but nothing else came out.

"Is there something you want to tell me?" He stared at her lovely face, trying to decipher her silence.

She shook her head. "Not now. Please."

"Wait here." He walked out of the sitting room and upstairs to his bedroom.

If she believed she'd disappointed him because she'd enjoyed herself, she was sorely mistaken. He had his own share of questionable nights and more questionable choices. Her safety was his only concern.

A pound should be more than enough for a cab. As for the clothes and shoes, he didn't have anything that would fit her, but that was the least of his problems. He snatched a pair of soft leather boots she could easily put on, a pair of trousers, a shirt, and a jacket.

His valet would be horrified at the mess in the wardrobe and his wet clothes.

After he selected a flat hat for good measure, since her hair was still wet, he ran downstairs. She paced in only the dressing gown, having dispensed with the blanket. She was a lovely sight; he couldn't deny that. Elegant and graceful even in the large dressing gown that trailed behind her like a gown's train.

"There." He put the clothes on the sofa.

"Thank you." She started to untie the sash of the dressing gown before giving him a sideways glance. "Do you mind?"

"I do. I mean, of course. I'll leave."

"Just turn around."

"Yes." He did as told and stoked the fire while she changed.

The swish of fabric came from behind him, and her shadow projected at his feet from the lamp behind her betrayed her movements.

"I've finished," she said.

He faced her, and his breath hitched. Even in an oversized pair of trousers and jacket, she was a stunner. With her hair under the hat, she could easily be mistaken for a young lad.

A little smile played on her lips. "Wearing these clothes is a little odd." She tugged at the jacket.

"You look beautiful," he said before he could stop himself.

A slow blush coloured her cheeks. "I don't feel beautiful right now, but thank you."

"Let's go." He offered her his arm, and a little shot of energy went through him when she accepted it.

In those male clothes, no one would guess who she was. Still, he wouldn't let her go alone. Maybe he'd been away from London for too long, but he saw dangers everywhere in this metropolis he didn't recognise. Hell, compared to the Town of the Squirrels, London brimmed with criminals, crooks, and threats.

As she walked next to him to the entry hall, the hem of her trousers shuffled against the floor.

Once outside on the pavement, he hailed a passing cab and opened the door. "After you."

"I might trip on the hem." She held out her hand.

He took it, and the moment their hands touched, time seemed to stop. London looked less dark and grim when she flashed a timid smile. Although even in the dim light of the streetlamps, her pallor was evident.

He helped her up and got her inside. "Harley Street," he said to the driver.

"Sir." The driver nodded, casting a curious glance at them.

Perry massaged his aching forehead, groaning in pain.

"Headache?" she asked.

"Always after a seizure, but it should go away after a good night's sleep."

She frowned. "I hope the cause of the seizure wasn't me. I know you have questions about my behaviour," she said after a pause.

"Yes, I do."

She avoided his gaze. "You told me to think more about having fun and less about books. Well...I followed your advice, and I'm happy I did."

"You seem far from happy."

"Sometimes it's difficult to be happy," she whispered. "And studying didn't make me happy anymore."

He was confused. "You talk as if you'd stopped studying altogether. But you're a doctor now. You must have worked really hard to achieve that goal. You haven't abandoned your dream. That's wonderful."

Her demeanour changed instantly. She slouched, shrinking away from him as much as the confined space allowed.

"I said something wrong." He touched her hand gently; it was cold.

"No, you didn't." She choked on the words.

He rubbed his neck where the muscles remained stiff after the seizure. He didn't know what to say. Years ago, he'd wanted nothing but to have fun. The incident had cured the hedonism out of him—extirpated it from him without anaesthesia was more like it—and before that, he hadn't appreciated his brother trying to tell him that life was more than a wild party. But Edith was different. She didn't lose herself in pleasure, did she?

The cab came to a stop in front of Edith's townhouse, breaking his confused musing.

"Are you going to tell your parents about what happened tonight?" he asked, worried again. "About your moment of panic?"

She hunched her shoulders. "I'm not going to say anything. They wouldn't care anyway."

"Bollocks. Your parents are nothing but proud of you." He tilted his head to stare at her face, but she avoided his gaze. "Edith." He took her chin gently and stroked the curve of her jaw with his thumb. "I hope you didn't argue with your parents and that they didn't expect more from you. You're a brilliant, amazing woman who will achieve great things. Think about all the people you'll save by being a surgeon. Your wonderful path has just started."

She turned her scared, teary eyes to him. Her bottom lip quivered. "Thank you for the cab, Perry. Good night."

"Edith. Wait."

She jumped out of the cab like a hare and ran towards her home, leaving him worried.

She'd proved to have the courage to graduate and overcome the trauma of the *Princess Alice* tragedy. Her parents had to be incredibly proud of her. Hell, he was proud of her and a little envious as well. He hadn't achieved anything as successful as her medical degree.

He found excuses whenever Oliver urged him to do his duty and be the next Earl of Ravenscroft, while Edith had rolled up her sleeves and worked hard to accomplish a great result. She was an example to follow and made him regret some of his choices.

Whatever bothered her, it couldn't be that serious.

ten

AFTER EDITH HAD run away from Perry with the strongest sense of embarrassment that had ever troubled her, she'd slid inside her bedroom through the window she'd left open, arriving home unnoticed.

Years ago, after Marianne got married, Edith had moved to a small bedroom on the ground floor, claiming she liked it more than her old bedroom upstairs. But in truth, the reason for her choice was that she could easily climb in and out of the ground-floor bedroom without being noticed if she timed her sneaking out and in carefully.

The 'sneaking in' part of the night had gone smoothly. The consequences of last night, both physical and emotional, were another matter, though. A headache drummed against her skull after the champagne, the scare in the swimming pool, and the shock of seeing Perry again.

She never drank a lot of alcohol because just one sip of champagne was enough to give her the temporary happiness she desperately needed and also a fierce wave of nausea. Father said she was particularly sensitive to spirits, which was fine with her. But she'd exaggerated last night. She didn't fully remember what she'd done before the shock of the pool had made her come to her senses.

Her worry was monumental, so thick she could use it as a cloak around her shoulders.

She felt small enough to pass through the eye of a needle after having met Perry and not confessing her lies. To her defence, he'd caught her off guard.

His praise rang in her ears, tormenting her. He was proud of her. He admired her. Goodness, if he only knew. Like a coward, she hadn't found the courage to tell him the truth. More than once, she'd tried to tell him everything, but staring at his kind blue eyes had destroyed her resolve. She hadn't wanted to see his good opinion of her crumbling in a moment, not when she'd worn wet undergarments and his clothes.

As she dragged herself to the dining room for breakfast, she ignored the ache in her sore body and the headache she deserved.

"Good morning, Mother," she said, controlling her voice.

Mother cast a glance over at her. "Good morning. The tea is growing cold."

"Sorry." She was so forlorn, her morning tea tasted like vinegar.

"You look so pale," Mother said, buttering her toast.

"I didn't sleep well." Or enough. Barely two hours before the maid had come to light the fire in Edith's bedroom.

"Are you going to the dispensary today?"

"It's my free day."

Mother pressed her lips hard. "Do you know what bothers me the most? The fact you believe I'm stupid."

"I've never said that." She sipped her tea, but it really had a bitter taste despite all the sugar she'd added.

"Tell me what you did." Mother shot her a scorching glare. "Are you using opium again?"

"Mother, no. I told you. It happened only once."

That was true; she'd tried and hadn't liked it, but ironically, Mother was convinced her daughter abused it.

Edith forced herself to swallow the tea. If she refused to have breakfast, her mother would grow even more concerned.

"I blame myself and your father as well," Mother said. "We should have been firmer with you. But no, I was sorry for what you went through, for what we all went through. We did everything you asked, and this is the result. And opium got the better of you."

"Mother, please."

Edith closed her eyes for a moment. The sunlight bothered her eyes, and her mother's words stirred something ugly in her chest. She didn't know what was worse, that her mother believed she was an opium addict or that she kept lying.

"I don't have the symptoms of an opium addict," she said. "No mood changes, chronic itching, or nausea. Do you think Father wouldn't notice if I took opium?"

"I don't know." Mother was flustered. "You're knowledgeable in medical science and work in a dispensary. You can easily find what you need to hide the symptoms."

Goodness. That was extreme. Edith wasn't that conniving.

"I'm all right, Mother. I simply didn't sleep well."

Sometimes the easiness with which she lied surprised herself.

"So you're all right, are you? Good." Mother buttered her piece of toast hard enough to break the slice. "Since you're all right, I have some news for you. The London School of Medicine for Women is going to open for new enrolment next week. Do you want to try this year?"

If Edith said no, Mother would get angry and lecture her on the importance of having an education and the fact Edith spent her days cataloguing drugs while she could be a medical student, which would lead to another lecture she had no patience for today.

So just to avoid an early morning argument that would go nowhere, she said, "I'll think about it."

"I heard the college changed the admission test. It's harder now."

Edith nodded.

Mother wasn't fooled if the way she narrowed her gaze was any indication. "Your father and I are tired of seeing you waste your talent like that."

She sipped more tea. Her stomach churned in reply. It seemed she couldn't avoid a sermon.

Mother's expression softened. "I understand the incident was harrowing. I barely survived it, too. We have to thank your father's knowledge of medicinal drugs for saving us. But if you don't want to study, then do as Marianne did."

Edith paused drinking. "Find a husband?"

"Why not?" Mother's tone became more high-pitched. "Why waste your time in a dispensary and be tempted by opium every day when you could start your own family and manage a house? Being the mistress of a house isn't a simple job. It requires organisation and expertise, hard work and patience."

Hard work and patience seemed things Edith couldn't afford anymore.

"Honestly." Mother shook her head. "I can't believe you're the same girl who spent all her time studying and reading books. I had to force you to stop reading. You dreamed of becoming a doctor, and now what do you do all day? You lie to us and go out with people I barely know. What a disappointment. Aside from Miss Ferguson, who's a fine lady, I don't know any of your friends."

Daphne had simply more experience than Edith in hiding her vices and her real personality. Edith pushed away her plate of toast. Her stomach didn't want food anywhere near it. Darn champagne.

Mother's words weren't new. At least once a week, she made the same speech about how Edith was a disappointment and how she should find something proper to do.

But that morning, those words hurt like red-hot needles piercing her chest. Maybe because Perry had told her the same things. No, his speech had been ten times more painful than Mother's because he believed Edith was a doctor. At least Mother, even though ignorant of all the things her daughter did at night, was aware of Edith's situation and lack of any accomplishments—medical or otherwise.

Mother lowered her voice. "You must think of Marianne as well. She's a viscountess now. Your behaviour reflects badly on her. Thomas might decide to send Marianne away if the rumours about you ruin her."

"My name has never appeared on the scandal sheet." She wasn't stupid enough to cause a scandal. She was careful not to make that mistake, and Marianne helped, too.

Marianne's reluctant complicity was another source of worry. More than once, she'd paid for Edith's mistakes, literally. Marianne's money had silenced more than one witness to one of Edith's wild adventures. Not that Marianne condoned her sister's behaviour, but between dragging her aristocratic husband into a scandal and spending a few pounds, she chose the latter.

"It's a matter of time before something terrible happens." Mother wasn't finished, but the door opening cut her off.

"Madam, miss." The maid carried a large, colourful bunch of flowers. "These have just arrived. They're for Miss Winkworth." She handed the bunch to Edith.

"Flowers?" Mother shifted her gaze from the maid to Edith. "From whom?"

"I don't know, madam." The maid curtsied and left.

Edith remained speechless, holding the ridiculously big bouquet. The display of colours brightened the room. There were roses, daffodils, baby breath, tulips, and beautiful, open-mouthed orchids.

"There's a message." Mother snatched the small envelope nestled between two roses.

"Mother, wait."

Mother opened the letter with eager fingers. Her expression of curiosity changed into that of confusion. "They're from Lord Ravenscroft."

Oh, no. Edith held her breath, hoping Perry hadn't written anything compromising in the message.

"I don't understand." Mother scowled at her before reading out loud. *"Dear Edith, I'm sorry for what happened. These flowers carry my apology and my congratulations on your new medical degree. I'm sure you'll have a wonderful career as a doctor. Yours sincerely, Perry."*

Heavens. Edith put the flowers on the table.

Mother lowered the letter. "What is the meaning of this? Why does Lord Ravenscroft believe you're a doctor? And why is he apologising?"

She cleared her throat. "There must be a misunderstanding."

"Obviously. I simply wonder how the misunderstanding started. This is serious, Edith. You can't lie to an earl who is also a family friend."

"Mother, I..." The lie she was about to tell, that she knew nothing about the misunderstanding, died a merciless death on her tongue.

Somehow, her mouth refused to tell yet another lie. It was a first. Perhaps she'd reached her lifetime's share of lies, and from now on, she wouldn't be able to tell a single lie, not even 'I love your parasol; it matches your eyes.'

"Well?" Mother prompted.

She was spared from giving an answer as the maid entered once again.

"Sorry, madam, miss. Miss Daphne Ferguson is here to see Miss Winkworth urgently," the maid said.

Thank goodness. Edith rose. "If you'll excuse me."

"Our conversation isn't over."

She turned towards the maid. "Please put the flowers in a vase. Thank you." She left the dining room in a hurry despite Daphne's visit wasn't exactly happy news.

Daphne was waiting for her in the sitting room, wearing a pristine lemon dress and showing a perfect complexion. She didn't look like a woman who had spent the night drinking champagne, dancing in her undergarments, and doing all sorts of debaucheries. Frustration flamed Edith's chest. Once again, Perry's words about who a real friend was echoed in her ears.

"There you are." Daphne hugged Edith, enveloping her in a cloud of expensive perfume. "I knew you were all right. What happened to you after the pool? You disappeared without a word. Tell me the truth. Did you find a nice gentleman to spend the night with?" She batted her eyelashes.

"Absolutely not." Edith disentangled herself from Daphne's embrace and shut the door. "I couldn't find you, Neville, or Valentine, and my clothes disappeared."

"I took them." Daphne laughed. "Don't look so shocked. It was a joke."

"A joke? I was naked."

"Heavens!" Daphne walked around the room, lifting vases and photograph frames as she went. "What happened to you? Honestly, you've become so boring. You're ruining my morning with your tone. I had such a lovely night in the Scarlet Room, and you're doing nothing but complain. How can you be so selfish?"

Edith didn't know if Daphne had changed and become cruel all of a sudden, or if she'd always been like that, but Edith hadn't noticed it until that moment.

"I wouldn't complain if Valentine hadn't tossed me in the pool, and you encouraged him." She forced her voice down. The last thing she needed was for Mother to hear about the Scarlet Room. "You know how terrified I am of water, and you didn't care."

Daphne scrunched up her face at a porcelain figurine of a shepherdess. "See what I mean? You're complaining again. The pool was shallow. I didn't think it would be a problem for you. Really, you should do something about this infirmity of yours. It ruins everything, and quite honestly, it's embarrassing. I'd be so ashamed of myself if I were you. I'd drown myself in the Thames." She laughed. "Oh, right. You can't get near it!"

"Daphne!"

"Shush. The dive in the pool was meant to be a joke, nothing more, and after all, you're all right."

"I don't understand why you're so mean." Edith paced as the headache pounded harder.

Perry had been right. She could have died in a stupid, shallow pool just because the panic had frozen her. And while Daphne had never been cruel, she certainly was now.

Daphne huffed. "I'm not mean. I'm simply tired of your complaints. You weren't so whiny before Neville's nephew returned."

"I'm not whiny. I'm tired."

Daphne flashed a wicked smile. "Excuses. I know what will make you feel better. Let's go."

Oh, no. Not now. Her mouth soured at the thought of yet another party. "No, I don't think I want to go anywhere. I need some time alone. I need to think."

Edith put a hand on the knob, ready to ask Daphne to leave. Her life needed a change. The night at the Scarlet Room had taught her that. Or rather, Perry had. Although she wouldn't know where to start to change aside from telling Perry the truth. If she didn't do something, the sense of void devouring her would leave only fragments of her soul.

"Don't be difficult. There's something I need to tell you." Daphne hooked her arm through Edith's. "Or rather, Valentine needs to tell you something. A surprise."

Maybe Edith was biased, but there was a mocking note in Daphne's voice.

"Surprises are the last thing I need," Edith said.

"You must come with me to Valentine's atelier."

"No." She removed her arm from Daphne's. "No more. I need to get ready for work."

"It's your free day."

"I want to go to the dispensary anyway."

"Valentine is waiting for you. Something exciting happened, and he expressly asked me not to tell you anything. He wants to tell you himself. I came here to take you to him."

Edith shook her head. "Not this time. Please, go. I need to get changed."

"You whiny—"

"I said please!"

Chin tilted up, Daphne walked out of the room. She paused in the hallway. "Well, I tried. Remember that."

eleven

THE POETS HAD lied to Perry. All of them.

He'd thought that sending a bunch of flowers to Edith with an apology would have brought her to him in a matter of hours. They would hug, apologise to each other, and start over. Instead, she'd sent a nice, polite, and rather impersonal letter to thank him for the flowers and tell him she was sorry too for the way she'd behaved, promising she'd talk to him soon.

That was it. End of.

Maybe she'd thought he'd sounded too annoyed last night. Maybe she hadn't liked how he'd pressed her to talk. They knew each other, but their sudden meeting after five years must have shocked her as well.

Hopefully, the beauty of art would give him an answer. His mother had firmly believed that art was the best source of inspiration and calm in troubled times, and that beauty would save the world.

The beautiful painting of a horse running through a green pasture surely gave him calm. Going to the latest art exhibition at the National Gallery had been Oliver's idea. Naturally. Perry had reluctantly followed, but he had to admit there were some extraordinary paintings worth buying.

"You needn't worry," Oliver said, keeping his voice down, even though the gallery wasn't particularly crowded. "No one is going to talk about your attack in the Scarlet Room. Besides, half of the people in the club were convulsing on their own for one reason or another. Your seizure could have easily been mistaken for the aftershock of a drug."

Perry's concern wasn't about who had witnessed his last seizure, at least not entirely. He didn't want to be branded as an unhinged person, who needed to be locked up in an asylum, but his situation with Edith concerned him more than anything else.

Although her resilience was proof of her inner strength. Damn, he loved her strength so much; it gave him strength as well.

"I'm not worried," he said, tilting his head to admire a dramatic depiction of the sea. "Well, a bit. But I haven't had seizures in almost a year. Why now? The cause can't be strong emotions. When Albert announced he was leaving for Brazil, I was utterly shocked. Yet no seizure."

"If only I could understand what triggers your attacks." Oliver scribbled on his inseparable notepad. "It's not anger. You're angry all the time."

"I'm not." He moved on to the next painting, a floral composition with delicate colours he approved of. "I get angry only when you tell me I'm angry."

"See, there are people who have suffered from seizures since childhood. They're born that way. Your seizures are the result of a head trauma. The key is to find what triggers them. It has to be an emotion, an event, or maybe a particular combination of different types of food. Or something else." Oliver went through the pages of his notepad. "Do you remember I told you about that young, promising doctor of medicine I met in Vienna during a conference?"

Perry shrugged, moving on to the next painting—a still life. "Not really."

Oliver released a long breath. "Do you ever pay attention to what I say?"

"Reach your point."

"I'm talking about Dr. Sigmund Freud. Does the name ring a bell?"

Perry arched his brow. "I'm aFreud not."

"Ha-ha. Yes, funny. Mock me." Oliver shot his gaze skywards. "Mock the work I do for you."

"I very much appreciate everything you do for me, and I believe I show my appreciation with the generous salary you receive from me."

Oliver waved a dismissive hand. "Talking about money is vulgar."

"You didn't think that when we discussed your salary. I remember you being very vocal about how much you wanted a raise."

"Anyway, Dr. Freud has some fascinating theories about the human brain and about how people can overcome traumas with time and mental exercises. He also thinks that traumas change the way we make decisions deeply and affect our soul or psyche."

Perry paused, intrigued by the theory. "What about Edith? Obviously, the *Princess Alice* incident changed the way she behaved."

"I'll be honest with you. I think you're overreacting. She's simply a young woman, wanting to try new things. She graduated recently after years of hard work. Now she wants a moment of freedom before she starts a demanding job in a hospital wing."

"Maybe you're right. It's that she didn't seem unfamiliar with excess and wildness."

Oliver shook his head. "Trust me. Once she starts working, she won't have time for extravagances. Of course, the incident changed her, but she's a doctor now. As a doctor, her life is going to be too busy for nonsense like the Scarlet Room."

"You're a doctor, and your life isn't busy enough if you have time for the Scarlet Room."

Oliver narrowed his gaze. "The excursion was part of *your* therapy. Purely scientific interest."

Perry stepped aside when a lady strode past him in a great hurry to reach the exit. He followed her with his gaze. He could swear she was Marianne, Edith's sister, or rather, she was Lady Lancaster now. The two sisters were nearly identical.

"Lady Lancaster," he said.

The woman and her maid came to a stop. Yes, it was Edith's sister, wrapped in fine velvet and silk. Her large eyes grew larger when she saw him.

"Lord Ravenscroft." She bowed her head.

The maid curtsied.

"I'm happy to see you again, my lady, and to offer my congratulations on your marriage with Viscount Lancaster."

"Thank you. I'm happy to see you as well, Ravenscroft." She twisted her reticule.

"Lady Lancaster, this is my friend, Dr. Oliver York," Perry said.

Oliver bowed. "My lady."

She gave him a nervous nod before turning to Perry. "Ravenscroft, I hope your health is..." Whatever she meant to say was cut short by her muffled sob. She blinked, clearly making an effort not to make a scene.

"My lady, is something the matter?" he asked in a low tone.

"I must apologise." Her voice broke. "But I need to leave in a hurry. It's an urgent matter. I promise I'll send an invitation for tea soon, so we'll have the chance to talk properly, but I can't stay now."

"By all means. Can I help?"

She shook her head, wiping her tears with a handkerchief.

"I wish you all the best." Perry had barely time to bow before she gave a quick nod and hurried away.

"What an odd encounter," Oliver said. "She must have received bad news."

"In a gallery?"

Perry resumed his stroll until he arrived at the end of the hall where a rope barrier blocked the path.

A uniformed attendant stood in front of a closed curtain behind the rope stand. "Do you gentlemen wish to visit the exclusive collection in this section of the gallery?"

Perry wasn't sure. Lady Lancaster's behaviour worried him. Perhaps he should find Edith and ask her if he could help.

"It depends. What's in there?" Oliver asked.

"Some of the paintings behind this curtain might offend your sensibilities," the attendant said. "Also, the entrance requires a one-pound fee."

Offend his sensibilities. Perry took it as a challenge. His sensibilities were quite low, as Edith had pointed out years ago.

"I'm curious. I wish to see the collection." He handed the man two pounds.

The attendant unhooked the rope barrier and held the curtain open for them. "I shall remind you that, should you wish to buy any piece, you need to take note of the lot number or title before claiming it at the reception area and place your order as soon as possible."

"Thank you." Not that Perry meant to buy anything. Albert had a passion for paintings, but Perry wasn't obsessed with them.

"Goodness." Oliver turned the colour of strawberries as they stood in front of a nude painting.

The woman in the painting wore only a flimsy tunic that played over her curves as if disturbed by a gust of wind. Excellent technique. Even Perry could see that. The painting had been sold for one hundred and fifty pounds. Absurd.

"Why are you blushing?" Perry asked. "You're a physician. You should be used to seeing the human body."

"Not like this." Oliver patted his forehead with a handkerchief.

"You were in the Scarlet Room with me," he whispered. "There were naked people everywhere."

"That was different." Oliver averted his gaze from the painting. "Those people got naked because they were in their cups, and if you wanted to watch them, it was your choice, but they didn't explicitly ask to be looked at. This painted lady is here because she *wants* you to look at her, but I don't want to."

Perry frowned. "That's the most twisted thought I've ever heard, and it doesn't make sense. Also, the lady is a goddess, Artemis, which explains the moon and the lack of clothes. A goddess doesn't wear clothes and doesn't care if you stare at her."

"Now, that doesn't make sense."

The next painting depicted another Greek goddess, Hera. Sold as well. She sat naked on a throne, wearing nothing but a tiara of sorts and holding a sceptre. A fan made of peacock feathers opened behind her.

Perry craned his neck to read the name of the artist. Mr. Valentine Carter. The man had talent, as far as Perry could tell. Talent and an obsession with Greek goddesses. The models were stunning as well.

"Mr. Carter is going to make a fortune today."

"Hardly." Oliver kept his gaze low. "I heard he's up to his neck in debt. Gambling, apparently. He owes money to the coal magnate, Sir Andrew Ferguson as well. He'll be lucky to get a penny after he pays his creditors."

"Pity. He's a great artist." Perry admired Artemis one last time before moving on.

"Oh, goodness." Oliver lowered his gaze again when it was Aphrodite's turn. "I can't, for the love of me."

Hmm. Yes, Perry had to admit that Aphrodite was rather bold. She stared directly at him with eyes hooded by pleasure, daring him to say she couldn't enjoy herself. Oliver kept his head down, conceding Aphrodite her victory. Needless to say, the goddess of love and beauty had been sold as well for five hundred pounds. These paintings wouldn't be there in a matter of hours.

"Let's move on," Oliver whispered.

The next painting was—all the breath was punched out of Perry's lungs.

He blinked a couple of times to clear his vision. The words 'not possible' echoed in his mind. The goddess Astrea stood with her arms spread against the backdrop of a dark-blue night sky. Only silver starlight dressed her. Her strawberry-blonde hair formed a halo around her in stark contrast with the night sky. Her forest-green eyes held both shyness and boldness—a combination that made her absolutely stunning. Her curves were one enticing swell after the other. He could spend the whole day tracing them with a finger or his gaze. She looked so real he felt he would touch her if he reached out.

"Tup me blind," he whispered.

"I'd rather not." Oliver stared at the tips of his shoes.

"Look." Perry shook his arm. "You must see this."

"I'm not sure I'm made for this sort of art. I'd rather stare at still life paintings."

"Oliver, please, just take a look at this. I need your opinion."

Scoffing, Oliver raised his head. "Ah! It's... Dr. Wink—" he hissed before lowering his gaze again.

"As I thought. It's her. Unequivocally." Perry ran a hand through his hair.

If he and Oliver had recognised her, anyone could. Hell, her reputation would be ruined forever. She would be mocked and shunned. Her family would suffer, too.

Now Lady Lancaster's hurry acquired a new meaning. She'd been terrified of someone seeing the painting. In fact, Lady Lancaster could be easily mistaken for Astrea. A disaster. Not that he'd care what a lady chose to do with her body, but he didn't make the rules. Edith and her sister would be ruined, scorned, and ridiculed. Edith would lose her job as a doctor. She would never find employment.

The price tag read the offers for the painting started at three hundred pounds. Not cheap, but he didn't have a choice. He couldn't leave her painting there where everyone could buy it.

He nudged Oliver. "Take note of the lot and title. I'm going to buy this damn painting."

twelve

EDITH TRIED TO concentrate on the list of drugs that needed a fresh supply. The dispensary in St. Brigid Hospital had tall, oppressive shelves, dark walls, and only one window. Not exactly cheerful.

Adding to the list the quinine, she couldn't even write without being tormented by her thoughts. She should see Perry. Absolutely.

The message she'd sent to him didn't convey what she wanted to tell him, starting with the whole truth. He'd encouraged her through the years of her fake studies. He ought to know his admiration for her was misplaced. Yes, she'd go right now. No more excuses. If she really wanted to change her life, she had to start with Perry.

As difficult as it was, it was the only way to turn a new page in her life.

She put the list down and untied her apron. Everyone said that Condy's fluid was odourless, but she could swear to catch a pungent whiff of the purple-coloured disinfectant when she left the dispensary. The white walls and bright light in the hallway caused her to blink after the darkness of the dispensary.

"You need to focus!" The angry voice of a nurse came from one of the patients' rooms.

She paused to peek inside. A nurse was sitting next to the bed of Mrs. Richards, a woman who had suffered a head trauma similar to Perry's.

"Oh, enough for today." The nurse scraped her chair back and left a bowl of soup on the nightstand. "I have work to do."

"Is something the matter?" Edith glanced at Mrs. Richards's pale and tense face.

The nurse wiped a large stain of pea soup from her apron. "It's taking me too long to help Mrs. Richards eat her lunch, and she isn't cooperating. I have my round to finish." She strode out of the room, muttering.

While Edith appreciated the nurses' hard work, every patient needed proper attention and care; that was what her father had taught her.

You must be quick in the operating room to save a life, but outside of it, everyone needs time, respect, and patience.

Edith sat on the chair the nurse had vacated and took the bowl. "May I?"

Mrs. Richards gave a jerky nod.

Holding the bowl with one hand, Edith helped Mrs. Richards take a spoonful. Mrs. Richards's arm shook, sending drops of soup on the bedsheet. Her eyes reddened with tears.

"A friend of mine suffered from your same condition," Edith said, taking another spoonful. "It took him time and patience, but now he can do everything." She helped the woman again. "The trick is to take as many pauses as you need." She stopped Mrs. Richards's hand. "Move again when you're ready."

Pausing and starting again, Mrs. Richards managed to swallow the spoonful without spilling the soup.

Edith squeezed the woman's hand. "Excellent. Try again."

An hour later, the stained bedsheet showed Mrs. Richards's effort, but the bowl was empty.

"Thank you," Mrs. Richards stammered but not as seriously as Perry had used to. She blinked fresh tears, and emotion tightened Edith's throat. "It's difficult."

"It is."

Mrs. Richards sighed. "I must get b-better. My husband isn't earning enough. I don't know how we can... the children..." The rest of the sentence was incomprehensible so much she stammered.

But Edith could guess what the woman meant to say. She hugged Mrs. Richards, worried about the woman's future. Perry's condition had taken years to improve, but he could afford the best specialists and a Swiss clinic. Mrs. Richards was a tailor's wife and a seamstress herself, but she wouldn't be able to work for a while.

"...children have not enough food," Mrs. Richards said. "We have debts."

The two sovereigns Valentine had given Edith were still in her pocket. She'd meant to give them to Marianne to repay one of the many loans Edith had enjoyed, but she'd changed her mind.

She handed the two gold coins to Mrs. Richards. "I don't mean to offend you, but please, accept these."

Mrs. Richards shook her head. "C-can't pay back."

"It doesn't matter." She put the coins in Mrs. Richards's palm and closed her hand. "Do it for me."

"Thank you," Mrs. Richards's voice cracked.

After Edith changed the dirty bedsheet, she sat on a bench in the corridor, wondering how she could help Mrs. Richards. For now, she ought to talk to Perry. A flurry of dark-red velvet distracted her.

Marianne marched towards her, her lips pressing in a grim line. "Come with me for a walk."

"Actually, I was—"

"Now!" Marianne said before striding towards the exit.

Edith jolted. Marianne shouting an order was a first. In a hurry, she retrieved her coat from the anteroom and put it on.

Marianne and her maid waited for her outside the hospital.

Since Marianne had become a viscountess, talking to her alone was impossible. Her lady's maid followed her like a shadow, often glancing at Edith with a disapproving stare.

"Here I am," Edith said.

"To the park where no one can hear us." Marianne headed to the small park in front of the hospital with the determination of a general going to battle.

"What is it?" Edith asked once they stepped into the park.

Marianne turned to her maid. "I need a moment alone with my sister." After the maid moved away, Marianne said, "I really don't know what you were thinking." She sounded like their mother.

Edith was at a loss. There were many things she'd done without thinking. She was spoiled for choice. "What do you mean?"

"I saw it."

"Saw what? What are you talking about?"

"The painting."

A moment of utter shock caught Edith. The whole world seemed to have gone silent and still. Aside from a distant buzzing in her ears, she didn't hear anything. What Marianne said couldn't be possible.

"I…"

"I knew it." Marianne took a few deep breaths, but she didn't look calmer. "It's you in that painting. At first I thought, I hoped I was mistaken, but your reaction dispels any doubts. Goodness, Edith. What were you thinking?"

Panic left a pungent taste in her mouth. That was it, the moment when all the lies she'd spun for years came crashing down on her.

"It's not…where did you see it?"

"The National Gallery, by chance. I was curious to see the paintings in the restricted section, thinking they were about protestors or other political matters. Never mind. The point is that there were many similar paintings, all by Mr. Carter, and *yours* stood out. The Star Maiden."

Edith's pulse slammed in her veins. "Mr. Carter said he wouldn't sell it, wouldn't show it to anyone. He promised."

"Well, he lied. But there's more. After I saw the painting, I left the gallery to talk to Thomas. I wanted to buy the painting before someone else did. But when I returned, it was gone."

"Heavens." So much for overcoming her fears. So much for starting over. She'd made a mess, and no, she couldn't blame Valentine or Daphne. She didn't need help to destroy her life. "What can I do? Marianne, I swear. I had no intention of putting you in trouble."

"You always say that, don't you?" Marianne pointed a finger at her. "You do whatever you want without thinking of the consequences."

"I was told the painting wasn't to be exposed."

Marianne ignored her. "We must find out who bought it. Do you realise what will happen if people recognise you? I might be mistaken for you, for goodness' sake. Thomas would be furious. Why did you do it?"

"It was because..." The reasons she'd agreed to pose seemed rather shallow now.

"You silly girl." Tears glistened in Marianne's eyes. "Mother is worried about you. She told me you've lost appetite, and some days you don't leave the bed. Father barely talks to you. And all this for what? Your personal enjoyment."

Edith lowered her gaze. Dozens of thoughts twirled in her mind. None of them pleasant. For someone who chased only enjoyment, she wasn't happy at all.

"The situation is serious." Marianne took Edith's hand. "Your behaviour reflects badly on all of us. I knew that sooner or later, you'd start a scandal."

"There must be something I can do."

"Edith." Marianne's tone became sharper. "Think about

Father. Even his reputation would suffer, and what will you and Mother do when his patients don't want to see him because his daughter posed naked for an artist?"

"I'll do everything to prevent a scandal." She sounded scared to her own ears, but she wanted to reassure Marianne a little. Surely, something could be done to avoid a catastrophe. "Listen, I'll go to the gallery and find out who bought the painting. Then I'll convince the buyer to give the painting to me or...something else. I'll work to get the painting from the buyer. I'll do anything to get it back. I promise."

"I'll come with you." Marianne patted her pocket. "I have enough money to bribe the whole lot of attendants at the gallery."

EDITH HAD TO ADMIT THAT, without Marianne, she would have had a hard time dealing with the staff at the gallery. The attendant was adamant about the fact a client's privacy was paramount. The gallery would never, ever, under any conditions, reveal a client's name. He threatened to send for the police if Edith insisted.

Marianne kept talking though. "You must understand. We're two ladies in need of assistance, and you aren't behaving in a very chivalrous fashion."

The attendant was flustered. "My lady, you must understand. I have my orders, and our clients are exclusive ones."

"This is a matter of life or death," Edith said. "Do you want someone's death on your conscience? You must believe us when we say it's of utmost importance that we find the person who bought the painting."

The man fiddled with his collar. "Please, my ladies, my job is at risk."

"We won't tell anyone you helped us." Marianne handed him a few banknotes.

Dash it. Edith would need to repay her sister, not only for today's bribe. "Please," she said.

The attendant gazed around before pocketing the money. "I'll leave the register open and unattended on the counter for a few minutes. If you take a peek at the list of buyers in the left column, it won't be my doing."

The moment he stepped away from the counter, Edith grabbed the register. The titles of the paintings were in alphabetical order. Astrea... Astrea... there she was. Sold for five hundred pounds and bought by...

"Oh no." Edith grabbed the counter for support.

Earl of Ravenscroft. Not him. Anyone but him.

Marianne read the column as well. "That's good news," she said. "He's a good friend, isn't he? You'll have only to ask him to have the painting back, or even better, to destroy it. Goodness, I'm so relieved."

No, Edith wasn't.

thirteen

NOT EVEN A day had passed since Perry had bought the Star Maiden, but he was already infatuated with the painting. More than infatuated. Obsessed. Which surprised him.

He'd purchased it only to protect Edith's honour, but now that the Star Maiden hung on the wall of his personal parlour, he found himself charmed by it, utterly mesmerised.

Mr. Valentine Carter was a true artist. His strokes could be both light and strong, depending on the effect he wanted to achieve. He brought out Edith's delicate beauty and caught the perfect shade of her forest-green eyes. Impressive. The more Perry looked at Astrea, the more it seemed she swayed her hips and smiled in a coquettish manner.

Of course, the fact Mr. Carter had seen Edith in that ridiculously transparent gown, tunic, or whatever the flimsy thing was didn't escape his notice.

He wasn't sure how he felt about that. Annoyed, perhaps. Envious, for sure.

The painting belonged to him, and only he would enjoy it. A set of curtains would protect it from prying eyes when he wasn't in the room. He'd instructed his servants not to peek under the curtains under the pain of being dismissed from his service.

Edith herself was a work of art as a woman. Her lines were delicate and stunning at the same time. The flare of her hips seemed so real he believed he could touch it, feel the warmth of her skin, or smell her fresh scent.

An urgent knock distracted him. "My lord."

He tugged at the rope and covered the painting. "Come in."

"My lord." The butler pushed the door open and bowed. "Lady Lancaster and her sister, Miss Winkworth, are here to see you. They said it's urgent."

"I'll receive them in the sitting room, thank you." He could bet the sudden, unannounced visit had to do with the Star Maiden.

He found the two sisters pacing in the sitting room. Lady Lancaster paced clockwise. Edith paced anti-clockwise. That surely revealed something about the two sisters, but he wouldn't guess what.

"Lady Lancaster, Edith."

"Ravenscroft." Lady Lancaster bowed her head. "Apologies for the intrusion."

Edith greeted him, too, but her gesture was less deep and more guarded than her sister's.

"Thank you for seeing us, even if we didn't send a card." Lady Lancaster tormented her hands while Edith pressed her lips in a hard line.

He gestured at the armchairs. "Please, take a seat and tell me what the matter is."

Lady Lancaster perched on the edge of the sofa. Edith sat next to her with her hands folded on her lap.

"We won't take too much of your time, so we'll go straight to the point." Lady Lancaster nudged Edith with her elbow.

Edith cleared her throat, her gaze on her hands. "We're aware of the fact you came into possession of a certain painting." She finally gazed up at him. "I'm sure you know what I'm referring to."

Oh, he knew very well. "The last time we met, we had a conversation. I'm sure you know what I'm referring to."

Lady Lancaster shifted her gaze from Edith to Perry. "The last time? What is His Lordship talking about?"

Edith ignored her. "This is different. That painting shouldn't have been sold. Mr. Carter is a friend of mine. He promised me the painting wouldn't leave his atelier. That was the deal we made for me to agree to pose."

He propped his elbow on the mantelpiece. "I'm sorry to hear that one of your friends lied to you. But yes, I purchased the painting from the gallery."

"I mean to buy the painting," Lady Lancaster said. "Whatever you paid for it, I'll give you that sum and more. Edith and I are ready to do anything to avoid a scandal."

"And I'll repay you, Marianne," Edith said with determination. "Not just for today, but for all the times you helped me. I swear it."

"All the times? What does that mean?" he asked no one in particular.

Edith stared at him as if begging him not to say more.

Lady Lancaster sniffled. "Edith is a very energetic young woman who is going through a difficult moment, and there were times when she went astray."

"Went astray," he said under his breath.

Edith sank her teeth into her bottom lip. The two sisters stared at each other as the air charged with tension.

"I have to say the painting is stunning," he said. "Mr. Carter is a great artist but a gambler. Rumour has it, he had to sell his goddesses to pay his creditors. Anyway, I bought the Star Maiden because I was worried about Edith's reputation."

Edith blushed. "Thank you."

"What a relief." Lady Lancaster exhaled.

"Besides, now that Edith is a doctor of medicine, she ought to be careful about how she spends her free time," Perry said, "and about the company she keeps."

Lady Lancaster angled towards her sister. "I don't understand. A doctor?"

Edith grimaced. She tried to speak a couple of times, but not a word came out.

"What is it?" he asked.

Lady Lancaster nudged Edith again. "Please. Explain."

Edith took a deep breath. "Perry, what I tried to tell you without success the other night is that I'm not a doctor. I never went to medical school. I lied in my letters." Each word came out with effort as if she forced herself. "I lied to you."

Perry took a moment to understand what she said. "You didn't go to the London School of Medicine for Women?"

Lady Lancaster's eyes widened. "Heavens."

Edith shook her head, her facial muscles tensing.

A moment of thick silence stretched as Perry mulled over her confession . She wasn't a doctor.

He didn't understand. "Why lie?"

"Because I didn't want you to think I was a failure," she said.

"Oh, Edith." Lady Lancaster pressed a finger to her temple.

"And lying was a better option?" He couldn't believe it. All that time, he'd admired Edith for her strength and resilience in studying for years, and it was all a lie.

"I'm sorry. Lying in a letter was all too easy. It was like writing my personal diary and writing about my dreams. It felt so liberating to put my dreams on paper." Her words came out softly, but the truth in them roared. "I know it doesn't make sense to you, but writing those letters made me feel better, and once I started lying, I couldn't stop. One lie pulled forth another, and the dream was too beautiful. The more time passed, the harder it was to tell the truth." She spoke faster now, the words tripping over each other. "At least there was someone, you, who didn't think I was a disappointment. But studying was too hard for me after the accident. I couldn't focus. I couldn't breathe when I picked up a book. Thinking about memorising names and facts was too overwhelming for me. It was a curse. The books I so adored were now my enemies. The harder I tried to study, the harder I wanted to run away." She swallowed hard, taking deep breaths.

"I had no idea." Lady Lancaster shook her head.

He ran a hand over his face. A combination of opposing feelings battled inside him. There was frustration, disbelief, and a healthy dose of sorrow for her. Edith's lies, combined with her behaviour in the Scarlet Room and the painting, displayed a rather worrying situation.

He handed her his handkerchief. "Here."

She didn't gaze up when she took it. "When I wrote those letters, I felt different as if I were someone who mattered."

"You do matter," he said, his heart aching for her. "A lot."

"I had no idea you still dreamed of becoming a doctor. If you want to study, why don't you start again?" Lady Lancaster said.

"It's too late." Edith wiped her face. "I'm not sure I can start studying again."

"It's not too late," Perry said.

"I'm sorry. I know I have no excuses." Shaking, she straightened. "I lost control of my lies and of my life."

Bloody hell. He needed to think about the revelation. He hated to admit he was deeply disappointed and felt like a fool.

The fire crackling in the hearth was the only sound for a few intense minutes.

"I'll make amends," she said with a determination that reminded him of the Edith he knew.

"I won't show the painting to anyone," he said.

"I know. I trust you. But I ought to take my responsibilities, and I'll start immediately." She bowed her head. "Thank you for your kindness, Perry. Marianne, shall we leave now? Please?"

"Of course. Thank you, Ravenscroft." Lady Lancaster seemed on the verge of bursting out crying as well. "At least we know the painting is safe with you."

He wished Edith's heart was safe from breaking.

fourteen

EDITH HAD MADE a few mistakes—many mistakes—
and it was time to pay for them, both materially and spiritually. She wanted to reimburse Perry for buying the Star Maiden, no matter what he said, and she wouldn't allow Marianne to buy the painting. Also, she ought to apologise to Perry again and have a private conversation with him.

But first, she needed a word with Valentine. So even though she wanted nothing more than to see Perry again and lay all her lies out, she went to Bloomsbury.

Loud voices and laughter came from the other side of the door to Valentine's flat. She knocked hard to be heard over the noise.

Valentine himself opened the door. "Dear Edith. What a pleasure. Please do come in." He held the door open for her, shouting over his shoulder, "Beautiful Astrea is here."

The cheek of him.

Daphne, Neville, and other people Edith didn't know crammed into the sitting room. An empty bottle of wine lay in a corner, along with discarded jackets, ties, and ladies' capelets. Plates with half-eaten sandwiches were scattered around. She twitched her nose at the smell of tobacco.

"Edith." Daphne rushed to hug her. "So you changed your mind and came here."

She removed Daphne's arms from herself. "I'm not here to stay."

Neville raked a long gaze over her, but it didn't seem to show appreciation.

"Everyone." Valentine filled a glass of wine and raised it. "Please, join me in a toast for Edith's beauty and the outrageous amount of money I made."

"Valentine, I need to talk to you." Before he could answer, she grabbed his arm and dragged him to the next room.

"What is it, my dear?" He polished off his glass with one tilt of his head. "Listen, if it's about the swimming pool, I'm sorry. I had no idea you hated swimming pools. Daphne said you'd be fine."

"You promised me you wouldn't sell my painting." Anger rose to the fore. She shook with it. "I demand you give me the money you made out of it." So she could pay Perry and take the darn painting, even though he didn't want her money.

Valentine turned serious. "Oh, that. I'm sorry, but I thought you knew. Daphne was supposed to tell you before the sale."

She let out an unladylike curse. "No, Daphne didn't tell me anything."

"I had a huge debt I needed to settle rather urgently. If I hadn't, I'd be in serious trouble."

"You broke our deal."

He ran a hand through his hair. "Try to understand. There were people who would have hurt me if I hadn't paid. I owed a large sum to Daphne's father, and he isn't a man you want to upset. Selling the goddesses was Daphne's idea actually."

Edith hitched a breath.

Valentine glanced at the door. "I told her the goddesses' series wasn't for sale, and it wasn't complete, anyway. I needed one more model for Astrea. Professional models aren't easy to find, and they're expensive. Daphne said she would find a model."

"She convinced me to pose, and I was cheap and foolish. You knew you were going to sell the Star Maiden before you started painting it, but you lied on my face. And you never wanted to paint me specifically. You merely needed a sacrificial lamb."

"Oh, no." He put a hand on her shoulder. "When I saw you, I understood immediately you would be perfect. If I hadn't liked you, I wouldn't have painted you."

"Wonderful. Really. I feel so much better now."

"I'm sorry for the deceit, but Daphne is like her father. You don't want to go against her."

She rubbed the aching spot between her eyebrows. "So you don't have any money now, I gather."

"Thirty pounds."

"Good gracious."

"I needed the whole set of goddesses before selling the paintings because all the goddesses together make an impression, and that raises the price, and I was right. Those paintings were a success. Your painting made hundreds of pounds. Will you pose for me again?"

The question shocked her. "Absolutely no. Never."

"I hope you'll change your mind."

She didn't need to hear more. She tried to leave the room, but Daphne and Neville blocked her path.

"What's the matter?" Daphne asked.

"Edith is upset because I sold her painting," Valentine said.

"I tried to warn you," Daphne said. "But you didn't let me talk."

A sudden fatigue caught Edith off guard. "You lied to me. You and Valentine meant to sell my painting from the beginning."

"Don't be sad, Edith." Neville caressed her cheek, and she recoiled away from him. "Sadness doesn't suit you. I would've bought your painting hadn't I woken up late the day of the exhibition. It's so difficult to be up and about before eleven."

"You're famous now. Aren't you happy?" Daphne asked.

"Ask me that again after I've slapped you." Edith sidestepped Daphne, but Neville coiled an arm around her waist and stopped her again.

"Not so fast, Star Maiden." He inched closer to her ear. "Who's the lucky bastard who has your nude painting? And don't think I forgot about our deal."

She removed his arm from her waist. "What deal?"

Daphne gave her a pointed look. "What do you mean? The dare we all agreed upon at the Scarlet Room."

"I didn't agree to do anything." Although she'd been in her cups, and she didn't remember everything about that night.

Valentine raised his eyebrows. "Yes, you did. We heard it and saw it."

"Whatever this matter is, I have a more urgent one." She tried again to leave the room, but Neville blocked her.

"Not yet. We need to talk." He held the door open. "I need a word with Edith. Alone."

"I'm in a hurry," she said.

"It won't take long."

The others filed out in silence. When he shut the door, the chatter from the sitting room died. "It's Perry, isn't it?"

"I don't know what you mean."

He leant against the door, effectively trapping her. "He has your painting, doesn't he?"

She folded her arms over her chest, waiting for the moment he moved away from the door.

"Perry isn't the good man you think he is. He's a spoiled, entitled brat."

She scoffed, outraged.

"When he was younger, it didn't matter what atrocious act he did, his parents always forgave him. They found his irreverent manners charming, his lack of respect for others a sign of strength. They scolded him, yes, but never too seriously because he was precious Perry."

"Let me go." She didn't understand what this family's story had to do with her.

He didn't let her reach the handle, taking her wrist. "Albert did everything by the book. The golden boy of the family. He never broke a rule. I used to be like him until he defended Perry when he charmed my intended, and she broke the engagement with me. He did it to spite me, to prove he could charm any woman. *I'm so charming, every woman does what I say*, he told me."

Those were exactly the same words Perry had used years ago to describe himself. Perhaps he'd been wild when he was younger, but he would never be cruel.

She wriggled her arm free; getting free from Neville's hands was becoming a habit. "I don't care about your quarrel with Perry. It's a matter between you two."

"He's doing it again. Now he's turning you against me."

"That's nonsense." She hadn't liked Neville well before Perry had returned.

"It's not if you think you can refuse to give me what's mine. I won the card game. We had a bet. You owe me a tumble." A hard glint shone in his eyes.

She shook her head. "I didn't agree—"

He took her by the shoulders, none too gently. "Not at first, but after the champagne, you did."

It could be. Her memories of that night were confused. She took advantage of the fact that he'd moved from the door to make a dash for it. She slipped out of his grip and flung the door open. Breathing hard, she crossed the room towards the front door.

"Edith!" Daphne started to follow her. "What happened?"

She strode out of the flat and rushed down the stairs. Her pulse spiked. The bet was nonsense. Did he really expect her to have a tumble with him only because she'd lost a stupid card game while she'd been drunk? Well, good luck with that. She had more pressing matters to deal with.

She sped up along the pavement, fuelled by her frustration, to catch an omnibus to Belgravia. By the time it drove close to Belgrave Square, her breathing was normal again.

She didn't have the money to pay back Perry. Knowing him, he wouldn't want a penny, but that wasn't the point. Paying for the painting was the first step towards owning back her life.

A bitter taste pitched up her throat as she climbed the short flight of stairs to his glossy black front door. A hint of fear, worry, and shame jumbled up together. But it was a necessary combination of feelings.

She rang the bell and waited, changing her mind a dozen times. Perhaps she should wear something else before talking to Perry, or write down what she meant to say, or she should stop being a coward.

"Madam?" The butler jolted her.

"Good afternoon. I wish to see His Lordship if he's receiving visitors."

The butler held the door for her, but his puzzled expression held disapproval. That was the second time that Edith had come unannounced to see Perry.

"Please wait here." The butler left her in the entry hall. Bad sign? Perry might order him to kick her out.

She remained still, watching the comings and goings of the maids and footmen as they worked through the house.

"Where's my stethoscope?" Dr. York said to no one in particular, coming out of a room. "I can't find anything in this—ah!" He skidded to a stop upon seeing her, his glasses askew on his nose.

"Dr. York." She gave him a quick nod. "Afternoon."

He straightened his glasses, removed them, and put them back on again. "Miss Star... I mean Winkworth. I shall..." He flushed.

Oh, goodness. Edith sighed. He must have seen the Star Maiden.

"See, I'm searching for my telescope. No, what am I saying? I'm not an astronomer, but I was thinking about the... silly me. Ha-ha. Look at the time! Well, it was nice chatting with you." He bowed and turned around in a hurry, only to hit the wall face first with a loud smack. A small painting hanging on the wall shook from the impact.

Edith cringed in sympathy as a phantom pain hurt her nose. "Are you all right, sir?"

"Yes, yes. Good day." Without looking at her, he disappeared into a room.

Poor man. The Star Maiden must have shocked him.

She craned her neck to see if he came out again, but Perry thudding down the stairs distracted her.

"Edith." He too came to an abrupt halt at the bottom of the stairs.

His sapphire eyes filled with surprise intimidated her; they lacked the usual sparkle.

"I'm sorry to trouble you, but I wondered if we could talk," she said when he didn't speak.

"Of course." He went to the parlour on the ground floor. "I was thinking about you."

Yes, she could easily believe that.

"Tea?" He put a hand on the knob. "I'll ask Mason to bring a repast."

"No, thank you." A cold sensation set on the bottom of her stomach. "I..."

"Please take a seat."

She did as told gladly because her legs quivered. "I'm really sorry to have lied to you." She had to let those words out as soon as possible.

He sat in front of her, staring at her intently. "I'm sorry, too. I thought we were good friends and that you knew you could tell me anything."

Oh, that hurt. But she understood him. "I didn't want to disappoint you, but I realise I disappointed you more by lying. It's that once I started lying, I couldn't stop. It became an escape of sorts if it makes sense."

"So what did you do in the past years?"

There was no reproach in his voice, only sadness, which pained her more.

"At first, I tried to get back to studying, but it didn't have the same meaning. I wondered what kind of experiences I had missed while I was reading and studying. If I'd died that day in the Thames, my whole life would have been about studying and nothing else. The answer scared me because aside from my books, I didn't have anything. No friends, no hobbies, no experiences. I thought of what you told me about enjoying life more. The near-death experience pushed me to try something new, and my life became worse from that moment on. I lost control of my life. It was so controlled before the incident, and it became the opposite afterwards. I didn't want you to think of me as a silly, shallow girl." She exhaled to take a breather. "I volunteer at St. Brigid Hospital in the dispensary, but aside from that, I don't deal with medical science anymore."

The whole speech sounded absurd to her own ears. Mostly, it sounded incredible that half a decade had passed between a party and a day in the dispensary.

She shivered when he gently took her hands and sat next to her on the sofa. For some silly reason, his concern for her sliced her chest open, and pain poured through the cracks.

A cold shiver slithered through her, leaving a trail of goose-bumps over her skin. In the past years, she'd never cried. After the incident, she'd shed her share of tears.

But that day, sitting next to Perry and his compassion, the dam holding her tears back broke. A tear slid down her cheek. She bit down a sob because she didn't want to fall to pieces.

"What about your parents?" he asked in a gentle tone.

"My father barely talks to me. He hates that I stopped studying. My mother tries to convince me to return to study or get married, but her disappointment is obvious. Marianne...I fear she might hate me."

"No, your sister and your parents love you." He rubbed her knuckles with his thumb. "You aren't happy. That's the problem."

"No, I'm not. The parties and excesses give me a glimpse of happiness that lasts a second. Then I'm empty of emotions, as if I didn't care about anything. A wraith until the whole circle starts again. And then there's the darn painting."

"Edith." He touched her cheek gently. "What is it? What do you want?"

"I don't know," she whispered in a cracking voice. "I don't know anymore. Even when I get something I want, satisfaction eludes me, and I start chasing a new thrill, an exciting new thing. It's exhausting."

"You know I won't let anyone see the Star Maiden. Hell, I'll destroy it if you want me to." He drew soothing circles over the back of her hand.

"Too many times people have had to repair the damage I've caused. No, I want to pay for the painting."

"There's no need for that. I don't want your money."

"I want to do it. It's only right. Somehow, some way, I'll find the money to buy the painting from you."

Perry reclined on the sofa. "I have a proposition. You'll work for me for the next six months. After that period, you can consider me reimbursed for the purchase of the painting. No money required. Then we'll discuss what you want to do with the Star Maiden."

"Work for you? Doing what?"

He stared into her eyes as if he wanted to see her soul. "We'll find something."

"I'm not good at anything."

"That's not true, and your skills are the least of your problems. But I have to tell you, I love the Star Maiden."

She tasted the saltiness of her desperation on her lips. "Do you really like the painting?" She had no idea why that comment intrigued her.

He looked surprised. "Of course I do. It's exquisite. Mr. Carter has talent, and you're stunning. I'd like to keep it, so it's not for sale. But if you work for me, I'll consider myself reimbursed."

"All right." She smiled, maybe for the first time in years. "I agree to work for you."

"Fantastic." He squeezed her hand. "You'll start tomorrow morning. Nine o'clock. Don't be late."

fifteen

IN A FEW minutes, Edith would be in Perry's study, and he couldn't stay still.

Sitting at his desk, he struggled to understand the letter in front of him. Some days, when a headache throbbed, reading and concentrating were difficult. The words were clear, but he didn't understand them. Or perhaps he was simply too nervous that morning.

He wasn't going to lie. Learning she'd lied to him had been a strong blow. For all those years, knowing she'd studied hard to achieve her goal had been a source of pride and inspiration. Also, her studies had been her excuse not to visit him in Geneva, and he'd never griped about that. Building a career as a doctor was a difficult task—that was what he'd thought.

But now, all her lies hurt. At the same time, he understood how easy chasing pleasure was; it was seductive, addictive, and never enough. He'd wanted to hug her yesterday during her confession, but he'd been unsure of her reaction.

A knock came, and Mason entered. "My lord, Miss Winkworth is here to see you."

"Please show her in. Would you see that tea is served?"

Mason bowed. "My lord."

Edith entered in a cloud of blue fabric. Her hair was dishevelled, and her cheeks were flushed. "Good morning."

Perry stood up and clasped his hands behind his back. "Good morning. What happened to you? Did you run here?"

"Almost. I didn't want to be late. My mother held me, asking me questions about my job here, and I didn't know what to say." She chuckled. "Telling my mother I posed for a nude painting that's now in Lord Ravenscroft's personal parlour and that said lord is offering me a job so I can reimburse him wasn't the right thing to say at breakfast."

"What did you tell her?"

She paced around the room, stopping in front of the bookshelves. "I was rather vague. I didn't want her to get the wrong idea about you as well and think ill of you. She has a fervid imagination, quite morbid at times. She asked me if you wanted me to do something inappropriate."

He nearly snorted a laugh as inappropriate but enticing visions flashed across his mind. "That can be arranged if you're game," he quipped. Mostly.

Her beautiful forest-green eyes became two narrow slits. "Lord Ravenscroft, you truly are *not* a gentleman."

"I beg to differ. A scoundrel would take advantage of you or show the painting to the world. Oh, wait, that's exactly what that painter, whom you claim is a friend of yours, did to make money and pay off his gambling debts. So I ask you, who isn't the gentleman?"

She smiled. He could easily become addicted to her smile. "*Touché.*"

"It's always a pleasure to converse with you."

A corner of her mouth quirked up, and a naughty twinkle lit her eyes.

Mason, carrying a tray with the tea, interrupted them.

"Please take a seat," Perry said when Mason left.

She sat on the chair in front of the desk, but he gestured to the chair next to him.

"This chair," he said.

"Why?"

He pinched the bridge of his nose dramatically, feigning outrage. "You work for me, Miss Winkworth. You'll do everything I ask."

"So inappropriate activities it is, then." She did as told.

"Careful, Edith. I might take up on your offer."

That naughty twinkle sparkled again. She perched on the edge of the chair. "What should I do?"

He handed her the letter he'd tried to read. "Read this out aloud."

She took it. "Does your condition cause you trouble reading?" The question didn't lack kindness.

"Sometimes, when my head hurts, I have problems understanding while reading. I can read the words, but they're meaningless. All I got is that the letter is from my uncle."

Her expression softened.

He poured the tea. "Usually, it doesn't last for long."

"I actually saw Neville the other day."

He perked up. "Neville? Are you two friends?"

"Well...did I say something wrong? You look flustered."

"I'm surprised you're so familiar with him." And a little concerned. Uncle Neville didn't have a terrible reputation; he didn't squander money, and his name didn't appear on the scandal sheet, but his liking for women and pleasure was known.

"He's friends with Daphne and Valentine, but he isn't my friend. I'm sorry he's your relative, but I find him upsetting. He was with Daphne, Valentine, and me in the Scarlet Room. Didn't you see him?"

Perry sucked in a deep breath. The man he hadn't seen at the gaming table had been his uncle. "Did he witness my seizure?"

"I'm not sure. I was focused on you and didn't notice where he was. Why? Is something the matter?"

He scratched his chin. The rules of the Scarlet Room were clear. Even if Uncle Neville had seen the incident, he couldn't tell anyone.

"Albert was very careful not to mention my seizures to anyone. Aside from you, your family, and the doctors, no one knows. My uncle is aware I needed medical treatment in Geneva but doesn't know about the seizures."

"Do you worry he might use the information against you?"

"We've always had a civil relationship."

She hesitated before speaking. "He told me the story of his intended, claiming you seduced her and convinced her to break up her engagement."

"Bollocks. My uncle and I discussed the matter many times years ago. Margaret broke up the engagement of her own accord when she realised she didn't love him. I simply happened to have listened to her when she was desperate and confided in me. Neville saw us together and drew his own conclusions, the wrong ones, of course. Nothing ever happened with Margaret. She's now happily married. The fact my uncle still believes I caused the incident is absurd. Anyway, please read."

She read the letter in a clear tone that helped him understand. "*Dear Peregrine, I received your previous letter about the possibility of ceding the title to me, and I'm more than happy to take the title of Earl Ravenscroft when you're ready. I appreciate how difficult the past years have been for you, and—*" She lowered the letter. "Are you renouncing your title?"

He fiddled with a pencil. "I've been thinking about it. Uncle Neville is next in line."

"Why do you want to renounce the title?"

He turned towards her. "My condition isn't a temporary situation. An earl is required to attend social events and meetings in the House of Lords, which means being constantly under scrutiny. If someone witnesses one of my seizures, I won't simply be considered unfit to hold the title but also a danger to society. I want a normal life and decide when I'm in the mood to see others."

"But you told me your seizures aren't frequent."

"But they still happen. Being an earl isn't like being a doctor."

"What do you mean?"

He waved at the pile of documents on his desk. "You can certainly become a doctor. You have the brain and the knowledge necessary for the job. I'm not sure I'm now fit for the job of an earl. I need help reading sometimes. Doctors don't understand the cause of my seizures. I don't expect people to understand them, either."

"People always fear what's different and not easy to understand. Your condition doesn't impair your cognitive ability. Look at the progress you've made. It's incredible."

She was talking like a doctor again. Good.

"From experience, I know people don't care about my cognitive ability. They think my seizures are the result of madness at best and witchcraft at worst. Many people think I'm not sane in the head." He tilted his head. "Which I guess is true, in a way."

She moved her hand closer to his. "Yes, some people would lock you up in an asylum only because you can't control the seizures."

"Trust me, sometimes I wish I were locked up in an asylum, too. At least my life would be simpler."

"You don't mean that."

He wanted to ask her if she would start studying again, but that would be pushing her. Her presence here was already good progress.

"Would you read the next letter, please?" he asked.

"Of course." Edith brought her chair closer to the desk, and he caught her fresh scent of jasmine. "Which one?"

EDITH HAD JUST FINISHED TELLING her mother about her new job, thinking that would put to rest any further unpleasant conversations, but Mother hadn't stopped asking questions. Questions Edith didn't know how to answer.

Why you? What's the pay? Do you work alone with him? What do you exactly do?

The dining room at breakfast had become an interrogation room. Edith couldn't sip her tea in peace without being questioned.

"It doesn't make any sense." Mother must have said that at least a dozen times. "Why would the Earl of Ravenscroft hire you as his secretary?"

"Because he knows me and trusts me. He's going through a difficult moment because he's just returned to London after years of absence, and he needs a friend to help him with his work. That's all." And it was true as well.

"So you spend the day alone with him."

"I work for him, Mother. And Perry and I are friends."

"I know, but a friend of mine told me that people who receive blows to the head might become dangerous, aggressive, or even be prone to indecency."

"Ridiculous. Mother, do you believe a friend's passing comment and not what Father says?" She rose from the chair. "I don't want to be late."

The maid opened the door. "Lady Lancaster is here, madam."

"Marianne, darling." Mother rushed to Marianne as if in need of being rescued from a dragon. "It's so good to see you here."

"Mother." Marianne kissed Mother's cheek and gave Edith a worried glance.

Edith couldn't blame her. "Good morning, Marianne. Tea?"

"Yes, please." She removed her gloves and eyed the newspaper. "Is it new?"

"Fresh from being ironed." Edith poured her a cup of tea.

Marianne went straight to the scandal sheet. "Any news?" A quivering note intruded in her voice.

"None, darling," Mother said. "Is something the matter?"

"No, no." Marianne let out a forced laugh. "Quite the opposite. I came here to announce we're hosting a ball next week. I would love to invite Lord Ravenscroft. We neglected our duty to invite him for too long."

Edith exchanged a glance with her sister.

"Splendid idea." Mother waved at Edith. "I was just talking with Edith about that. Lord Ravenscroft hired her as his secretary," she said 'secretary' as if it were an absurd job.

"Did he now?" Marianne said. "Interesting."

Edith cleared her throat. "Yes, he needs help with his work. Apparently, headaches plague him."

Mother softened. "Poor man."

"Will you pass my invitation to him then?" Marianne asked. "I'll send him a formal card, but you might want to tell him first."

"Of course." Edith finished her tea, wondering if Perry would be interested in going to a ball. "I'll see you later."

"I'll walk you out." Marianne followed her to the entry hall.

"Everything is all right," Edith whispered, checking Mother was still in the dining room. "Perry won't show the painting to anyone."

"It's not that." She took Edith's hand. "It's about what you told us the other day. I had no idea you were suffering so much."

"Because I didn't tell you."

"I should have asked you how you were faring more often. I'm so sorry, Edith."

"Don't be." She hugged her sister. "You helped me a lot."

"How? Lending you money? Some help." Marianne shook her head. "You've always been the strongest one between us. I didn't think you needed a different type of help."

"Me, the strongest? You did all those exercises to overcome your fear of the water. I'm still as scared as a kitten."

"I neglected you. I was a terrible sister."

"You got married."

Marianne's bottom lip quivered, and she took a deep breath. "I love you, Edith."

Even Edith needed a deep breath. "I love you too, Marianne."

sixteen

EDITH HADN'T SEEN Perry for the whole morning.

He'd left instructions for her to arrange the books in his library and hadn't shown himself, which was a little disappointing. But a more pleasant task didn't exist because, while her relationship with books had been troubled as of late, she'd never stopped appreciating them.

Among cups of tea and oat biscuits, she'd spent the morning dividing part of Perry's extensive book collection into groups by author and title. He owned a few first editions; she was nearly scared she might ruin them by touching them.

She couldn't remember the last time when she'd enjoyed herself with a quiet, solitary task. The dispensary was oftentimes chaotic with nurses constantly coming and going.

The downside was her thoughts spoke louder in the silence of the library, and not all of them were pleasant. Marianne's apologetic face kept flashing through her mind; Mother's disbelief at her new job never failed to worry her; Neville's words made her uncomfortable. Not to mention she hadn't talked to her father about her new job yet.

She was standing on the step, balancing herself on her tiptoes to reach the top shelf, when footsteps approached.

"Good afternoon," Perry said.

"Bother." She lost her balance. The book she wanted to put on the shelf dropped on the floor with a thud. She gasped. "Oh no!"

The step quivered, and she slipped, only to end up in Perry's welcoming arms.

"Careful." His clean scent of soap filled her nostrils as he held her.

She put a hand on his chest, right over his quickening heartbeat. "You caught me off guard."

"Apologies. I thought you'd heard me."

His Adam's apple bobbed up and down when he talked. Fascinating. Had he always had those thick eyebrows, or those emerald specks in his irises? Or those hard muscles in his arms? His *pectoralis major* wasn't bad, either.

"I was too focused."

He swallowed. "I'm sorry I couldn't be here this morning." He released her and put some distance between them, but his smouldering gaze remained on her. "I had my exercise session with Oliver. He likes to record everything I do. I feel like the prime minister followed by journalists."

She smiled and crouched to pick up the book. "I hope I didn't ruin it."

He knelt as well, and they reached out for the book at the same time, their hands touching. She met his gaze, and for a second, the air between them was charged with tension, but not of the angry type.

"Don't worry." He took the book and straightened. "If the spine breaks, I'll have it repaired."

"Thank goodness there are things that can be repaired easily." She smoothed a crease on her skirt.

"Some things require more time than others, but eventually, any damage can be repaired."

She didn't share his confidence. "My sister is giving a ball next week, and you're invited."

His expression changed as if she'd told him he would meet the queen without wearing clothes. Dash it. Why did she think of Perry naked? Maybe because she wondered how those muscles looked at closer inspection.

"Is something the matter?" she asked.

"I'm not keen on attending balls." He put the book on the top shelf without even rising on his tiptoes. "But I don't want to be rude to your sister, and I can't spend my life as a recluse. Meeting people bothers me, but I want to go."

"It won't be a crowded ball. Marianne doesn't like it when there are too many people. But she's fond of trying foreign or unusual foods. All delicious. Her parties are famous for the most extravagant hors d'oeuvre."

His nod lacked determination.

"I prefer small gatherings as well. Too many people ruin the party," she said.

"Have you attended many parties in the past years?" he asked, leaning against the shelf, carelessly handsome.

"More than I'd care to count." She brushed a speck of dust from another book. "I found parties to be a good distraction from worries and thinking too much."

"You must have had many experiences." A hint of sadness slipped into his voice.

"None of them are worth remembering, and in fact, I don't remember many of them."

He chuckled. "Still, I guess you have better memories than being prodded by doctors and pricked with needles while sweating to speak your name."

She put the book aside and closed the distance between them, stopping a couple of feet from him. "I must apologise. Of course, my troubles can't be compared with what you went through."

"No, I didn't mean it in that way. It's me who should apologise." He pinched the bridge of his nose. "Forgive me. I'm tired," he stammered the last words.

She cupped his cheek without thinking. Her hand moved of its own accord, but she needed to touch him. The conversation she had with Marianne echoed in her head.

"I wish I'd been a better friend. You needed me, and I was here, lying and carousing from one useless party to the next. I've been very selfish."

Perhaps Edith imagined things, but she could swear Perry's glances at her were particularly heated. Since he'd bought her painting, she believed his attitude towards her had become more sensual. Or maybe it was her imagination.

No, she didn't regret having posed for Valentine, not the act itself, but what had happened afterwards. The painting was personal. It was her personal journey towards... right. She didn't know where she was going, to be honest.

Her journey wasn't about freedom because her parents had always given her freedom and support to follow her dream, or what had been her dream. Even when she'd spent her days doing nothing, they'd been patient with her. But they weren't stupid. They were aware something was wrong with her. Yet they'd never sent her away. And she'd abused that freedom for unimportant things while Perry had gone through a real struggle.

He covered her hand with his and tilted his head just enough to brush his sculpted lips against her inner wrist, shooting a bolt of lightning through her.

In her wild nights, she'd kissed many a gentleman, but the blast of pure excitement his gentle kiss triggered was unprecedented. One soft peck from Perry, and her whole body sizzled with pleasure. The sensation had nothing to do with the shallow, fleeting thrills she experienced when drinking or spending a night out. This excitement reached her heart and curled up comfortably there.

"I don't bear a grudge against you. I never have." His warm

voice was the perfect match for that little kiss. There was chastity in that kiss and sin in his gaze. "But it breaks my heart to know you suffered, too, and didn't have a true friend next to you."

"It's not as dramatic as I let you think. Marianne has always been ready to help me. My parents would have helped me as well, had I let them. But at the same time, I think my wild years are part of a journey I had to take alone." She caressed the line of his strong jaw, feeling the light stubble. "I confess I feel the need to do something wild and lose myself, not to think even now. It's like a drug."

"I know. I was you a long time ago." He leant into her palm. "Will you resume your studies?"

She stiffened and removed her hand because one thing was to admit her past mistakes and make amends. Picking up her medical books was quite another. She doubted she had the skills to become a doctor. That dream was long gone.

"I'm not sure."

"I didn't mean to upset you," he said.

"Nothing of the sort." Her lost opportunity upset her. "It's difficult for me. It's too late. I missed the opportunity to get a medical career."

He took her hand and kissed it. "It's not too late. You only need time to realise that."

Not picking up studying was what she wanted; she wondered if it was what she needed.

seventeen

THE SMALL GATHERING in Marianne's house wasn't that small after all.

Edith hoped Perry enjoyed himself a little in the crowded room. Marianne had invited many young ladies of the Season, a couple of members of parliament, and peers. There were lots of foreign drinks, outlandish food, matrons, and gossiping ladies. Unfortunately, even Neville was present, but he'd blissfully ignored her so far.

Among graceful nods of her head and half curtsies, she sauntered across the brightly lit room towards Perry. Marianne must have used a year's worth of wax and gas to illuminate the ballroom because not a corner of the room lay in shadows. Tucked between a large philodendron and the banquet table, Perry was on full display, even though he likely did his best not to be noticed. Judging by the glances the guests tossed in his direction, he wasn't succeeding.

"Are you enjoying yourself a little?" she asked, looking at the plates of hors d'oeuvre on the table.

His scowl softened. "Too nervous to enjoy myself. I don't want to have a seizure here in front of everyone."

"You should focus on something else other than your worry. Try one of these delicious starters. Quite unusual. There are caviar nibbles, tiny artichoke pastries, oyster tarts, shrimp sandwiches...a bit of everything."

"Not now, thank you."

"Do you want to go home?"

He shook his head. "I need to get used to parties."

She took a bite of a smoked salmon canapé shaped like a small rose; Marianne's cook was a true artist. "Anxiety doesn't help."

He shifted his glass of champagne from one hand to another without drinking it. "That's what Oliver always says."

"What do I always say?" Dr. York walked over to them, an artichoke pastry on his plate. "Surely, something clever and remarkable."

"That anxiety doesn't help my condition," Perry said.

"No, it doesn't. I was talking about the effect of anxiety on people with Sir James Harris, the physician-in-ordinary to the queen herself. He agrees that anxiety is the malady of this century." Dr. York cast a furtive glance at her, his face reddening by the minute. "Oysters! Don't trust them. They're very shellfish." His laugh sounded forced. "Sorry, I say silly things when I'm nervous."

"No, not only when you're nervous," Perry said.

The good doctor regarded her in a different way since the affair of the painting. His cheeks flushed as he bit into the artichoke pastry.

"I'm glad Perry has a valid, loyal physician like you, Dr. York," she said. "A physician who's also a friend. I admire everything you do for him."

His flush intensified, and he started to cough into his fist. Awful, gagging noises came out of him as he clamped his handkerchief over his mouth.

"Deep breaths." Perry gave a few strong pats to Dr. York's back. "Don't die here, please. It'd be a great inconvenience."

Tears shone in the doctor's eyes as he coughed on the handkerchief until he finally breathed normally again.

She poured a glass of water for him from the banquet table. "Here."

He didn't look at her. "Thank you, miss. I was arti-choking." He laughed but started coughing again before gulping down the water in one go. "Apologies." He hurried away, staggering a little.

"Poor man," Edith said.

"You ruined my physician." Perry gave her a lopsided smile. "He isn't himself when you're around."

"I'll be more careful then. I don't want him to hurt himself." That had been the second time.

"I'm not myself either when you're with me." All the amusement was gone from his voice, and he gave her that intense blue stare that made her quiver inside.

"Why wouldn't you be yourself?"

The conversation had taken a sudden, serious turn she didn't know how to handle.

"I appreciate the way you found the courage to talk to me and admit you lied. Not everyone would have done that. It takes a lot to acknowledge we're wrong, need help, or are addicted to something. Your lies hurt me, but I've never doubted your courage and resilience, and I admire you." His condition caused him to hesitate and stammer out a few words, but the honesty and passion in them were undeniable.

His fierce approval of her brought a lump of emotion to her throat.

"Your admiration is misplaced," she said. "I feel anything but brave. I'm scared all the time and a coward at heart. The *Princess Alice* incident proved that."

"You're too harsh on yourself."

Sir James, the queen's physician, walked over to them, breaking the moment.

"Miss Winkworth." The short physician stroked his goatee and gave her a wide smile. "Lord Ravenscroft. Apologies for the intrusion."

Perry gave a nod, clenching his jaw.

"Sir." She bowed her head.

"May I talk to you for a moment, miss?" He turned towards Perry. "Would you mind terribly, Ravenscroft? I have an urgent matter to discuss with Miss Winkworth."

"By all means. I don't mind at all." It sounded anything but.

"I'll see you later," she said to him.

The gentleman ushered her to a quiet corner, glancing around in a furtive manner. "I'm deeply sorry to have interrupted your conversation with Lord Ravenscroft, but I couldn't contain my excitement."

She smiled, thinking about a polite way to tell him she didn't have the foggiest idea what he wanted from her. "About what, sir?"

He gazed around. "As the queen's physician, it'd be better if my interests didn't become common knowledge."

"Sir?"

He fiddled with his gloved hands. "See, art is my passion." He stared at her as if she were supposed to understand whatever he wanted to say from that simple statement.

"That's admirable. Why would you keep that interest a secret, sir?"

He inched closer. "Mr. Valentine Carter is my most favourite painter."

Oh, blazes. She had a hunch about where the conversation was going.

"I absolutely adore him. I have almost all his paintings in my house." His speech became passionate. "I spare no expense when it comes to acquiring one of Mr. Carter's masterpieces. You likely know that Mr. Carter's paintings, well, let's say that some of them are considered quite scandalous. That's why he doesn't show all his paintings to everyone. Sometimes he asks the National Gallery to display his most provocative works in a secondary wing with restricted entrance."

Yes, Edith knew something about that. She searched the room for someone she might use as an excuse to leave. Perry stared at them from the other side of the room as if he wanted to stride to them and take her away.

"To be brief," Sir James continued, "I acquired some paintings in a special series on Greek goddesses. They're, ahem, rather explicit paintings. They sold like hot cakes the very same day they were put on display."

"Really?" She feigned surprise.

"I managed to buy a few of them, but I couldn't buy them all, which is frustrating. I love to have a full set of everything. I have..." He counted on his fingers. "Aphrodite, Hera, and Athena, but to come to my point." He lowered his voice to a whisper. "I heard that you posed for a stunning painting, the Star Maiden."

Edith wanted to crush her glass of champagne. "Who told you that?"

"I'm afraid I can't tell you the name."

Her face flamed. Her entire body did. "Well, I'm sorry to say that whoever gave you that information is seriously misinformed because I have never, ever posed for any paintings. Now, if you'll excuse me."

"I won't judge you, miss." Sir James blocked her path. "It's all about art. So did you pose for it? Do you know who bought it? How big is it? The clerk at the gallery refused to give me the name or any other information. I'm confused. Does this painting even exist?"

The suggestion of bribing the clerk at the gallery was swiftly suppressed.

"The Star Maiden has become a myth," he said. "No one seems to know if it's real or not. I even talked to Mr. Carter himself, and he didn't confirm or deny any rumours. So frustrating! Oh, but I understand the game Mr. Carter is playing. By acting all mysterious and shedding rumours about his paintings, he's increasing their value. The higher the interest, the higher the price."

Actually, she thought Valentine didn't want to stir more trouble than he'd already done by blabbering about the darn painting.

"Do you know anything about the Star Maiden?"

"Apologies, sir, but I can't help you." She strode away before he could say anything.

What had she said about not regretting posing for Valentine? Well, she'd been wrong.

PERRY WORKED his jaw as Edith strode away from Sir James. Whatever the doctor had told her must have bothered her if the way she closed her fists and hurried out of the ballroom was any indication.

He started to follow her, but his uncle swept in front of him, blocking him.

"Perry, I know this isn't the right place, but we should discuss the details of your renunciation."

He craned his neck to see Edith disappear behind a corner. "I'll ask my secretary to arrange a meeting."

Uncle Neville's expression became serious. "You know I care about your health. What you went through was horrible. Of course, you won't lack anything afterwards."

"Thank you, Uncle. Your affection for me is touching although I don't understand why you told Miss Winkworth I'm the cause of your broken engagement."

His uncle didn't flinch. "I've never said such a thing. I merely told Edith about my past. She came to whatever conclusion she pleased. So shall we discuss this affair?"

Bollocks. "I'm afraid I can't now. If you'll excuse me." He ignored Uncle Neville's narrowed eyes.

He traced Edith's steps as discreetly as he could, weaving through maids, footmen, and guests. The hallway was empty and, thankfully, wasn't as brightly illuminated as the ballroom. His eyes were grateful. At the end of the corridor, the door to the conservatory stood ajar.

"Edith?" He slid inside, breathing in the scent of wet soil and blooming jasmine. "Are you here?"

"Perry." She was sitting on a bench in a froth of pink fabric. Her forlorn expression gave a dramatic tone to the sight.

"What did Sir James tell you?" He sat next to her.

Roses and orchids created the perfect frame around her and her lovely pink gown. The moonlight added the last magical touch to her profile.

A little crease appeared between her eyebrows. "He's after the Star Maiden. Apparently, the rumour of me posing for Valentine has spread, and Sir James is interested in buying the painting."

"Not bloody likely." He nearly growled.

A quick smile smoothed down her frown. "The rumour worries me."

"I wouldn't be surprised if Valentine himself spread it. He's quite unreliable, and gossip is the best source of publicity. I'm sure Sir James isn't the only one who wants to buy the Star Maiden."

"I didn't choose my friends well as of late." She tugged at a ribbon on her skirt. "I have so many regrets, and the worst thing is that I ignored my inner voice telling me not to do certain things when I was reckless."

"I went through your same journey, and I can tell you this, the sense of guilt will go away after a while. Give yourself time to heal."

"You're always so kind." She held his hand.

He couldn't ignore the little shiver dancing down his neck. Exactly as it'd happened in the library, even a small touch started a stir in his chest.

"There's one thing I regret to this day, though," he said.

"What is it?"

"Not having kissed you that Christmas night." He pointed up to where a branch of mistletoe hanging right over their heads. "Mistletoe."

"Actually, that's snowberry."

"Does it matter?"

"It depends. What do you want to do?" She grinned, teasing him.

"Well, the short version is that I want to kiss you. The long version is that I really, really, really want to kiss you."

She laughed and tilted her head. "What are you waiting for then?"

He didn't rush to kiss her, not because he wasn't eager to, but because he wanted to savour every second. He inched towards her. The smile vanished from her lips as she moved towards him.

His heart lodged somewhere in his throat, and his breathing quickened. He hadn't kissed a woman in years. But when he pressed his lips against hers, he felt he could roar like a lion.

She kissed him back, putting her soft hand on his cheek. Her sweet scent seemed to reach his heart because it was the only thing he sensed. She parted her lips and darted out her smooth tongue. The first lash over his lips was like a bolt of energy going through him. A deep groan escaped him. And just like that, something changed between them.

The kiss took a wild turn. They moved at the same time and with the same passion. He thrust his tongue into her welcoming mouth as she tangled her fingers through his hair, pulling him closer with eagerness.

Hell, he needed that. He needed her softness, her fingers in his hair, and her body pressing against his. But it wasn't just passion. A sweetness he hadn't foreseen beat in his chest.

Their tongues danced together, exploring and teasing. He coiled an arm around her waist and held her, feeling the warmth of her body through the layers of satin.

Finally. A kiss years in the making.

The time he'd spent waiting for it was worth every second. He ran a hand down the curve of her waist and up again to touch the underside of her breast. They both gasped when he caressed her gently. Then her mouth was over his again, demanding and eager, but she drew in a breath when he rubbed her nipple with his thumb. Feeling her shiver under his touch was the most intoxicating sensation he'd ever experienced.

They broke the kiss, and he rested his forehead against hers. Their uneven breaths mingled in that moment of silence and moonlight. He wanted to say how much the kiss meant to him, how much he cared about her, but any word he thought of sounded inadequate. He'd ruin the moment if he said something meaningless, or worse, if he stammered, so he held her instead, letting his heartbeat speak for him. He held her for a time that seemed both long and too short.

She laid her head on his chest, her shoulders stooping. "I liked it so very much."

"So did I. For a parasitic plant, the mistletoe is quite generous when it comes to creating the right atmosphere. Sorry, snowberry."

She laughed. "Being surrounded by flowers and sweet scents is the most romantic setting ever."

"I'm sure we aren't the first guests to find their way here. Who knows how many romantic encounters happened in this conservatory? If that palm tree could talk, who knows what it'd say."

She laughed harder. "It'd say it's a fern."

"Really?" He glanced at the tall green plant. "I suggest we spend more time kissing in a conservatory to improve my knowledge of plants."

She wrapped her arms around his neck. "Excellent suggestion, Lord Ravenscroft."

He wanted to kiss her again but paused, simply staring at her large eyes filled with moonlight. "I'm glad you told me the truth."

"So am I. You made me face my bad choices. I needed that."

He stood up, holding her hand. "We'd better return to the ball-room separately. You go first."

She laced her fingers through his before releasing his hand. "I'd rather stay here, but the last thing I need is the rumour of another scandal."

She rested her head on his shoulder as they walked to the glass door opening to the hallway. Such a simple but intimate gesture.

"I'll see you in a moment." She slid her hand out of his slowly, leaving a path of fire on his palm.

He stood behind a... whatever plant it was while she walked out of the conservatory, fixing a wayward curl. With the moonlight pouring through the windows, she really looked like a goddess bathed in silver light. A goddess he'd been lucky enough to kiss.

She paused in the middle of the hallway to wave at him. He waved back, not sure she could see him.

For the first time in years, he experienced other emotions than worry and anxiety, and it was wonderful.

Perry was still thinking about Edith and their secret moonlight kiss hours later when he returned home with Oliver. Her body had left a trail of perfume, warmth, and passion over his, and he loved it.

"Pleasant evening, wasn't it?" Oliver waited for Perry's answer, holding his pencil over the notepad. How he could write while in the moving carriage was a mystery.

He reclined his head. "Very."

"Great. Was there a moment when you feared a seizure might come?"

"No. At first, I was anxious, but then I enjoyed myself."

"Excellent." Oliver nodded, scribbling on a page. "I'm afraid Miss Winkworth didn't fully enjoy herself at the end."

He straightened. "What do you mean?"

Oliver slid the notepad into his pocket. "Well, I caught a bit of an odd conversation between Miss Winkworth and your uncle. She was waiting for her carriage when he walked straight to her, meaning business. They chatted with quick words. She looked upset. I didn't hear the whole exchange, but I'm sure your uncle told her that her payment was overdue, that they had a deal, and she had to honour it. After that, she left, visibly bothered."

"A payment." Perry scratched his chin.

"She replied they didn't have any deal, to which he said he could *force* her."

"What the hell did he mean?"

Oliver shrugged. "Don't need to worry. If she needs money to pay your uncle, you're going to help her, aren't you?"

Of course he would.

eighteen

NEVILLE'S WORDS HAUNTED Edith the day after the ball as she volunteered at the hospital early in the morning. More than Neville's words, his tone bothered her. He'd been completely serious when he'd talked about her overdue payment, even straight up telling he was ready to force her if he needed to.

"You seem upset," Mrs. Richards said with hesitant words.

"Only a bit worried. Silly personal problems I won't trouble you with." She pulled her chair closer to Mrs. Richards's bed and raised a hand. "Squeeze my hand."

Edith was helping Mrs. Richards practise the same exercises Perry had done to improve mobility. As a seamstress, Mrs. Richards needed to regain the use of her hands. The woman frowned, closing her fingers around Edith's. Her cheeks reddened, but the pressure applied by her hand was rather light. A sign she needed to exercise more.

"Well done." Edith held the woman's hand. "You're making progress."

Mrs. Richards sagged on the pillow. "I'm tired."

"We'll continue another day."

She shook her head. "They asked me to leave. They need the bed."

Edith paused while standing up. "But you haven't recovered yet."

She shrugged. "My husband will take me home this evening."

Staying at home with her family had its benefits, but Mrs. Richards's condition required care. Her husband needed to work to support his family, and Mrs. Richards wouldn't have anyone to watch over her, help her exercise, or stimulate her speech.

Edith hugged her, careful not to hurt her. Every word of comfort coming up in her mind sounded like a lie, so she simply hugged the woman.

There had to be something she could do.

"Thank you," Mrs. Richards said.

But Edith hadn't done anything.

Later, after she left the hospital, she took her time to walk to Perry's house. The day was particularly bright, and the sunlight warmed her cheeks. It was the first time she'd enjoyed the sunlight in years, as strange as it sounded. Intense nightlife and walks in the sunlight weren't good companions.

On top of everything else, she couldn't stop thinking about the kiss. The beautiful, sweet, wonderful kiss. It'd been a chaste kiss compared to other kisses she'd shared. She'd experienced more savage kisses that had led to messy tumbles and awkward moments, but Perry's kiss had left a shock of sensations through her body like the aftermath of an earthquake. The ripples still tickled her.

She entered his study, inhaling the scent of freshly brewed tea and scones. "Good afternoon," she said.

He stood up, hands clasped behind his back, handsome in a dark suit. The sunlight agreed with him. It made his inky hair glossy and his eyes a deeper blue.

"In time for tea." A fleeting smile graced his lips—lips that she knew were soft and demanding—and was gone in a blink, which made her realise how rarely he smiled. "I trust you're well."

"Yes. Last night was unexpectedly pleasant, especially when I was in the conservatory."

He gave her a mischievous grin. "I agree. The conservatory was one of the best moments of the past years. Unforgettable. I'll always cherish it."

She sat on the chair next to him. He sat down as well. For a few moments, neither of them spoke. They stared at each other, smiling and letting the happiness of being together speak for them.

"What are we going to do today?" she asked.

"Reading shouldn't be a problem for me, but I need to go through these documents." He deposited a thick folder on the desk. "We'll share it."

"Great."

"But I must warn you. They're rather uninteresting. Agricultural reports from my estates. Please take note whenever barley is mentioned."

Uninteresting was an understatement.

After a couple of hours of reading boring reports on the fluctuation of the price of barley, potatoes, and cabbage, Edith was about to either fall asleep on the desk or scream out of boredom. Whenever she blinked, visions of vegetables floated through her mind.

The worst thing was that the day had remained perfect. Not a cloud marred the absolute blue sky. A light breeze cleaned the coal dust from the air and carried a hearty scent of wet soil. Days like that were a rarity, and she longed for a walk in the park, some sunshine, or listening to the birds' song.

"Right-o." Perry set aside the documents they'd finished and selected a new folder. "We can start with the reports on..." He opened the folder and read. "Changes of the values in extraction coal production."

Oh, goodness. "Can we take a walk?" She propped her elbow on the desk and rested her chin on her palm. "Please?"

He scrunched up his face as if she'd spoken in a foreign language. "A walk?"

She gestured at the window. "Look at the sunshine. The sky is a solid blue. The temperature is delightful. The breeze is perfect. We've been sitting here for hours."

He furrowed his brow. "Yes, that's called working."

She rolled her eyes. "I'm sure even workers are entitled to a break. It's good for one's health."

"You may go if you want. I don't take walks in the park."

"Yes, I gathered that much." She rose, and he stood up as well. "But I'd like to go with you. Just an hour. We might buy something to eat from a street vendor and enjoy it on a bench in the park, watching the birds flying around."

His eyes flared wide. "I don't eat street food."

"Baked potatoes are delicious, or we can have a slice of pork pie or a Cornish pasty. Come on, Perry. Take a walk with me. It'll be fun."

There was a quick knock on the door, and Dr. York entered the study. "Perry, I brought you a few bottles of camphor oil. Great for muscle pain." He came to a stop upon seeing her. His face blanched. "Miss Winkworth." He bowed.

"Dr. York." She nodded. "I trust you recovered well from the incident with the artichoke pastry."

He scrubbed the back of his neck. "I did, thank you. I can't complain. I tried, but no one ever listens, especially Perry." He let out a nervous chuckle.

Edith laughed as well while Perry shot his gaze skywards.

"I was trying to convince the earl to take a walk," she said. "Surely, Dr. York agrees with me about the benefits of exercising."

"I do. Absolutely." Dr. York gazed everywhere but in her direction. "Miss Winkworth is right. Perry needs to take a walk. Well, it's always a pleasure to chat with you, Miss Winkworth." He put a basket of bottles filled with an amber liquid on a table and left in a hurry.

Perry exhaled as if answering made him tired. "All right. It sounds like madness, but fine. Let's take a walk."

"There was a time when you wouldn't have hesitated to agree to a walk in the park."

"That time is long gone." He held the door open for her.

After a footman helped a muttering and scoffing Perry slide into his coat, they headed out. The ride in the hansom cab would be a short one, but she had every intention of enjoying it.

She closed her eyes for a moment, letting the warm sunlight from the window caress her cheeks. When she opened her eyes, he was staring at her.

"Isn't it lovely?" she asked.

He averted his gaze. "It is."

She touched his hand. "You'll see, it'll be great. And as a general rule, ladies are always right, and gentlemen are always wrong."

"So if I say, 'by Jove, Edith, you're right!', does it make you wrong? We have a paradox."

She narrowed her gaze. "You truly are a scoundrel."

He laughed, a deep, rumbling laugh she loved; it calmed the restless feeling always bothering her.

When he helped her out of the cab, deep lines marred his brow again. Children ran along the pavement and the gravel paths of the park. Pretty parasols twirled in the sunlight. Everyone chatted and laughed. The happiness was contagious, at least for her.

Instead, Perry walked with his tall hat down over his face, shoulders hunched, and a scowl that would terrify the most hardened highwayman.

"Perry." She touched his arm.

He stiffened. "What?" He cleared his throat. "I don't feel comfortable. Too many people."

"Do you want to return home? I'm sorry I insisted on taking a walk." She turned around, ready to leave the park, but he took her arm.

"No, I don't want to leave. You and Oliver are right. I need to go out more. My only concern is my condition." He glanced around. "I don't want any witnesses."

"We'll find a nice path that's not too crowded." She hooked her arm through his although he remained stiff and tense.

"Thank you."

His muscles loosened a little when she took one of the less crowded paths. The tree branches were mostly bare, but the warm breeze held the promise of a lovely spring. The scent of wet soil and pine resin was a feast for the senses.

"Do you feel less tense?" she asked.

"I do." He sounded anything but.

But it was her turn to tense when she spotted the Serpentine. Every time she saw it, no matter how far away, her knees weakened with fear of the water. The sunlight glinted off its smooth surface, glittering with gold. A pretty sight, but fear never failed to chill her.

She hitched a breath as the memory of the rotten smell of the Thames's water choked her. Swimming through the murky water of the river had been like shoving boulders. Her arms and legs had grown tired quickly because the water was heavy, and the currents had been strong. The smell had almost caused her to faint. To this day, it made her gag. Perhaps coming here had been a mistake.

"Edith." Perry's concerned face filled her field of vision. "You're safe."

"What?"

"You were shivering." He caressed her shoulder.

"You know, rabid dogs suffer from hydrophobia, fear of the water." She focused on the limpid blue of his irises. "I hate the water now. I'm scared of even taking a bath. I've been taking only showers for these past years. It's ridiculous, isn't it?"

He gave her a rueful smile. "You're talking with a man who doesn't want to see people."

"But you have a good reason."

"So have you. I'm not fond of rivers myself."

Edith focused on a pretty sparrow singing from a tree branch, not to be troubled by the Serpentine. "Marianne had the same problem. She too couldn't stand the sight of a lake, sea, river, or swimming pool. But she practised every day. She started with small bowls of water where she would sink her foot. Then she used larger containers. It took her a year to take a bath. She has almost overcome her fear of the water altogether."

"Why didn't you try it as well?"

She shook her head, remembering those days when Marianne had wanted to convince her to try. "I was tired of feeling pain or being scared. I didn't care about torturing myself with gruesome exercises. Sometimes, Marianne would cry and shiver when she forced herself to sink into the water. Mother held her hand, crying too and encouraging her. Marianne would become ill, so difficult the contact with the water was for her. Once, she fainted. Another time, she didn't sleep for days or eat anything. It was awful to watch. I didn't want to go through that. I'm not as brave as she is."

Compassion glowed in his eyes. He caressed her cheek. "I have only sympathy for you. I also trust your strength."

"Your opinion means a lot to me."

"You can be everything you want," he insisted. "Even a doctor." He froze, catching a breath.

"Perry." She straightened. "Is it a seizure?"

He shook his head slightly. "Blimey, Edith. A snake has just slid under your skirts." He barely moved his lips when he spoke.

"Honestly?" She scoffed, rolling her eyes. "This stupid trick will never work with me."

He held her shoulders with a firm grip. "I swear it's not a trick, and don't make hasty moves."

"I wouldn't have fallen for your silly technique to convince a woman to show you her undergarments years ago. I won't fall for it now. Besides, you have my very revealing painting at your disposal. You have already seen my legs. Let's find some baked potatoes. I'm famished." She started to walk, but he stopped her.

"Don't move!" He licked his bottom lip, remaining really still. "I swear on my honour. It's not a trick. I'm going to lift your skirt very slowly and remove the snake if I can."

"You're hopeless, but a good actor." She burst out laughing. "I won't—"

Something quite muscular and narrow coiled around her calf, slithering up her leg. It couldn't be a snake. Snakes were supposed to rest under the ground at that time of the year, weren't they? Although the day was indeed unseasonably warm, and quite honestly, she knew nothing about snakes' routine.

"Good Lord," she said.

"Stay still." He inched her skirt and petticoats up.

"I feel it." A hysterical note crept into her voice, and tremors crawled down her back. "It's going up."

"Stay still and be quiet. Control your breathing." He pulled up her skirts.

Cool air hit her legs through her stockings as the fabric of her skirts went up. The snake coiled around her knee; she could tell by the pressure around her kneecap.

"Is it a *Vipera berus*?" she asked without looking down.

"What the hell is that?"

"An adder."

"Then say adder, for crying out loud! No, it's not an adder. It's an 'I have no bloody idea.'"

"Perry!"

"It's a snake. We don't need to know more. Hold up the skirts and don't move." He stepped towards the bushes, and a wave of panic hit her.

She shivered, holding her skirts up while the snake tightened its grip around her leg. "Don't leave me."

"I'm not leaving you. I'm searching for a stick. There." He walked to her slowly. "Stay calm." He dipped his head, holding a broken tree branch.

She winced as whatever Perry was doing disturbed the snake that reacted by squeezing her leg more tightly. "Hurry."

The snake hissed.

"Please." And she thought the water was terrifying?

"Come here," he said in the gentle tone she would use for cute puppies. As if the snake would behave. "Almost there."

The tip of the stick scratched her skin through her stockings, but then the pressure of the snake vanished after Perry made a wave gesture with his arm.

He tossed the stick behind her. "Done. It's gone."

Edith released her skirts and turned around in time to see a green and brown snake slithering towards the bushes. She shivered from head to toe, her hands cold.

"Heavens."

"It was shocked, the poor thing." Perry wiped his hands with his handkerchief.

His comment pulled her out of her shocked stillness.

"The poor thing? What about me? I could have died. Adders are venomous."

He shook his head. "I don't think so. Adders are rarely lethal. Even I know that."

"I had a snake around my leg."

"But nothing happened. You and the snake ruined each other's day. You're even." He hugged her and rubbed her back. "You've been very brave."

"No, I was terrified. I'm shaking." She rested her head on his chest, snuggling closer to him.

"Let's go home and have a nice cup of tea."

∾

THE DRIVE HOME was a blur because Perry was worried Edith might faint, so pale she was. She stared out of the window without saying a word and gripped his hand with surprising strength, almost crushing his fingers.

He sighed when she sat in his study with a hot cup of tea in her hands, in front of the warm hearth.

"Better?" he asked, peering at her from his armchair.

She shivered. "Yes, thank you. I think I'll follow your example and avoid going to the park from now on. Too dangerous."

"I doubt an incident like that will repeat itself."

She blew on her cup, disturbing the steam. "Were you scared?"

He added a sugar cube to his tea. "To be honest, not really. The snake moved sluggishly; it was cold, I guess, and even if it bit you, I doubt it would be lethal. And Oliver or your father would intervene promptly."

"I didn't share your optimism. I'm not sure what scares me the most now. The water or the snakes."

"So I saw." He twirled the teaspoon in the cup, pondering for the umpteenth time if he should bring up the conversation between Edith and Uncle Neville.

"What troubles you?" She snuggled in the armchair. "Something has been bothering you from the moment I came here. What is it?"

He worked his jaw. "My uncle is causing you trouble, isn't he?"

"Oh, that." She rubbed her forehead. "Did you hear my conversation with him?"

"Oliver was a few yards away."

"Neville..." She cleared her throat. "Apparently, while I was in the Scarlet Room and in my cups, I lost a silly bet against him, and he now demands I stick to my part of the deal."

"How much do you owe him?" He dipped his head to catch her gaze. "Tell me the sum, and I'll pay him today. He won't bother you again."

Her cheeks turned crimson. She stared at her tea for a long

moment. "I don't owe him money. The stake wasn't money." She shifted on the armchair.

A hot flare bothered him. "Hell. It's you he wants."

"It was a stupid wager done in the Scarlet Room. I shouldn't have agreed, but between the champagne and the excitement of the night, I said yes, or so Daphne and Valentine said. Although I do remember something about a bet with Neville."

A bitter taste soured his mouth. "When he said he could force you, he meant that."

"I don't think he did. He was bluffing." She gave him a fleeting smile before returning her attention to her cup.

"I beg to differ. My uncle is usually very determined."

She nodded. "He's always tried to grope me, but—"

"Excuse me?" He leant forwards. "How dare he!"

"Nothing has ever happened aside from a few brushes and unwanted touches. He teases but never pushes too hard, and I've always managed to keep him at bay."

"That's hardly better." He clenched his cup. "Edith, you'll forgive me if I don't think that his despicable behaviour means nothing. You made me change my mind about him."

And about renouncing the title. Albert would be furious to know a man like Uncle Neville was the next earl. Had his parents been alive, they would have been horrified at the thought. Hell, Perry was horrified.

"His actions are troubling, but I can deal with him," she said.

"He's my uncle." He sipped his tea to get rid of the bad taste in his mouth. "I feel responsible for the way he behaved towards you and not at all proud. I could have been like him had the incident with his fiancée never happened."

"I don't think so."

"I firmly believe that responsibilities make us stronger. That's why I proposed that you work for me." He paused to finish his tea and control his irritation. "Will you write a letter for me? I have a bad headache."

She gave him a sceptical look. "Is it for Neville?"

"I mean to tell him that I don't wish to renounce the title. What you just told me changes everything. Also, I really want to take my responsibility as the new earl. It scares me, but I want my brother to be proud of me."

She closed her hand around his. "You'll be a great Earl of Ravenscroft."

He grinned. "But not a gentleman."

nineteen

PERRY GLANCED AT Edith working at the typewriter. For someone who had never used one, she learnt fast, and he wanted the letter to his uncle to be as formal and clear as possible. No handwriting.

"How are you doing?" he asked, pausing from dictating the letter.

"It's not easy, but if I go slowly, I don't make mistakes."

"I think we've finished. Just add a salutation, and I'll sign it."

She stopped beating the keys. "Done." She pulled the page out of the machine. "Short but polite. Neville won't have any reasons to complain."

Perry signed the letter and sealed it in an envelope. "I'm sure he'll find one." He rose, letter in hand, to pull the cord to summon the butler.

Mason appeared in a moment. "My lord."

He handed him the envelope. "This needs to be delivered with urgency."

Mason bowed and left as quietly as he'd come.

After that, he had another subject to discuss with Edith. She gathered the pieces of paper in a neat stack, and he got lost admiring her elegant hands. If she wanted, those hands would save many lives when she became a surgeon.

"Will you join me in my personal parlour for a cup of tea?" he asked.

A little crease furrowed the space between her eyebrows. "Of course. You sound serious."

"I am."

They left the study and went upstairs in silence. Silence aside from Oliver's voice echoing from downstairs.

"I can't find my catgut. Has anyone seen it?"

Perry sat in the plush armchair in front of the covered Star Maiden. "I want to talk to you about what happened the other night."

She took the sofa. "The conservatory."

He took a moment to consider his words because that kiss meant a lot to him. He wanted to court her properly, ask her father's permission, and see her regularly, not just to work in his study. After that, they might get engaged if she agreed. He hoped she would because the warm, fluttery feeling in his chest couldn't be simply attraction or friendship. He cared about her. A lot.

"I don't want to..." he stammered. Great. The absolute worst moment for his speech to become hesitant.

"Perry." She reached out from the sofa to put a hand on his. "You don't have to say anything. That kiss was nothing, really."

"Nothing?" He ignored the quick pang in his chest.

"I mean, it was special, but we don't have to get married because of a kiss. It happened, and it was wonderful, but you don't have to feel responsible for my reputation or worry about my delicate feelings. It wasn't my first kiss. I'm not some young, blushing debutante who needs protection from a scoundrel or a rake." She laughed. "I might be considered a lady rake."

"Ah..." That kiss had been everything for him.

"Do not worry about me," she said.

"I do worry about you. I care about you." That was why his heart broke a little.

"I know, and I'm grateful for that." She squeezed his hand. "But see, I don't care about finding a husband. What happened in the conservatory won't ruin my chances of getting married because I'm not interested. Marianne has always wanted to be a wife and a mother. Not me."

That wasn't how he'd planned the conversation to go.

"It's that...I mean I took some liberties in the conservatory," he said.

No, that wasn't what he'd wanted to say. Not like that. But when his speech stumbled, his control diminished. He'd meant to ask her what her opinion on a proper courtship would be. She wasn't interested in marriage, but her opinion might change if he courted her.

She removed her hand. "I enjoyed the kiss and was more than willing to be kissed. If you took liberties, it was because I let you. In fact, I wouldn't mind being kissed again. Would you kiss me again?"

"Yes." No hesitation. Curious how he didn't stammer now.

She patted the space next to her on the sofa. "Come here."

Anticipation caused his pulse to spike as he sat beside her, his shoulder brushing hers.

"Kiss me, Perry. Hard."

The headache vanished when he cupped her face and kissed her. Her lips against his felt too good. He did as told and devoured her mouth while holding her head. The kiss was a battle for dominance among clashes of lips and teeth.

They kissed open-mouthed when she invited him in. The tension bothering him was silenced by a shot of pure pleasure rushing down his body. Sod his proposal for now. He wanted to kiss her and get lost in her softness.

He stroked her thigh through the layers of her skirt. When he reached her hip, he pulled her closer, and she sat on his lap. The jumble of sensations the contact with her ignited in him was almost laughable.

Putting a firm hand on her nape, he deepened the kiss, caressing her tongue with his, exploring, making her his. A little moan came out of her, and he captured it with his kiss.

She straddled him in a bold move that had him shivering with need. When she rolled her hips and rubbed against him, his trousers became uncomfortable. She held his face in a savage grip, and he was more than happy to return her passion.

He wanted more than a kiss. He wanted to worship her lovely body and make her feel all the pleasure he could give her. But when she slid a hand between them, he stopped her. If she touched him, he'd take her on that very sofa.

Breaking the kiss required every ounce of his strength. "Edith." He sounded breathless.

"Yes?" She shifted her hips back and forth, tormenting him.

With her lips swollen from the kiss and her eyes glowing from within, she looked exactly like the Star Maiden.

I want more.

Three easy words that scared him. Not because he was afraid of what he felt, but because she wasn't ready to hear them, and he wasn't ready to hear her *no, thank you.*

He held her face, memorising every single line, curve, and feature of it. "Hold me. Just that."

Each word required a ridiculous amount of energy and concentration as the headache pounded with renewed strength, but this time his condition had nothing to do with it.

She caressed his cheek with too much tenderness. The caress tasted like a goodbye. "Of course."

Then she hugged him with desperation as if fearing he would vanish into thin air in a moment. He held her back, inhaling her flowery scent and getting drunk on her sweetness.

Stealing kisses was pointless when she was stealing his heart.

PERRY'S WORDS kept echoing in Edith's mind, and each time they rumbled louder, making their way through her thoughts.

Hold me. It sounded like a prayer.

She replayed their last conversation as she arranged the bottles of the recently delivered medicinal drugs in the dispensary. Apparently, new antipyretics to reduce fever were becoming popular replacements for laudanum.

Focusing on the labels was difficult though. Kissing Perry was...special for lack of a better word. He was an excellent kisser, passionate and determined, but that wasn't the reason a quiver started in her chest at the thought of kissing him again.

He cared for her, and she cared for him. Was that all? Once, she'd enjoyed a tumble with a man who had really cared for her. There was nothing new about the act.

But Perry was different. He'd tensed when she'd told him the kiss had been nothing. She'd made a mistake, thinking he'd wanted to be reassured she didn't expect him to marry her.

To her defence, she'd had many similar conversations with men the day after a tumble. The awkward silence, the stumbling words, the fleeting glances—just to tell her, 'It was enjoyable, but I don't want to court you, least of all marry you,' which was fine with her.

She'd wanted to put Perry out of his misery by anticipating his 'I don't want to marry you' speech, but the joke was on her because she'd disappointed him, which made her wonder what he'd wanted to tell her or hear.

"Edith." Her father's rumbling voice jolted her.

She straightened, almost losing her grip on a bottle, quickly wondering if she'd done something to anger him. "Father, what are you doing here?"

His eyebrows knit together as he eyed the bottles of morphia. "I came here for a consultation. How is your work for Lord Ravenscroft going?"

"Very well."

His harsh expression hardened further. "The London School of Medicine for Women has closed for enrolment."

To be honest, she wasn't thinking about that.

A long exhale came out of him. "If you want to enrol, you still have a chance to do so. You'll have to find a qualified teacher, approved by the college, to take the admission test with, in private. You'll start your classes late, but you aren't completely ignorant of medical science. A late start shouldn't be a problem for you."

She pressed her lips together. "We have had this conversation many times, Father."

She expected the usual outburst. *You can't throw away your future like that. You disappoint me. You wasted years of studying...* and so forth.

Instead, he released a breath and slouched as if caught by sudden fatigue. He seemed to have grown old in a moment. He didn't say anything and left the room, nearly dragging his feet.

For some reason, his silence and quiet dejection hurt more than his outbursts. It was as if he'd given up on her.

She rubbed an aching spot in her chest. No, she couldn't go to medical school only to make her father happy. If she had to start a medical career, or any other career, it would be because she really wanted it. But there was something else she wanted to discuss with him.

She followed him. "Father."

He stopped and turned around.

"I wanted to talk to you about a patient, Mrs. Richards. She was discharged a few days ago," she said all in one breath. "She sustained severe head trauma, similar to what Perry endured. She needs help with her physical exercises and to buy drugs. I think she's eligible for funded care. She needs it."

"Did a doctor visit Mrs. Richards and give a diagnosis and a prognosis on her condition?"

"No. I spent some time with her and noticed the similarities between her case and Perry's. She's a seamstress, and her livelihood depends on her ability to move her hands."

He looked like an executioner. "I understand, but since you aren't qualified to provide a diagnosis, your words have little meaning. If the doctor who followed her care doesn't believe the patient needs anything else, then there isn't anything I can do."

"Father, please. She needs help." She kept her voice low as a group of nurses passed by.

"You're a volunteer in a dispensary."

"Don't use Mrs. Richards's condition to punish me."

A muscle in his jaw contracted. "I'm a doctor, and I'm doing my job. You do yours." He spun towards the exit and left her in the middle of the hallway.

"That's unfair," she said to his retreating back.

Frustration bothered her when she returned home. If Father didn't want to help, she might ask Perry. He would help Mrs. Richards. Although Father had a point when he said Edith wasn't qualified. Mrs. Richards's condition could be less serious than Edith thought. She didn't have any clinical results to support her claim aside from her instinct.

She had barely time to enter her house and hand her coat to the maid when a knock came from the door.

Daphne's smiling face came into view when Edith opened the door.

"Edith."

She closed her eyes for a moment. "I'm not sure I want to talk to you."

Daphne brushed past her and entered. "You aren't still angry with me for the story of the painting, are you?"

"No, I just need to change a few things in my life."

"Since when are you so pesky?" She leant against the wall, disregarding her bustle. "Valentine and I are going to a dinner party tonight."

"I'm not coming."

The words came out of Edith's mouth before she could think. But she didn't regret them. The affair with the painting had been a lesson she wouldn't forget.

"Neville will be there, too."

Edith folded her arms across her chest. "One more reason for me not to come."

Daphne scrunched up her face. "You lost a bet. I think you should give him what he wants."

"And I think you should leave."

Daphne burst out laughing. "You're joking."

"I'm not." She held the door open. "I have no intention of going anywhere or being anywhere near Neville."

Daphne pushed herself from the wall and walked to the door with measured steps while keeping her sharp stare on Edith. "Is it because of Perry?"

"Please, Daphne, leave."

Her eyebrows spiked. "I would give Neville what he wants if I were you. He can be quite frightening when provoked. Not to mention that he's going to be the next Earl of Ravenscroft soon."

"No, Perry isn't going to pass his title to Neville."

"He will, and Neville will get everything. Ask yourself if you want to remain on the side of the loser or be with the winner." She patted Edith's cheek before heading for the entry hall.

Edith closed the door and leant against it. Despite the bravado she'd shown when she'd been with Perry, she was worried; she couldn't deny it. And what was all that talking about Perry being the loser? As if it mattered. She would always remain by his side.

twenty

A NIGHT SPENT thinking of Edith hadn't brought any counsel to Perry.

Years ago, when he'd been a scoundrel, he wouldn't have thought for more than a second about a kiss with a willing, beautiful lady. But since the incident—or rather, since spending years in a clinic for his rehabilitation, showing respect to others had become an absolute, constant necessity.

Besides, Edith wasn't a woman he barely knew. She was special. She captured his attention whatever she did, and he cared for her too much to choose to have a quick tumble with her.

The fact she was a few feet from him right now didn't make his situation easier. A new headache bothered him that day, thus he'd asked her to write the bank cheques for the bills he had to pay. He'd write his signature at the bottom of them, but at least he didn't have to read long records of numbers and copy them in very small characters.

"That's the tailor." She handed him the next cheque. "It's ten pounds only."

"A new waistcoat, but not for me. It was for Oliver." He signed the slip of paper and set it aside.

"A silk bow tie."

He signed the next. "Oliver again."

"The last one. Grocery. Five pounds."

"Thank you, Edith." His hand hurt from all the writing.

"You don't spend a lot." She opened another register. "Dr. York spends more than you."

"I'm trying to be frugal on principle. A gentleman doesn't spend ostentatiously, according to the *Gentlemen's Book of Etiquette and Manual of Politeness*. Have more than you show, speak less than you know."

She stretched out her arms over her head. The movement pushed forwards her breasts, straining the fabric of her shirt. Surely, a gentleman shouldn't notice that; it had to be written somewhere in the manual.

"You're taking being a gentleman very seriously," she said.

"In my youth, I never did, but I now see the point." He set aside the pen. "After the incident, I was surrounded by compassionate people who did nothing but support me. So many people were kind to me, and not because I was the brother of an earl. They felt sorry for me and wanted to help me. Believe it or not, that changed me. Your family, you, my brother, Oliver, and the nurses and medics in Geneva helped me get better. Being at the receiving end of love and compassion is a wonderful feeling, and I want to return the favour."

She touched his hand. "You're a good man, Perry."

Not really. A good man wouldn't want to grab her by the waist, sit her on the desk, and kiss her until she moaned again.

Their heated second kiss had been a mistake because he was under a spell now. And he wanted to bloody court her.

"Thank you, Edith. I try to be a good man."

"About that." She frowned. "I'd like to ask you a favour."

"Anything."

"I met a woman at St. Brigid Hospital, Mrs. Richards. She fell off a ladder and hit her head hard. After that, she was in a state of prolonged loss of consciousness for weeks, and now she has problems moving and talking properly."

"Disturbingly familiar." He smiled.

"She was discharged from the hospital a few days ago, but she needs help. She isn't wealthy, and her husband is struggling." She put her hand over his. "Would you help her? You understand better than anyone how important medical support is in a situation like that."

"Edith." He brought her hand to his mouth and kissed it. "Of course, I'll help Mrs. Richards."

"You're wonderful." She threw herself at him, wrapping her arms around his neck.

He held her, smiling at her enthusiasm. Her willingness to help others was undeniable. If only she would resume her studies.

She kissed his cheek. The difference between this chaste kiss and the one they'd shared in the parlour was so vast there shouldn't be any comparison between the two. But his heart didn't seem to agree. Both kisses caused it to thud faster.

"Thank you, Perry, for caring about her," she said.

"I care about everything that makes you happy."

He must have said something shocking because her eyes widened and her lips parted. But he had something even more shocking set aside for her.

He was about to tell her that he wanted to court her properly when his very agitated butler opened the door.

"My lord, Lord Neville is here and wishes to see you." Mason patted his forehead with a handkerchief. "I'm afraid your uncle seems quite insistent, my lord."

"Show him in, Mason, thank you."

Mason had barely time to bow before Uncle Neville strode inside. His gaze flickered over Edith for a glacial moment. She stiffened.

Uncle Neville straightened his fine jacket. "Perry, Edith."

"Miss Winkworth." Perry stood up. "You will address Miss

Winkworth appropriately when in my presence, or you may leave now."

Edith trapped her bottom lip between her teeth.

A muscle in Uncle Neville's face twitched. "I'm very well acquainted with *Edith*."

More than Perry would like.

He clasped his hands behind his back. "If you refuse to be civil with my guest, I'm afraid I'll have to ask you to leave without allowing you to tell me why you came here in the first place."

"Very well. I won't address her at all." Uncle Neville produced a folded letter from the inner pocket of his jacket. "I'd like to discuss your late letter with you."

Edith rose. "I'll leave you."

He was about to tell her to stay, but perhaps she was uncomfortable in Uncle Neville's presence. "Thank you, Miss Winkworth."

She gave him a little smile before walking out.

Uncle Neville turned his head to stare at her in a fashion not at all gentlemanly.

"Uncle," he said, frustration burning the back of his mouth.

"What is she doing here?" Uncle Neville jabbed a finger in the direction of the door.

"Reach your point. I don't have much time." Perry sat on his chair, but his uncle remained standing.

"We agreed about you renouncing the title. And then you send me this?" He waved the letter.

"I've had a change of heart and realised how cowardly it was of me not to face my duty. That's all. Albert and my solicitor support my choice. It's nothing personal." Actually, it was.

Uncle Neville placed his hands on the desk. "I beg to differ. You shouldn't be the earl. Your health is too delicate."

"Thank you for your concern, but I'm well. I've fully recovered from the incident."

Uncle Neville arched a sceptical brow. "I heard rumours about you."

"Oh, I heard rumours about you, too. I can tell you exactly what I heard." Perry held his uncle's stare.

"I'm incredibly curious." His uncle put aside a pile of documents to lean closer. "What did you hear?"

"Leave Miss Winkworth alone."

He tapped the letter. "Renounce your title, and I'll oblige."

"Don't be ridiculous."

Uncle Neville pocketed the letter again. "Then I'll do what I want with Miss Winkworth, and the outcome will be your doing." He stressed the last two words.

Over his dead body. "You don't deserve the title. You put the Ravenscroft name to shame."

"We'll see who is the one shaming the Ravenscroft name, Nephew. You and Miss Winkworth will hear from my solicitor."

Perry clenched his jaw when his uncle left. His uncle's threats didn't worry him; the law was on his side regarding the title, but Edith was another matter.

twenty-one

T HE REST OF the day slogged through more cheques to sign and letters to answer.

Edith had worked so hard that week Perry had decided to treat her and mistreat himself just to make her happy. Because what he wanted to propose to her was one of his nightmares.

So he asked her to go to...

"Dancing?" Excitement rang in her voice. "You want to go to a ball?"

"No, not a ball. When I was younger, I used to go to Saffron Hill and take part in one of the many dancing parties in the public houses at night. I would wear plain clothes and dance all night among pints of ale and laughter."

It sounded absolutely crazy now.

Her face brightened. "It sounds wonderful. You aren't worried about someone witnessing a seizure then."

He shrugged. "No one will know who I am. I'll be just another patron."

"What are we waiting for?"

"Dusk. The dances won't start until nightfall."

"I'll change and see you later." She hurried out of the room, humming a happy tune and tearing a smile out of him.

He drummed his fingers on the desk, wondering if he'd be able to finish a whole dance before wishing to go home. Her smile was worth his sacrifice.

After he changed into a plain brown suit and a flat hat that horrified his valet, he hailed a cab to Edith's house. Chased by the lamplighters, darkness crawled over the wet cobbles as he waited for her.

She emerged from the shadows, wearing a pretty dark-green dress that exalted her eyes, and his mood lifted in a moment.

She sat next to him in the cab, shifting constantly as if she couldn't stay still. "I'm ready."

He couldn't hold back a smile at her happiness. "Saffron Hill," he said to the driver.

"So you're incognito now."

"I disappeared from London years ago, and when I lived here, Albert was the earl. Everyone paid more attention to him."

"Do you resent him for his choice?"

"At first, I did. But now I don't, really. He's truly in love with Gabriela. Albert chose love."

"Yes, but you..." She fiddled with a fold of her skirt. "I'm sorry."

"I'm not fit for the job. Is that what you wanted to say?"

She shook her head. "I didn't mean it like that, but you went through a lot and needed to recover."

"Albert gave me time. He didn't leave me alone when I was still in the hospital. He waited for me to recover before marrying Gabriela. But I'm aware of my limits. Not to mention the constant worry of having a seizure in front of everyone."

She put her hand over his, and the simple contact sent a shock through him, as usual. "The seizures are sporadic now. In a few years, they might be gone altogether."

He laced his fingers through hers. "Oliver thinks the same. He says the seizures are caused by a trigger, and if I identify the trigger and control it, they will stop."

She nodded. "I read that strong smells, like that of kerosene, can trigger seizures in some people. Sometimes it could be a flash of light, thunder, or even a type of food. It's fascinating, isn't it?" Her eyes flared wide. "I'm sorry. I didn't mean to offend. I was talking from a purely scientific point of view."

Hell, he loved it when she talked like a scientist. "Don't apologise. Your brain works in that way, and it's a beautiful brain." He laughed. "That's an odd thing to say."

She laughed as well and rested her head on his shoulder. He loved these simple moments of intimacy, too. They were deeper than the kisses they'd exchanged so far.

Saffron Hill's alleyways were lit with dozens of lanterns hanging from the many public houses. Loud music came from the open windows, and the air was thick with the smell of ale and wine. Holding Edith's hand, Perry led her to the nearest public house. The patrons were dancing, playing instruments, and clapping their hands in the tap room in a chaotic and colourful party.

"It's fantastic," she shouted over the din.

"I told you."

Edith didn't waste time. She tugged at his hand and pulled him towards the middle of the hall. The patrons pressed him from every side. Loud voices buzzed in his ears, and a cold sensation crept over him despite the stifling temperature. He dragged his feet until he came to an abrupt stop.

"Wait." He took a shaky breath. "Maybe you go ahead, and I'll follow."

"We can leave if you don't feel comfortable."

Her concern warmed his chest, but he needed more time to get used to the crowded room. "It was my idea. I'll dance with you but not immediately."

"It's not fair for you. I don't have to dance."

He smiled. "I want to see you dance. Don't worry about me.

I'll get a mug of ale, find a nice, quiet corner, and watch you for a while until I get used to the crowd. Really. Go. Have fun."

"If you want to leave, let me know." She kissed his cheek, and he found he could breathe more easily.

She didn't wait for a partner but jumped into the middle of the dancing crowd. The other dancers welcomed her with loud cheers and raised mugs of frothy ale.

He watched her dance across the room because for some reason it was difficult not to, and he didn't want to deprive himself of the pleasure. The more he focused on her alone, the less the crowd bothered him.

Edith twirled around, laughing and clapping her hands in rhythm with the upbeat music. Her skirts flapped around her legs, and her cheeks were flushed. He leant against the wall and drank her in, his blood humming in his veins.

She locked her gaze on his, swaying her hips. If she hadn't already charmed him, she would now.

In the warm light of the lamps, her skin glowed from within. He understood what Mr. Carter had seen in her when he'd painted the Star Maiden. She looked like a goddess of light and charm, and he was utterly smitten with her. She headed to him, dancing across the distance separating them. The closer she came, the louder his desire roared.

"Your turn now." She tugged at his arm. "I've been dancing for an hour, and you've been sitting here, watching me. Are you ready?"

"Yes." He was under her spell, and the fact didn't bother him in the least.

He put his mug of ale on the table and led her towards the middle of the room. "It's a contredanse, isn't it?"

"This one is out of fashion. You won't find it in any fancy ball-room, but it's one of my favourites."

He followed her steps and copied the other dancers. He was slow compared to the others, but his brain surprised him because the instructions on the routine he'd learnt with his dance master resurfaced. Once he remembered the sequence of steps that had to be repeated a few times, he let the dance flow.

He laughed with Edith, holding her in his arms.

"Too many people?" she asked.

"Yes, but if I focus on you, I don't mind."

"Get off me!" a man yelled from behind him.

Loud voices and insults erupted from the back of the room. People shoved each other. Someone bumped into Perry's back, and he ended up smashing against Edith.

"Ouch." She lost her balance.

He held her up and led her away from the jostling crowd.

"What's going on?" she asked.

"A brawl. They often happen after a few drinks. It's better if we leave."

The sound of wood smashing came along with that of punches and glass shattering.

More people joined the fray until mugs were thrown across the room and the tables were overturned.

"Stop fighting!" the publican yelled over the chaos.

Not that anyone paid him the slightest bit of attention. Perry and Edith had almost reached the door when a chilling shout rent the air.

"Blood," someone cried out.

"We need a doctor! Help!"

Edith came to a stop. "What happened?"

"I bet someone got stabbed," he said.

"Perhaps we should take a look."

"Of course." He didn't hesitate.

As the fight died down among mutters and whispers, the patrons formed a circle around a grovelling woman on the floor.

"I didn't mean to stab her." A man raised his bloodied hands. "It was an accident."

"Is there a doctor here?" the publican asked.

"There's one over there," the man said.

Perry and Edith turned towards the doctor in question. The man was slumped over a chair with an empty bottle on his lap and his glasses askew on his nose. He snored so loudly Perry could hear him from across the room.

"Someone sends for a sober doctor," the publican said.

"It's going to be too late. She'll bleed out," a man said.

Perry tugged at Edith's hand. "Can you help?"

Her chest rose and fell quickly. "I haven't practised anything in years, and when I practised, my father was always with me."

"That woman is going to die. There's no time to wait for the doctor." He took the leather bag lying at the feet of the drunk doctor and handed it to Edith. "Please."

She was breathing harder now than when she'd danced. "I'm not a doctor."

"Take a look at her."

"She's the mother of two," the publican said. "Nice woman, she is."

"Please," Perry said.

"I'll see what I can do." She took the bag and straightened. "She's unconscious. Lift her gently and put her on a table. I need hot water, clean cloths, and lots of light."

The change in her voice and posture fascinated Perry. One moment, she trembled and paled. The next, she hardened and took charge.

She waved the people away. "Give her space. Perry, will you help me? You'll need to clean your hands with carbolic acid."

That caught him off guard. "Yes."

She cut the woman's shirt, untied the worn corset, and lifted the chemise revealing a slash in her abdomen. Perry twitched his mouth at the coppery scent of blood. The publican brought what Edith had asked and made sure people kept their distance.

After washing the wound with carbolic acid, she wiped it with a cloth soaked in hot water.

"The cut is not deep, but she needs stitches."

Despite the blood, Perry watched intrigued as she washed the cut and stitched it from the inside out while he handed her the shiny surgical tools she needed.

"Is she going to live?" the publican asked.

"I hope so."

She worked quickly without raising her gaze from the woman. Silence lingered in the room. The only sound came from the snoring physician.

After she stitched the wound, Perry helped her wrap a tight bandage around the woman's belly. A round of applause rose from the crowd once they finished. He sagged against the table, hands shaking.

"She'll need a proper doctor anyway." She wiped her hands.

"He should be on his way." The publican spread his arms. "Ale on the house."

Perry covered the woman with a blanket the publican produced from behind the counter while Edith sat on a chair, her hair dishevelled and her eyes wild.

He squeezed her hand, and she flashed a little smile.

They waited in the public house for the doctor to arrive in an eerie silence. After the outburst, no one chatted, the music had stopped altogether, and only the sound of the patrons sipping their drinks could be heard. It took the doctor a good half an hour to arrive. Without Edith's help, the woman would be dead by now. The patrons formed a circle around the improvised operating table again.

"Out of my way. Let me see," the doctor said.

Perry held his breath for both the woman and Edith. She had to see that medicine was her call after the incident.

The doctor examined the woman and inspected Edith's work. "Who attended to the patient's wound?"

Edith stood up. "I did. It was a penetrating abdominal trauma, two inches from the spleen. The patient went into shock approximately two minutes after the event. I believe the shock was due to the fright and the pain rather than to a severe laceration of an artery or hypovolemia. I performed a ligation of a branch of the splenic vein, using the smaller haemostat clamp, although the laceration wasn't as deep or serious as I feared, but I thought it wouldn't harm," she said all in one breath.

"Blimey." Perry scratched his chin. "I wish I understood what you said." But it was bloody arousing.

She blushed, looking adorable. "I just said the patient lost a lot of blood, but she didn't faint because of that."

The doctor nodded, a wide smile stretching his moustache. "I'm impressed, miss. The patient needs absolute rest, and I'll have to inspect the wound every day, but, miss, you did a good job." He offered his hand to her, and she hesitated before shaking it.

"Did I?" she said in a low tone.

"Absolutely. Your quick assessment of the patient's condition saved her life. You should think about becoming a professional." He checked the woman's pulse. "Perhaps you don't know, but there are a few medical schools that accept women. It's your moment, miss. Take advantage of it."

Perry beamed, but Edith's mouth didn't contract; it remained strained as if she were smelling something foul.

When they left the public house, Edith shivered despite the fact she was wearing a thick cloak and that no chilly gusts blew.

"You saved her," Perry said, shrugging off his coat to drape it around her shoulders.

"I was so scared. Look." She showed him her shaky hands. "I haven't touched a book on surgery in years, and the last time I practised was before *Princess Alice* when my father showed me the different suturing techniques on animal carcasses he got from the butcher. Mother hated our practice. She thought it was horrific. Only a few times, Father let me practise on unclaimed cadavers in the morgue."

"I don't need all these details. Thank you." He put a hand on his chest.

"Tonight, it was the first time I stitched a human, a living one, that is." She wheezed.

"Even the doctor said you did a good job." He swept a curl from her face, feeling her cold skin.

"I'm not sure how I feel right now, but I know I was lucky."

"That's not true. You were used to studying and reading years ago. All the knowledge you gathered didn't go away. It's there in your brain, waiting for you to decide to pick it up again."

She leant against his shoulder, and he wrapped his arm around her.

"You should start studying again, become a doctor, and help more people survive a stabbing."

She smiled, but the smile didn't reach her eyes. "I can't return to study."

"Why not?"

"That time has gone. Now I'm..." She seemed to choke on air with a shuddering breath.

"What?"

"I'm scared."

He pointed in the direction of the public house. "Thanks to you, two children didn't become orphans tonight. You can't be scared of that. You're a brilliant, brave woman, and the fact you don't see it makes me angry. Why do you think I asked you to work for me? Not for the damn painting or the letters I can't read. I did it because I believe you can be a great doctor. Hell, you've just proven it."

"My father was very disappointed when I stopped studying." Each word came out slowly as if she forced herself to speak. "How can I start studying without disappointing him again? If I fail, I'll completely lose his respect, or what's left of it."

"I don't understand. You can't disappoint him by studying again. That's what he wants for you."

She nearly hid her face in his chest. "I might not be good at studying anymore. What if I start again, and it turns out my brain can't keep up? He'll be so disappointed. I'll be disappointed."

"No, he won't be." He stopped walking to take her face in his hands. "He would never be disappointed by your trying. He'll be right next to you, cheering you up and helping you." He caressed the top of her head. "But the most important thing is what you want to do. Do you want to become a doctor?"

She pressed her cheek to his palm. "You know how difficult it is for a woman to be accepted into society as a surgeon. Female doctors are bullied and made fun of. Not to mention the years of studying and the cost of the fees."

"I didn't ask you to analyse society. Do *you* want to become a doctor?"

For a long, horrible minute, she didn't say anything but stared at him with a lost expression that broke his heart. Then she gave the slightest, tiniest nod.

He leant closer. "I'd like to hear you saying it, please."

"Yes," she whispered lower than a little mouse.

"Louder, please?"

"Yes." She raised her voice by only half an octave.

"Louder?"

"Yes." There was no change in her tone.

"For Pete's sake, shout!"

She let out a high-pitched scream that pierced his ears. He burst out laughing.

She laughed too, sagging against him. "Yes, yes. I want to be a doctor. I love medicine. I love working in a hospital. I want to study again."

He picked her up and twirled her around. "Yes!"

She wrapped her arms around his neck and whooped at the sky.

"Be quiet, you bloody drunk!" a man yelled from a window before pouring a bucket of icy water on them.

The sudden, unwelcome cold and wetness silenced Perry.

"There are people who want to sleep here. Go home." The man slammed the shutters closed.

Edith's mouth hung open as drops trickled down her soaked hair. "Goodness."

He brushed her wet locks from her cheeks. "Are you all right?"

She laughed but clamped a hand over her mouth to muffle the sound. "Never been better."

twenty-two

EDITH COULDN'T STOP shivering once in the cab.

Between the icy water and the emotions of improvising surgery on the dirty table of a public house, her body was too shocked to keep its warmth.

Perry rubbed her hands. "You're freezing."

"Why do we always end up soaked?"

He chuckled. "I'm cold as well. We need to change."

She snuggled closer to him, taking a moment to close her eyes and not thinking about anything. Perry's arms were that powerful. His strength was contagious, and the closer she was to him, the stronger she felt. He rubbed her back when she shivered again, her teeth chattering, but not just with cold.

When the cab stopped in front of his townhouse and he offered her his hand, the smile brightening his face warmed her with a flutter in her chest. Yet another strong emotion to deal with that night.

"I'll escort you home when you're warm and dry. As usual," he said, reaching out for the bell.

"No key?"

He shrugged. "Never had it."

Mason opened the door, shooting a worried glance at them. "My lord. Miss Winkworth. What happened?"

"Just a normal evening," Perry said.

"Mason," she said, brushing past him.

"What do you need, my lord?" Mason took their wet coats.

"Tea, please, in my room. No need to rouse Mrs. Davidson, and discretion, please."

The butler bowed. "My lord."

Perry held her hand, going up the stairs. "I'll give you something to wear while your clothes get dry."

"We shocked Mason." She exhaled in relief when she entered Perry's warm bedroom.

"He gets worried easily." He searched through his wardrobe.

Mason knocked and waited for Perry's permission before bringing in the tea. After tossing another worried glance at them, he left them alone. Oddly enough, she hadn't thought about being alone with Perry in his bedroom until that moment.

How scandalous. How perfect.

"Here. It's the warmest garment I have." He handed her one of his dressing gowns. "The screen is over there."

Goosebumps covered her skin as she peeled off her wet clothes from her body. His hearty scent wafted from the soft fabric of the dressing gown, and she closed her eyes when she slid it on. Warm and gentle, like Perry.

"Are you done?" she asked.

"Bring your clothes."

He wore another dressing gown that matched his sapphire eyes. His wet hair enhanced his fine features and that devilish smile of his; it still held the secrets of his former scandalous life.

He stretched her clothes on a chair in front of the roaring fire. The heated gaze he gave her warmed her more than the flames. He wasn't the first man who had looked at her scandalously with hunger, but he was the first man who had made it count.

"I won't forget this night." She sat on the thick carpet and stretched out her legs towards the fire.

He sat next to her. "I'm glad you decided to start studying again." He touched her hand with a finger, sending shivers up her arm. "Although you have a future as an art model."

She laughed. "You really like that painting."

"No. I really like you." He held her chin for a moment, and she got lost in the intensity of his stare. A stare that didn't belong to a gentleman.

She didn't think; she didn't need to. She kissed him hard. His response was immediate. A moan left her when he tangled his long fingers through her hair and pushed his tongue past her lips as if taking his right place. The cold wasn't a problem anymore. Sensations burned her from the inside out.

The kiss became a battle of lips and tongues as she ran her hands over the hard slab of his chest. The way he held her head in place with authority had a dominating quality she swooned over.

She fiddled with his sash until it yielded and she touched his smooth, naked skin. He was all sharp ridges and hard muscles. She could count each one of them with her fingertips. They broke the kiss at the same time, their breaths mingling.

She caressed his broad chest and firm abdomen again to reach underneath. That was her personal Rubicon because once she touched him, she'd crossed a line with no going back.

His lips parted, and she waited for him to say something, perhaps to stop her. But the hunger in his gaze couldn't be mistaken. A groan rumbled from his chest when she closed her hand around him. Of their own accord, her legs squeezed to soothe the throbbing ache between them.

He sucked his teeth as she stroked him carefully until he moved her hand aside and pulled off her dressing gown with one smooth move. Her nipples hardened under his eager stare because he paused to watch her in awe.

"You're so beautiful," he said with ferocity.

She didn't have time to reciprocate the compliment before he dipped his head and closed his hot mouth around her nipple.

All her breath swished out of her with a moan. He tongued and sucked at her, and the more he did that, the more wetness pooled between her legs. The ache was consuming her. As if reading her mind, he slid a hand between her thighs, pausing again to stroke her skin before rubbing her with surprising kindness. Slow, lazy circles that made her pant.

She widened her legs, and he used his whole palm to rub her. The sensation was like nothing she'd experienced, which was strange. It wasn't the first time a man pleasured her, but with Perry, everything was different. Everything seemed new.

He was relentless in his sweet assault, somehow guessing exactly what she needed at the perfect time. The right stroke, the right pressure, the right spot. Perfect.

The release came with enough strength to make her arch her back and shut her up. The scream she meant to let out remained trapped in her throat. She wrapped her arms around him as she enjoyed every ounce of the pleasure spasming through her. He held her in a sweet, sweet hug that melted her heart.

"Let me court you," he whispered against her skin, his lips brushing a sensitive spot on her neck.

His words shocked her back to reality. She inched back from him, needing to see his eyes. They were glowing with passion and determination that didn't leave room for doubts.

"I want to court you. Properly. Talk to your father." He took her face, his chest heaving. "After I court you, I'll propose. After that, I'll give you the most luscious wedding ever given, and then I'll do everything to keep you happy."

"Perry." She put her hands over his. "You don't have to do this. You aren't ruining me."

"But you are ruining me." He closed his eyes for a moment. "I'm not asking out of a sense of duty. I want to court you."

Goodness. He was serious. He wanted to propose.

She squeezed his hand. "I'm grateful, but you must admit that I'm certainly not the bride you want to share your title with."

"Why do you say that?"

"The fact huge scandals haven't involved me yet, it's a matter of time. There are plenty of rumours about me. I've spent the past years doing all sorts of things. Things that will ruin your reputation as well if they come out and you marry me. You saw me in the Scarlet Room. You saw how I behaved. I'm not a maiden, and I tried opium."

"I don't care about your past. I've trodden the same path. I only care about our future, a future together. I want you. I want more, Edith. I want everything."

"You can have me. Anytime you want. Even now." She started to open her dressing gown, but he stopped her.

"No, not like this." He took her hands although his hungry gaze told a different story.

"I don't know what to say." Her voice quivered, but she had to be honest. His proposal was a bit overwhelming at the moment.

"I understand." Sheer, undiluted pain radiated from him. "With my seizures—"

"Heavens, no! It's not that." She scattered kisses on his hand. "I don't care about your seizures. It's me. I've just recently found my way back to a normal life. I want to start studying again. I feel... whole again, with a purpose. But everything is happening too quickly. Give me a little time. Let me walk on my feet for a while."

He smiled, but his smile was sad as if he believed she was asking for more time only to sweeten the rejection.

"All the time you want."

"There's something else." She lowered her gaze. "Even though the Enabling Act has been approved, unmarried female doctors are scorned. A married woman and a countess at that won't be employed as a surgeon by any hospitals."

"So if I propose, your answer will always be no, no matter what." Too much sadness rang in his voice.

"I'm sure we'll find a solution." She hugged him and kissed his cheek. "You're wonderful, Perry. Everything about you is wonderful. I feel wonderful when I'm with you. The world is wonderful when we're together."

He squeezed her, burying his face in the crook of her neck. "You know, I won't forget this night either."

LET ME COURT YOU. Those words had tormented Edith for the whole night.

She couldn't imagine a better suitor than Perry. He had every reason not to trust her or be resentful. Instead, he'd been nothing but kind to her. Not just kind but passionate, generous, lovely, and understanding. She was running out of positive traits to describe him.

But exactly for his kindness, she wanted to start afresh and prove herself she could work hard, as she'd been used to doing, and achieve something. He inspired her to be a better person.

Although she'd be lying if she said she had everything planned out about her studies. One moment, she was determined to try the admission test as soon as possible before even that chance would be gone. The next, fear gripped her by the throat, and she wished to have more time to get ready and reacquainted with the medical books.

She was at home, sitting in front of the warm hearth in the drawing room with her battling thoughts for company.

After last night's bucket of icy water, she kept shivering. Or maybe it was her worries. She couldn't deny the strong emotion of having successfully operated on a human, the excitement of doing something she loved.

"Miss, a letter for you." The maid interrupted her dark musing, handing her an envelope.

"Thank you, Anne."

The letter was from Perry, but when she opened the envelope, there was only a journal article. She unfolded the piece of paper and read it.

The article praised the work of a female surgeon, Dr. Emily Barber, who had successfully avoided a man's leg amputation by applying a new technique to clamp the damaged artery and suture the wound. Her achievement was called revolutionary for the history of medicine by the journalist.

How had Perry known she needed a little nudge to make her decision? A lump of emotion thickened her throat. He managed to cheer her up even when he wasn't with her.

No more excuses. She stood up and marched towards her father's study without thinking too much.

"Father?" She inched the door open, her legs turning into blancmange.

He raised his gaze from his documents, his brow furrowing. There had been a time when he'd smiled whenever she'd entered his study.

"What is it? If you need money, I'm afraid you'll have to wait."

That hurt, but at the same time, it steeled her determination. Father was right. In the past few years, she'd sought him out mostly to ask him for money.

"I don't want money, Father." She left the door open in case he wanted her to leave.

He sighed and rubbed his forehead. "If this is about the case of Mrs. Richards, I've already told you my opinion."

"I made a decision."

"Yes?" he asked without looking at her.

"I want to resume my studies and become a doctor." Her voice quivered through her short speech, and she sounded utterly terrified to her own ears.

Father remained still. His hand, holding the pen, hovered over the document. He was so frozen she worried he might be sick.

She stepped closer to the desk. "I know I've disappointed you.

But I decided I want to become a surgeon, and I'll be grateful if you could help me get the books I need to pass the admission test. So I can start over."

He removed his glasses, his expression stern. Not the bursting enthusiasm she'd dare to hope for.

"If this is what you want, I'll absolutely help you in any way I can. Medicine has advanced considerably since you stopped studying. You'll have a lot to cover, both in anatomy and surgical procedures. After that, you'll need a proper teacher who'll administer your test. It's a huge commitment that requires an equally huge sacrifice. Are you ready for this?"

"Yes."

"I mean it, dammit!" He slammed a hand on the desk, causing the ink bottle to shake. "This is not a game. We're talking about your future and the future of the people who will be your patients. Becoming a doctor is difficult for a man, but it's especially difficult for a woman. Many people will shun you, even though the number of female doctors increases every year. You'll face a long, arduous battle, and you won't win unless you're completely committed to your goal."

"I am." She forced herself not to shiver.

His expression didn't soften. "You'll forgive me if I don't trust your word. You'll prove yourself through your results. Yes, I'll help you, but I expect you to put every effort and every waking moment of your life into this venture. No more late nights with your friends. No more spending the day in bed, sleeping. No more seeking only what pleases you. I want discipline and honesty."

Tears threatened to spill, but she blinked them away. She didn't want to cry in front of him. That would mean starting her new life on the wrong foot.

"Yes," she croaked out.

"Good." He picked up his pen again and gestured at the shelves loaded with books behind him. "You may start studying human anatomy again."

"Yes." She seemed unable to say something different.

She selected the latest edition of *Human Anatomy and Surgery*. Goodness, it was heavier than the edition she'd studied before. Scientists must have discovered so much in the past years.

"Thank you, Father."

He gave her a nod, but she longed for a hug or a comforting word that never came.

twenty-three

EDITH MASSAGED THE back of her neck. Her body
wasn't used to reading and focusing all day anymore.

Since she'd made a deal with Perry, she was reading in
his study while he read more boring agricultural reports at his
desk. Also, she preferred the quiet of his house to the chaos of the
constant visitors her parents received. Not to mention that Edith
didn't want to be disturbed by Daphne. Dr. York worked next to
Perry, avoiding looking at her whenever he raised his gaze. Still, the
fact he stayed there without blushing was an improvement from
their last encounters.

She yawned. "I'm rusty."

"I'm sure you'll do great. Do not worry," Perry said, putting
aside a folder.

"Medicine is the most noble pursuit," Dr. York said. "Your
father must be proud of you."

"I love him, and he loves me, but to be honest with you, I
expected to see him happier or that he would have hugged me. If
anything, he looked angry when I told him I wanted to study
again."

"Because he cares about you and is worried." Perry reached out and took her hand.

She acknowledged the little quiver at the bottom of her stomach. "At least he promised me to search for a qualified teacher for the test."

The butler opened the door. "My lord, there's a Mr. Simmons who wishes to see you and Miss Winkworth."

Edith tensed. "I've never heard the name."

"Please show him in, Mason." Perry stood up when a man in a fine, tailored suit walked in.

Mr. Simmons carried a leather bag under his arm. "Lord Ravenscroft, thank you for seeing me. I'm Mr. Simmons, senior solicitor at Thomson & Passmore."

A sickening lump crawled into Edith's throat. That firm was the oldest and most famous in London; its solicitors were employed by the top echelon of aristocracy and politicians. Mr. Simmons had to be there for a serious reason.

"Please take a seat." Perry exchanged a glance with her.

The solicitor sat down and opened the bag. "I represent Lord Neville St. George, Master of Tallbridge, and Mr. Jonathan Clarke, the owner of the Scarlet Room."

Edith suppressed a gasp. Dr. York scowled.

Mr. Simmons spread a few documents on the desk. "Miss Winkworth spent a night in the Scarlet Room in the company of Lord Neville. Is that correct?"

She cleared her throat. "Yes."

"Do you recognise your signature in the Scarlet Room's contract?" He showed her the ten-page contract she'd signed weeks ago.

"I do," she said.

He flipped through the pages, muttering under his breath. "This section"—he showed her the part in fine prints—"is a binding contract between you and not simply the Scarlet Room's owner but its customers. I believe you lost a bet against Lord Neville while playing a card game in the Scarlet Room."

Perry gave her an encouraging nod.

"I did, but what does that have to do with this?" she asked.

Mr. Simmons steepled his fingers together on the desk. "The verbal contract you agreed upon with Lord Neville can be enforced by virtue of the contract you signed."

"I don't understand," she said.

"In other words," Perry said, jaw tensing, "unless Miss Winkworth honours the terms of her agreement with Lord Neville, she might be fined."

"Or go to prison for breaching the agreement," Mr. Simmons completed.

"This is absurd." Perry furrowed his brow. "It was a nonsensical bet, and Miss Winkworth has no intention of yielding to Lord Neville's demands."

"I don't really remember having agreed to the bet," she said. "I was drunk."

The solicitor raised a quizzical eyebrow. "I have two witnesses, Miss Daphne Ferguson and Mr. Valentine Carter, who claim you only took a few sips of champagne. Hardly drunk."

"I'm very sensitive to alcohol."

"I'm afraid that's not enough. If you truly were incapacitated, then yes, the contract would be null. But as of now, there isn't enough evidence to support your claim." Mr. Simmons lifted his shoulders. "I'm here as the legal representative of the Scarlet Room and Lord Neville, and I'm afraid the contract is perfectly legal. Miss Winkworth does risk going to prison for a period between three and ten years, depending on what the judge decides."

She drew in a breath that burned all its way down to her lungs. "No."

"There's a way out of the obligation, of course." Mr. Simmons held up a hand. "Lord Neville is willing to withdraw his demand if Lord Ravenscroft renounces his title."

She clamped a hand over her mouth.

"This is blackmailing." Dr. York scoffed.

"Business, I'm afraid." Mr. Simmons fished out another document from his infernal bag. "I have everything ready here. My lord, if you wish to read the document and inform your solicitor, we can arrange a meeting tomorrow with the barrister. The alternative is that Miss Winkworth honours the agreement. Lord Neville will be satisfied with any of the two outcomes."

"I'd rather be involved in another shipwreck than ask Edith to honour something dishonourable." Perry snatched the document from the solicitor's hands. "I'll talk with my solicitor."

"No." Edith stopped him by blocking his hand. "You can't consider renouncing your title. I won't allow you to ruin your life because of me."

"You're more important." He gave her a sad smile. "You're everything," he whispered so low she was likely the only one who heard it.

She drew in a breath as she closed her fingers around his. "Don't. Please."

"Lord Ravenscroft?" Mr. Simmons prompted.

Dr. York scraped his chair back and shot up to his feet. "I must speak my mind," he said. "I have something to say. The contract Miss Winkworth signed in the Scarlet Room isn't valid."

Everyone turned towards him. His firm voice and clenched fists were a shock for Edith.

"Yes?" Mr. Simmons asked when Dr. York didn't say anything. The solicitor's tone was that of someone losing his patience quickly. "What's your evidence of the invalidity of the contract?"

Dr. York wiped his hands on his trousers. "It's not valid because... I have a confession to make."

Mr. Simmons exhaled and rubbed the bridge of his nose. "Then please, do go on. We're all ears."

"What are you doing, mate?" Perry whispered.

"I was in the Scarlet Room that night. You may ask for

evidence from its owner." Dr. York pointed a finger at Edith. "I drugged Miss Winkworth before she signed the contract. She was unfit to plead at the time she signed that document."

Dr. York's attempt to save the situation was admirable, but surely, it was too ridiculous to be taken into account.

"That's not true," she said. "It's absurd."

"With what did you drug her?" Mr. Simmons asked.

Dr. York jutted out his chin. "I administered her a dose of two hundred milligrams of cocaine, fifty milligrams of opium, and twenty milligrams of an experimental substance called phomine right before she entered the Scarlet Room without her knowledge. While we were waiting in the anteroom in the dark, I approached her with a ready syringe and drugged her. As a consequence of the drugging, she became confused and drowsy, incapable of understanding what the contract entailed. The contract is invalid."

Mr. Simmons narrowed his eyes to slits. "Why would you do such a thing?"

"Please. This is absurd," Edith said.

Again, everyone turned their attention to Dr. York. Edith was genuinely curious to hear his answer.

He opened and closed his hands. "An experiment. I needed to test a new drug combination on a healthy young female of the same weight as Miss Winkworth. Opportunity met need in the Scarlet Room, and hey presto! I drugged her."

"An experiment?" Mr. Simmons's brow spiked with disbelief.

Perry rubbed his eyes, muttering something under his breath.

"For my personal enjoyment," Dr. York said. "And scientific knowledge."

A moment of thick silence stretched. She could bet everyone was thinking the same—*rubbish*.

She huffed. "Dr. York, please. What are you doing?"

The solicitor didn't even glance at her. "Are you ready to put your declaration on paper?" Mr. Simmons handed him yet another document produced from his leather bag.

"Absolutely."

"Oliver," Perry said. "Don't."

Dr. York shut him up, lifting a hand. "I had to confess. The truth was weighing me down." He wrote on the piece of paper under the watchful eye of the solicitor.

"Dr. York, please," she said. "Don't do this."

"Please, Miss Winkworth, don't interfere. Now you know why you felt dizzy and nauseous that night. It was my fault."

Mr. Simmons read Dr. York's confession and added his signature. "Very well. Everything seems in order."

"So is the contract invalid now?" she asked, sceptical.

"Well, I have to deposit and file Dr. York's confession to my barrister's office and have it examined by a judge, but I guess the contract isn't valid."

She grinned at Dr. York, who flushed red, fiddling with his collar.

"Naturally," Mr. Simmons added, "Dr. York's medical licence will be reviewed by the barrister and most likely rescinded today. Should Miss Winkworth wish to press charges against Dr. York I suggest she visit the nearest police station. I'll supply a copy of the confession for Miss Winkworth's perusal."

"Excuse me?" Dr. York said.

Mr. Simmons stared at him as if Dr. York were a particularly slow dog. "You drugged an unaware woman without her consent, without a proper, previous medical examination just for your entertainment. Miss Winkworth could have died as a result of the drug injection. There could have been unexpected effects on her health. You'll agree with me, Dr. York, that this behaviour is particularly despicable, not to mention dangerous, for a medical professional, and against your Hippocratic oath. The Royal Medical Council will be notified immediately of your deplorable conduct and take any actions they see fit for your case, which will certainly include a hefty fine, the revocation of your license to practice, and depending upon the barrister, you may be facing imprisonment, no matter what Miss Winkworth does with the charges."

Dr. York paled. "But..."

"Unless," Mr. Simmons said, sweetening his voice, "you wish to retract your statement." He pushed Dr. York's written declaration towards him. "Your choice, Dr. York."

"Dr. York," Edith said at the same time as Perry said, "Oliver, think carefully."

"Mr. Simmons," Edith said. "Dr. York is lying. Obviously. He didn't drug me. For goodness' sake, the whole story is ridiculous. He would never drug anyone."

"I can confirm that," Perry said. "Oliver is the best man I know."

The solicitor shrugged. "Your opinion doesn't matter, I'm afraid. If Miss Winkworth was indeed drugged, as Dr. York claims, then her memories aren't reliable, and Lord Ravenscroft, your judgement is biased and unsubstantiated."

Dr. York's lips quivered, but then he straightened. "It's my decision. No, I will not withdraw my statement. That's what happened. Miss Winkworth's contract is null, and... and Lord Neville's claims are invalid. Lord Ravenscroft will keep his title."

Mr. Simmons let out a long breath. "As you wish." He collected the documents and rose. "Good day, my lord, Miss Winkworth, Dr. York."

The moment he shut the door behind him, Dr. York covered his face with his hands.

"Oh, Dr. York, you shouldn't have done that." Edith patted his shivering shoulder. "It was very brave of you, but..." A sob escaped her, too. A good man lost his profession to protect her. "I'm so sorry."

"Ollie." Perry hugged his friend, patting his back. "What the hell were you thinking?"

Dr. York wiped his face with a handkerchief. "What choice did I have?"

"Wait for me to talk to my solicitor," Perry said. "Make a plan together."

"I couldn't let you renounce your title or let Miss Winkworth be blackmailed by your uncle. Although I admit I didn't think my plan through. Oh, well. I guess it's my fault." Dr. York's face was ashen.

She choked on guilt. "It's not your fault, Dr. York."

He dropped himself onto a chair. "Apologies for sitting, Miss Winkworth, but my legs don't hold me."

"Dear Dr. York." She took his hand. "I'll find a way to help you."

He waved dismissively.

"I'll contact my solicitor immediately," Perry said.

"All my dreams..." Dr. York shook his head. "Years of studying and sacrifices. My father sold our horse to pay for my studies."

"Goodness, Dr. York. I'm so sorry."

He sniffled. "Do not worry, Miss Winkworth. It was my choice. You didn't ask me to sacrifice myself, but I did it gladly. Perry is the best friend I've ever had, and you, Miss Winkworth, are a fine lady." He rested his forehead on his closed fist. "If we don't fight for what is good, then for what?"

Edith held his hand again.

There was only one person she could ask for help.

twenty-four

I N THE PAST few days, Edith had spent more time with her father than in the past years, and each encounter had been charged with tension.

Yet the next conversation with him couldn't be avoided. She shivered when she knocked on the door to his study.

"Come in." His deep voice rumbled.

There had been a time when his voice had soothed her anxiety. She inched the door open. "Father, may I have a word?"

Mistrust tightened his features. "What happened?"

Well, she wasn't surprised by the welcome. "I need to talk to you."

"Let me guess, you changed your mind about your studies."

"No." She returned the harsh stare. "Honestly, you could stop being so aggressive. I don't deny I made mistakes, but I'm serious about wanting to become a doctor, and I'd appreciate it if you showed some respect for my decisions."

Was it her imagination, or did he give her a nod of approval? "Fair enough. What is it?"

"It's about Dr. York."

"Lord Ravenscroft's personal physician? What about him?"

She ran her palms over her skirt. "There was a misunderstanding, and his medical licence has been challenged and might be revoked, and he needs help now to get it back."

"Having a licence revoked is a serious business." He leant back. "What did he do?"

Both Perry and Dr. York were ready to sacrifice themselves for her. She had to return the favour and swallow her pride. "I made a mistake..."

He steepled his fingers together on the desk and gave her a 'No, you? Really?' gaze.

"To help me get out of a legal situation, Dr. York falsely declared to have drugged me. As a consequence, he will be forced to go before a judge, and the medical board. But, in truth, he didn't do anything. He invented a story and took the blame only to save me. If he hadn't helped me, I might have ended up in in court and possibly sued for breach of contract."

There. She hoped her father wouldn't ask for further details because she didn't want to talk about her stupid bet with Neville.

"Good Lord, Edith." He removed his glasses and rubbed his eyes. "When is this endless string of troubles going to end?"

"I'm trying to make the situation better, Father, but Dr. York needs help. Can you intercede for him with the Royal Medical Council? He's a brilliant physician who worked very hard to obtain his degree, and he's specialising on alienism. He doesn't deserve to have his licence revoked."

"What did you do exactly?"

"Father..."

"I want the truth." He tapped the desk with a finger. "If you want me to vouch for Dr. York, I must know what happened."

She took a deep breath. Her throat burned with emotion. As she told him about the Scarlet Room, the awful contract, and Dr. York's sacrifice, she skipped the part of Neville's request. Still, the whole affair sounded horrible.

A long sigh came out of her father. "Do you realise now how your actions have ramifications and touch other people's lives?"

She gave a curt nod, not trusting her voice.

"You do something without thinking, and good people get hurt. This isn't reasonable conduct for a physician."

"I know."

"What were you—" He slouched back in the chair. "Never mind." He remained silent for a long time.

Edith stood there, waiting, on the verge of running out of the room.

"Let's make a deal," he finally said in a grave tone. "You pass your admission test with flying colours, and I'll vouch for Dr. York. I'll do my best to help him."

"Thank you, Father." She itched to hug him, but his harsh expression wasn't encouraging.

"The fate of Dr. York is in your hands." His tone didn't leave room for relief.

"Yes, thank you." She hurried out of the study, her legs shaking.

She closed the door and leant against it, waiting for her pulse to slow down.

Now she had even more pressure and...a new reason to pass the test.

~

PERRY COULDN'T SMILE when Edith gave him the good news about Oliver because of yet another pounding headache.

Too much tension tightened his neck muscles. Not even the quiet and dim lights of his personal parlour helped soothe the ache.

"Is something the matter?" she asked, tilting her head. "You don't seem relieved to know my father is going to help Dr. York."

"I am." He massaged his forehead. "Apologies. It's a headache."

"Come here." She patted the spot next to her on the sofa as she'd done the other night.

He did as told.

"Lie down." She patted her lap.

He sighed when he laid his head on her lap.

They'd gained a victory over Uncle Neville, but Oliver had jeopardised his career. Not that Perry would dismiss him and leave him alone, but the threat of prison, loomed over Oliver like Damocles's sword.

"I have to pass the test though," Edith said, rubbing his temples with gentle fingers.

"Then Oliver has nothing to worry about. You'll pass."

"I'm not so confident. I need to keep up with all the new findings in medical science."

"I have complete faith in you." He closed his eyes, enjoying her touch.

Her hand wandered down his neck and over his chest. "Your faith in me is the best thing that has ever happened to me. I owe you my new confidence."

"Then I want a kiss," he said as a joke, but it came out more serious and demanding than he meant.

She bent over and gave him an upside-down kiss that worked better than a numbing potion for the pain. The kiss was sweet and slow, exactly what he needed. But when she straightened up, breaking the kiss, he was far from satisfied.

"My turn," he said.

After sitting up, he inched her skirts up, uncovering her lovely legs. Her stockings smelled of soap and wild jasmine. He inhaled deeply before slipping off the sofa. Keeping his gaze on her, he pushed her legs apart and nestled between them.

Her breathing sped up. He was glad she was experienced

because they both could be themselves and do what they wanted with each other.

"Perry," she whispered, all breathy.

He kissed her knee and inner thigh through the stockings. The garter at the top was a simple pink satin ribbon he promptly unfastened. The delicate fabric of the stocking slipped down her leg when he tugged at it. Another inhale.

The sweet fragrance of jasmine drove him mad with need. There was no better scent for the star goddess.

He traced the curve of her thigh and followed it to her drawers. She was all silky skin and tempting curves. He caressed her leg, widening her thighs until the slit of her drawers opened. They both paused. Her chest rose and fell quickly as he stared at her beauty. When he dipped his head and kissed her, she moaned loudly.

Her thighs tightened around him in a scented embrace as he lavished her with his tongue. He wanted to hear her scream and feel her fingers through his hair, so he deepened the kiss, tasting her sweetness. Her hips jolted, but he held them in place.

As he added two fingers, her warm velvet squeezed around them. Her moans became quicker and louder until she sagged against the sofa with a scream. The sound seized his chest with a yearning so deep he was sure he could never desire a woman more than his Star Goddess. The pulse of her flesh sent a stir of desire through him.

He smiled against her pink skin, kissing her inner thigh. "I could do this all day."

"Oh, I'd like that."

He kept his gaze on her as he crawled back onto the sofa. She pressed a finger on his sensitive lips, tracing them. That was all the warning he had before she kissed him, pressing her mouth against his. No more sweetness or slowness. The kiss was raw and unapologetic. But it held a familiarity that enhanced it.

He tangled a hand through her hair and pulled her closer, his headache vanishing. She poured all her passion into the kiss, pressing her body against his. The heat and hunger in her kiss made his body clench with an unbearable ache.

When her hand searched for the falls of his trousers, he growled and couldn't stop himself from kissing her deeper.

She didn't want to be courted now, and he wouldn't press the matter on her, but the truth was he desperately wanted her to be his wife, which was selfish of him. He'd have to wait until she passed the test at least.

"I love you, Edith," he said because he couldn't keep the truth to himself any longer. He cupped her stunned face and stared into her lovely forest-green eyes. "I love you, and I'll wait for you, whatever you decide."

"Perry." She hugged him with enough strength to squeeze him against her body.

She didn't say anything else, and it was all right for him. Because it didn't matter if she didn't love him as much as he loved her; he would still help her become the woman she wanted to be. He would still wait. She was worth the wait.

I LOVE YOU. Now a new set of Perry's words echoed in Edith's mind as she walked to his house the next day.

After he'd declared his love for her, they'd held each other until they'd fallen asleep under the watchful gaze of the Star Maiden. Then he'd escorted her home, and it'd been sweet and beautiful.

Why was everything that he said so devastatingly powerful and beautiful? She wanted nothing more than to be with him, but she wanted to rebuild her life first. She wasn't sure she could embrace all the feelings she had for him, not until she sorted out her life, which included passing the admission test, becoming a medical student, and saving Dr. York's licence.

She entered Perry's study with her heart thudding in her throat.

"Edith." He rose from the chair, smiling so widely to brighten the day.

Not an ounce of hurt or frustration came from him. He'd told her he loved her, and she'd asked for time. Yet here he was, smiling at her, happy to see her.

Something broke in her chest, and all the pain and loneliness of the past years came out, like water from a crack in a dam. She'd never been surrounded by people as much as in the past years, but she'd never been more lonely. Perhaps she didn't need all of them, only a selected few.

She rushed to him, and he opened his arms. Without asking questions, he held her, surrounding her with warmth and comfort. He caressed the top of her head.

She raised her gaze to his. Her love for him suddenly could no longer be contained. "Perry."

The butler, knocking on the door, interrupted them. "My lord?"

Edith disentangled from Perry's embrace.

"Mason," he said.

"Dr. Winkworth is here and asks to see you," Mason said, opening the door.

"My father?"

Perry frowned. "Is something the matter?"

"I don't know." Edith stiffened when her father strode into the room like a stormy cloud.

Father eyed the closeness between them, not at all pleased. "Lord Ravenscroft."

"Dr. Winkworth. You wished to see me?"

"I must speak my mind, my lord."

Edith moved towards the door. "I'll leave you to talk then."

"No. I wish to speak with you as well." If Father had looked stern the other day, he was positively furious now.

"I hope I can assist with whatever happened," Perry said.

"I'm glad you're eager to assist, Ravenscroft, because it's a matter that involves you." Her father put both hands on the pommel of his walking stick. "I spoke with a few colleagues and friends of mine this morning, respectable physicians who would be the perfect examiners for Edith's test."

She didn't allow herself to be relieved.

Father twitched his hands over the pommel. "My friends categorically refused to have anything to do with *my* daughter because of a rumour circulating recently. Witnesses claim to have seen Edith and you, Ravenscroft, in a scandalous...position in Hyde Park, of all places. My daughter was seen with...." He paused, anger flashing red across his face. "With her skirts up while you...I can't end the sentence."

Oh, no. The darn snake incident. "Father, nothing untoward happened."

"The incident is not what it seems," Perry said. "A snake slid under Edith's skirts, and I was assisting her in taking it out. Safety, not debauchery."

"Do you expect me to believe this story?" Father raised his voice. "A snake? In Hyde Park in early spring? Please, do not insult my intelligence, Ravenscroft."

"We aren't lying, Father. That's exactly what happened. Do you think I'm stupid enough to behave in such a wanton manner with an earl in a public park?"

"You've changed so much in the past years. I'm not sure I know you at all, Edith." His words were like a punch in her stomach.

She swallowed past the lump in her throat. "I would never do that, and Perry would never behave in such a fashion."

"Many people are now saying Lord Ravenscroft isn't a gentleman," her father insisted.

Perry paled, and a tremor went through him. He fiddled with the collar of his shirt, taking deep breaths.

"Do you realise what will happen to your sister's reputation when the rumour reaches her?" Father huffed. "There was a time when you cared about Marianne."

"I do care, and maybe it escaped your notice, but such a rumour would ruin me as well."

"Dr. Winkworth," Perry said. "Tell me what I can do to make the situation better."

Father turned his glacial stare to him. "You should know there's only one solution to end the rumours and save my daughter's reputation."

Marriage. Edith closed her fists as worry flared in her chest. Perry would surely do the honourable thing and marry her, which wasn't the reason she was worried. They shouldn't be forced to get married because of a rumour.

Perry cleared his throat. "But if Edith marries me, she won't be able to find employment."

"Edith's medical career will end anyway if her reputation is nothing short of impeccable," Father said.

"Rumours come and go, Father. If I stay quiet for a while and avoid going out, people will stop gossiping about me."

"What about your tutor? I don't have the qualifications to examine and validate your admission test. You need a certified professor. How will you find a tutor who wants to work with you? I've exhausted my rather extensive list of friends."

"Dr. Winkworth." Perry held up his hand. "I've been around physicians, hospitals, and doctors of all sorts. Plus as Ravenscroft, I have some influence. Allow me to ask the people I know. I'm sure I'll find someone, and needless to say, I'm more than willing to marry Edith, should this be the most suitable solution. No, even if it shouldn't. I want to marry your daughter."

Father's stance slouched a fraction. "I didn't expect that, Ravenscroft." He glanced at Edith. "I'm pleasantly surprised."

Perry bowed his head. "You can count on me. I'll do everything to protect..." He barely finished talking when he dropped to the floor, his body stiffening.

"Perry." She rushed to him.

Her father copied her. "Ravenscroft."

Perry lay stiff on the floor. His legs spasmed, and his eyes flared wide open. Edith held his head on her lap while Father blocked his legs and arms.

"We're here, Ravenscroft," Father said. "Breathe deeply, if you can hear me. Control your breathing."

"Perry," she whispered, caressing his forehead.

The spasms slowly died down. His muscles relaxed, and his eyes rolled back into his skull.

"Open his mouth lest he choke on his tongue," Father said. "If he casts up his accounts, make sure he doesn't suffocate."

She did as she was told and gently opened Perry's mouth. "I know you don't trust me, Father, but I've changed. Perry is helping me, and nothing happened in Hyde Park."

Perry blinked slowly, his breathing returning to normal.

"He's an honourable man." She caressed his cheek. "I trust him, and so should you."

Perry swallowed a couple of times.

Without saying anything, Father rose to pour a glass of water. He helped Perry drink it. "Do you know what I want more than anything for you?"

"That I stop being wild, I guess."

"No." He scowled. "I want you to be happy. I don't care if you become a doctor or not, or if you get married or become a spinster. I want to see you do whatever makes you happy, and in the past years, you've been anything but. That worries me more than gossip or your medical degree. I know I'm grumpy, and it's not easy to talk to me, but I love you, your mother, and your sister more than anything else, and it pains me to see you sad and lost. I can stitch a wound or fix a bone, but I can't mend a soul."

"I'm not sad anymore. I know what I want."

He moved to hold Perry up. "Help me lay him on the sofa."

She took Perry's legs up while Father carried him to the sofa.

"Thank you," Perry said in a quivering voice. "I'm better now."

"You're welcome, Ravenscroft," Father said in the compassionate tone he used for his patients. He covered him with a blanket before facing Edith. "Whatever you choose, be sure it's what you want. I can live if you decide you don't want to be a doctor. I can't live if you're miserable." He hugged her. It was a crushing bear hug that filled her with love and hope.

She rested her head on his chest. "Thank you."

He patted the top of her as he'd used to do when she was a child. "And just so you know, Mrs. Richards will receive fully funded care for her recovery."

"Oh, Father." She returned the hug, squeezing him as hard as she could.

Her father's love was the best motivation to pass the test.

twenty-five

ALL THE ATTENTION Edith gave Perry spoiled him. After his last attack, she hadn't left his side, giving him tea and buttered scones, and making sure he was comfortable. He loved every second with her.

Sitting on the chair next to his bed, Oliver took notes. "At what time did the attack happen?"

"Around two o'clock." Perry winced as he sat up, his muscles sore and aching.

"Do you want another pillow?" Edith asked.

He smiled, even though he was in pain. "No, thank you."

"What did you feel the moment before the attack?" Oliver asked.

"I was worried about Edith and what her father had told her." He still was.

"*Worry.*" Oliver cradled his chin. "Interesting. I have to check my diary and see how often you've been worried before an attack."

"You don't have to worry about me." Edith patted his hand.

"I beg to differ. The whole situation involves me as well. And now you need a new professor."

"I'm really sorry, Miss Winkworth," Oliver said. "I'm not the type of doctor you need. But I'll do everything I can to help you."

"Thank you, Dr. York. You're a godsend."

Oliver blushed up to the roots of his hair. "Well, I have to consult my notes." He left, muttering about worry and triggers.

"I need to talk to you," Perry said once alone with her.

"I know what you're thinking." She puffed up his pillows. "I'm sorry for what my father said. He doesn't know you. He jumped to conclusions."

"I perfectly understand your father. You're his daughter, and he wants to protect you. I'm not offended by his mistake. I wanted to talk to you about something else."

Her eyes grew larger in alarm. "You're worried about your reputation. It's understandable. I've caused you nothing but trouble."

"You and your father have the habit of jumping to conclusions and making assumptions. I was referring to finding an examiner for you. Sir James Harris, the queen's physician."

She narrowed her gaze. "He's after the Star Maiden."

"But he's a doctor I personally know, and he's a member of the London School of Medicine for Women's board. Being associated with him will silence any gossip about you. I'll send him a letter immediately."

"Thank you, Perry." She kissed his cheek, lingering.

"There's something else." He took a deep breath. "You know how I feel. You know I want to marry you and make you happy, but becoming a surgeon is your dream, and I can't ask you to choose between marriage and your career. I'll always support you, and I don't care if we don't get married. You'll always be my only one."

"I love you, Perry." She hugged him. "I love you so much. I should've told you a while ago."

He held her, kissing her cheek, neck, and lips. They fought

over who gave more kisses to the other until she laughed and had to stop while he kept kissing her.

"It's fear!" Oliver exclaimed, flinging the door open and causing Edith to gasp. "Fear is the trigger." He waved a few pages of his notepad in the air.

Edith moved away from Perry.

"I analysed all the data, and the only common factor among Perry's attacks is fear. When he gets scared, a seizure starts. Isn't that wonderful?"

Fear. It could be.

"But before his latest attack, he wasn't threatened," Edith said. "He wasn't scared."

"I think he was," Oliver said with an air of triumph. "He was worried about you. The same thing happened in the Scarlet Room. You fell into the pool, he pulled you out, and afterwards, he had a seizure. Fear, worry, and anxiety for someone he cares about."

Perry reclined on the pillow. "What am I supposed to do, then?"

Oliver's enthusiastic expression settled down as if he were disappointed that Perry didn't share his ecstasy. "It's obvious, isn't it? Don't get scared."

"Oh, thank you. Why didn't I think of that?" Perry scowled at his friend. "Remind me how much I pay you."

Oliver rubbed the back of his neck. "We can work on techniques to control your fears and anxiety. Perhaps we can find a medicinal herb that helps. But you have to do the biggest part of the job and work on your emotions."

Perry stared at her, sending her all the warmth of his love. "Nothing more simple."

EDITH COULDN'T SIT STILL in the carriage as they rode to Sir James's house.

Perry had been right. The prestigious physician hadn't hesitated to express his support for her. She suspected Sir James's help had more to do with the Star Maiden than her medical skills. Anyway, beggars couldn't be choosers. Only two days were left before the possibility of trying the admission test ended. But the urgency wasn't why she was so nervous. Above all, she wanted to do a good job.

"Stay calm," Perry said from the seat in front of her. "You've studied so hard. I'm sure everything will be fine. However it goes, I'm proud of you."

He sounded so honest and determined that some of his calm seeped into her.

"There's something else I wanted to ask you." She shifted her weight and cleared her voice. "It's about our marriage and my career. We've always said they're incompatible, but I might have found a solution."

He held her hand. "I'm listening."

"Well, don't be offended, but I was thinking, if I become your countess..." It was more difficult than she thought. "I won't need to work."

He drew his eyebrows together. "You won't be happy if you renounce your career, and I'm worried this choice might cause you to resent me over time."

"No, I mean, I'll study, get my degree, and then I'll volunteer. I care about helping people, and I can do that in every hospital as a volunteer if I don't have to earn a salary to live. Florence Nightingale had a staff of female volunteers, some of whom were titled ladies, and Elizabeth Garrett Anderson manages an all-female hospital in Mayfair where many volunteers work."

"You won't become a consultant surgeon, be part of any medical associations, publish articles in prestigious medical journals, or attend conferences."

"It's the price to pay to be a doctor and your countess, and it's a good compromise."

He burst out laughing and kissed her hands. "You're a genius!"

She laughed as well, the tension leaving her. "Now I only have to pass the test."

"I propose a bet. If you pass the test... no. When you pass the test, you'll spend a night with me. All night."

"You're on."

Thank goodness the queen's physician lived on the outskirts of London where the traffic was non-existent. Edith had the opportunity to concentrate on her exam without distraction.

Sir James seemed unable to stay still as he welcomed them.

He smiled broadly, gazing from her to Perry. "Lord Ravenscroft, what an honour to have you here in my humble home."

The *humble* home was a two-storey manor house with at least a dozen bedrooms, a deck surrounded by Grecian columns, and a garden that stretched for yards in every direction. Not even Perry's townhouse in London had such a grandiose garden. Not to mention the stunning paintings hanging on the walls. Paintings by Turner, Delacroix, and, of course, Valentine brightened the hallway with their beautiful rural views. She guessed the most explicit paintings were hidden somewhere.

"Thank you for agreeing to see us." Perry gave a polite nod.

"My pleasure. I love encouraging young people to study the noble science of medicine. Let's begin the test then. I believe the opportunity to enrol in medical school is going to close tomorrow. We must be quick." Sir James stretched out an arm towards a cosy study. "Everything is ready."

"I'll wait outside," Perry said. "Good luck."

Worry tightened her stomach as she sat in the small study with her forty-question test on the table. Sir James got himself comfortable in a chair, smoking a pipe and reading the newspaper.

"I hope after this test, you'll tell me the truth about the secret painting," he said between puffs of smoke.

No, she wouldn't use the Star Maiden as leverage. "I'm afraid the test won't change the fact that I didn't pose for any paintings, sir."

He scowled. "Right the other day, I was talking with Miss Daphne Ferguson, who, I believe, is a friend of yours."

Edith perked up. "She is, sir." Or was.

"I told her about your test and mentioned the Star Maiden, and she said that you posed for it."

Thank you, Daphne, for blabbering. "Daphne loves making jokes. I'm afraid she was jesting."

His scowl deepened. "The test begins now. You have an hour, Miss Winkworth."

Focus. She took the pen and started the test.

PERRY KEPT GLANCING at the window of the study where Edith was taking the test.

She wasn't going to fail. He had no doubts.

Walking through the garden should help soothe his inner turmoil and control his emotions. In summer, the garden had to burst into life with roses and begonias, but now it was all dull and brown with shy, budding leaves. Not exactly inspiring.

Wandering, he arrived at the stable and watched a groom taking care of his horses. Another groom or stable hand was fussing around his carriage for some reason. The road to Sir James's house was in pristine condition. No mud, gaps, holes, or bumps. His carriage couldn't possibly have been damaged by the smooth ride. Yet the man remained crouched next to the back wheel, doing something Perry couldn't see.

"Is something the matter?" He strode towards the two men.

The groom kept wiping the sweat from the horse's neck, but the other stable hand straightened with haste.

"Lord Ravenscroft," the groom said. "There's no problem at all. Your coachman and footman are taking a cup of tea in the kitchen, and I'm attending to your horses. They're in excellent shape. I gave them some water and a bit of oat."

Perry focused on the other man. "What about your companion?"

The second man shrugged. "No problem, my lord. The axle just needed some lubricant." The man showed his dirty hands. "Not much, but it's all done now."

Perry worked his jaw. His coachman zealously checked the carriage before every trip. Although the last few miles to Sir James's house stretched on a narrow road that ran along a steep escarpment. One couldn't be too careful. A carriage could easily roll down the slope; all it took was a small mistake.

A maid walked over to him, interrupting the conversation. "My lord." She curtsied. "Sir James sent me to fetch you. Miss Winkworth finished her test."

His heart gave a quick thump. So much for controlling his emotions. He returned to the house as fast as he could go without breaking into a run. He found Edith pacing in the sitting room, hands on her hips.

"How did it go?"

She threw a hand up. "I don't know yet. Sir James is checking my test. Oh, goodness, what if I made a mistake in listing all the bones in the wrist? There are so many, and I think I forgot one of them. I'm not sure if I described the Jackson-Norton procedure correctly, either."

"Don't fret. If you get nervous, I'll be nervous as well and get a seizure."

That got her attention. She stopped pacing and pressed her lips hard as if making a decision. "Whatever the result is, I have to thank you for your support. I wouldn't have come this far without you."

"You would have. I only gave you a nudge."

She paled a little when Sir James entered the sitting room, his gaze on her test. "Miss Winkworth." He removed his glasses. "You passed your test with flying colours. Congratulations."

She let out a funny noise halfway between a squeak and a yelp. "Heavens."

Sir James smiled. "I have no qualms about supporting your enrolment in the London School of Medicine for Women. Gossip doesn't matter when someone possesses such dedication. Use it well, miss."

She clamped her hands over her mouth and stayed in that position, her eyes wide as if in horror.

"Edith?" Perry touched her arm. "Are you all right?" He removed her hands from her mouth. "Congratulations."

She finally thawed and showed the biggest smile he'd ever seen. "Thank you. Thank you."

"I didn't do anything, Miss Winkworth," Sir James said, "merely checked your test— Miss Winkworth!" He stiffened when Edith hugged him.

"Apologies, sir. This test meant so much to me."

"I gather that." Sir James straightened his glasses. "You must bring the test with my assessment and signature to the school as soon as possible, or you won't get another chance until next year. Chop-chop."

"I'll fly." She almost snatched the test from the doctor's hands.

"I guess you're more excited than when you posed for Mr. Carter." He raised his eyebrows.

Edith's smile disappeared. "I didn't pose for any paintings, sir. I'm sorry."

He exhaled. "Off you go."

Edith's happiness was contagious, and Perry couldn't stop smiling as they drove in the carriage.

"I'll need a proper leather bag for my notepads and a new set of pencils. Goodness, Father will be so happy." She shifted on the seat, swaying her hips. "I could start next week if the school answers immediately. I'm looking forward to starting."

"I wouldn't have guessed."

"Oh, Perry, thank you so much." She threw herself at him from across the seat.

He laughed, welcoming her into his arms. "A celebration is in order."

"Two celebrations. We're engaged, right? And I've never been happier to lose a bet—" She didn't have the chance to finish the sentence as the carriage gave a mighty jolt.

A loud screech followed. Then the seat dropped from underneath Perry as if the ground itself had vanished. The rest was a blur of thuds, rolls, and painful bumps. The ceiling and the floor swapped places. Edith screamed. The world turned upside down, and he couldn't stop the rising fear in his chest.

Before the seizure took hold of him, he thought Oliver was right.

PERRY WOKE up in a hospital bed in yet another bright white room smelling of disinfectant, which threw him back to the day after the incident.

For a moment, he wondered if everything that had happened in the past years had been an illusion, and he'd woken up just now from the *Princess Alice* disaster. At least his head didn't throb, and his limbs were all in the right places. His hands were covered in cuts and bruises though. Surely, his face looked the same, judging by how sore it was.

"Perry." Oliver walked over to him from a chair in a corner. "How are you?"

"Sore." He was glad he could talk. "Edith?" His pulse spiked, and a buzzing noise rang in his ears. "What happened?"

"Calm down. She's all right. Your footman, coachman, and horses are all right as well. A few bruises but nothing serious. Like you. You were lucky. You could have broken your necks. Miss

Winkworth lost consciousness as well, but aside from that, no injuries. A wheel broke, and the carriage rolled down a slope, tearing the shaft and the breeching dee. The horses were dragged down, but once the carriage snapped free, they scrambled back up to their feet. The bushes stopped the carriage before it reached the bottom of the scarp. You were also lucky there was another carriage passing by. Its coachman sent for help immediately."

He exhaled. "May I see her?"

"She's with her family. Give them a moment." Oliver glanced at the door. "See, between the incident and the loss of consciousness, two days have passed."

All the blood flowed down from Perry's head, making him dizzy. "She missed her opportunity to enrol." He pushed aside the covers, ignoring the room tilting.

"Wait. There's something else we need to discuss." Oliver closed the door.

He had a hunch. "It was no accident, wasn't it?"

Oliver nodded. "Someone tampered with the wheels and the shaft."

"I saw one of Sir James's stable hands working on the carriage." He rubbed his eyes. "Hell, I had the feeling something was wrong."

"Someone tried to kill you."

"There's only one person who would benefit from my untimely death. But how did he know about our trip to Sir James's? I didn't tell anyone."

"Yes, it's a mystery," Oliver said. "I took the liberty of mentioning your uncle to the police. They're interrogating him as we speak, and an officer was sent to Sir James's house as well after it was clear the axle had been tampered with."

"I doubt the police will find that stable hand. He'll be out of London by now. Surely, Uncle Neville must have given him a hefty sum to sabotage my carriage."

"Hopefully, the police will catch him."

"I don't like the idea of hoping. We'll hire a private detective. I want to get to the bottom of this story."

"Fair enough." He patted Perry's shoulder. "I'll help you get dressed. We need to go home."

Perry slid on a fresh set of clothes with Oliver's help. His body was a map of dark bruises and swells, but his concern for Edith overcame his physical pain.

Staggering on his feet, Perry walked to Edith's room. She was sitting on her bed, pale and quiet in a dark gown. Dr. Winkworth, his wife, and Lady Lancaster were talking in hushed tones. They fell silent when Perry entered the room.

He nodded at everyone, his focus on Edith.

"Perry," she said in a small voice.

"Ravenscroft, we're happy to see you up and about," Dr. Winkworth said, shaking his hand.

Mrs. Winkworth wiped her eyes with a handkerchief, and Lady Lancaster held Edith's hand.

"At least no one got seriously hurt," Lady Lancaster said.

"Edith." He touched her head.

She didn't look better than Perry did, although her face showed only a couple of bruises. The problem was the shadow darkening her gaze. Her dishevelled hair and paleness enhanced her lost expression. The long dark dress didn't help.

She gave him a timid smile, standing up. "I'm glad you're well. We were worried."

He squeezed her hand.

"In a hospital again," she said. "We should stop having these incidents."

Perry kissed her hand, not caring about the fact her family was present. "I love you, Edith."

She wrapped her arms around his neck and hugged him without hurting him though. He hugged her back, so very happy he could do so.

Soft gasps came from Mrs. Winkworth and Lady Lancaster. Dr. Winkworth grumbled something Perry didn't understand.

"You'll try next year," he said when she released him.

Her next smile brought some colour to her cheeks. "It's a good thing that I can."

Mrs. Winkworth, clearing her throat from behind Edith, broke the moment. "Apologies, my lord, but we're taking Edith home."

"We'll take good care of her, Ravenscroft," her father said. "Thank you for everything you did for her."

He released her reluctantly and stepped back from her.

"I love you," she whispered, giving him a new smile only for him.

twenty-six

EDITH'S MOTHER HAD fussed around her for the past few days, doing her best to make her comfortable, and she appreciated it. But Father had been busy at the hospital, leaving early and returning late. Aside from mundane chatter about her health and the weather, they hadn't really talked, and she was eager to.

Mother hugged her the moment she stepped into Edith's bedroom, barely giving her time to slip into her dressing gown. "Darling. How are you?"

"I'm all right." She patted her mother's back. "Father?"

"Still out, but he should be back soon."

"Will you tell him I want to talk with him when he's back?"

Mother nodded, caressing her cheek. "Let me help you dress."

Edith winced when she walked to the sitting room. Her back was still a bit stiff, but the bruises were fading.

She was rearranging the books she needed to read—since she'd have more studying to do—when footsteps approached.

Her father appeared on the threshold. "Edith. Your mother told me you wanted to talk."

"Father." Her hand shook when she set aside an old book on human physiology.

He cleared his throat. "I trust you feel better."

She shrugged. "Only a few scratches and a big fright."

He walked in, his shoulders hunched. A sickening lump crawled in her throat in anticipation of his speech.

He let out a long exhale.

She cleared her voice. "What troubles you? The carriage accident or the fact I couldn't enrol?"

His face transformed from tense to surprised to compassionate. "Oh, darling." He crossed the room with two long strides to give her one of his bear hugs.

She'd forgotten how good it was to be held by her father. The combined scents of his bergamot cologne and disinfectant from the hospital lingered on his clothes, bringing her back to those years when she would listen to every word he said about his surgical procedures while Marianne and Mother were horrified.

"You did what I asked you. You passed the test with flying colours," he said, his voice cracking as well. "The accident was an unfortunate affair, but in a way, it doesn't matter. If you want to enrol in medical school next year, I'm sure everything will go well. I'm very proud of you."

"Oh, Father." She sobbed as he patted her back. It felt like coming back home after a long journey in the dark.

"Don't worry. You kept your part of our deal. I'll do my best to help your friend, Dr. York." He wiped her tears with his handkerchief. His eyes were red as well. "I've missed you."

"I've missed you, too, Father."

He released her, caressing her cheek. "Chin up. You're going to be a surgeon." He kissed her forehead, deleting the past years of solitude with it.

She kept smiling when he left the room, energised by the conversation.

She started to sort her books again when Marianne came as

well. In a rich-brown afternoon dress, she looked every inch the viscountess.

"Fancy a walk?" she asked. "Unless you're too sore."

"The last time you asked me to go out for a walk, you delivered some bad news and got angry with me."

She laughed. "Not this time. Our conversations have been tense as of late, but I just want to spend some time with you." Her eyes shone suspiciously. "And we nearly lost you. That made me think."

"It made me think as well."

"Yes, I...oh, Edith." Marianne rushed to hug her, enveloping her in a cloud of expensive perfume.

For the second time, emotion thickened Edith's throat.

"I'm sorry for all the problems I caused you," she whispered.

"Oh, shush." Marianne wiped her eyes quickly.

"You literally paid for my mistakes. I'll repay you."

Marianne grinned and took Edith's hand. "Let's take a walk."

"You know there's a rumour about Perry and me circulating, don't you?"

"Yes, a few ladies have been enthusiastic enough to inform me of the latest gossip." Marianne lifted a shoulder. "We'll discuss that."

With a perfect blue sky and a warm breeze, the day was indeed a fine one, not merely from a weather point of view.

"The best way to kill gossip is to show yourself, not to disappear. If you disappear, people will make up more stories," Marianne said as they promenaded in the park.

Marianne's lady's maid followed them as usual.

Marianne gave nods and polite smiles to other promenading ladies. "If you disappear, people will think the worst, and the gossip will become a certainty." She winked. "It wouldn't harm if you announced your engagement with Lord Ravenscroft, too."

Edith's face flamed as love warmed her chest. "The engagement isn't official yet. But if we announce it, everyone will believe we're engaged because of the scandalous rumours, not because we love each other."

"Does it matter? Needless to say, you should be careful when talking to Daphne."

"I haven't seen her in a while, and I'm not planning to."

Marianne leant closer. "A friend of mine told me Daphne is quite close to Lord Neville, which worries me. He's openly against his nephew, and I can't help but think that Daphne is working by his side, maybe to the point of being involved in the carriage accident."

Edith came to a quick halt. "You're right. Sir James told me he met her, and during their conversation, he mentioned to her I would take the medical test with him. Daphne must have told Neville. That's how he knew where Perry and I were going."

"Well, that doesn't prove she's involved in Lord Neville's plan. Perhaps she mentioned the test to him in all innocence."

"Possible. Besides, I'm not sure what she would gain from the incident."

"If she hopes to become the next Countess of Ravenscroft by marrying Lord Neville, then she has a good reason to help him. Her father is eager for her to marry a lord."

Speaking of the devil. Daphne was walking with another woman towards them. The moment Daphne saw Edith, she sped up, the ribbons in her hat flapping.

"Careful," Marianne whispered. "Whatever happens, don't make a scene. It'll make things worse."

"Edith, Lady Lancaster." Daphne bobbed a curtsy to Marianne. "It's a pleasure to see you again. I'm so sorry for what happened to you, the carriage accident, I mean." She sounded honest.

"Daphne," Edith said, "I don't wish ill on you, but it'd be better if we avoided each other."

Marianne gave a nod of appreciation. "Have a good day, Miss Ferguson."

They started to sidestep Daphne, but she touched Edith's arm.

"Wait, please. I know I did wrong to you, but I'm here to make amends." Daphne closed her parasol.

"May I ask how?" Marianne lowered her voice. "Every time my sister gets involved with you, something unpleasant happens."

Well, if Edith had to be honest, she was partly to blame, too. Daphne had never forced her to go out partying. Edith had followed her willingly.

Daphne bobbed another curtsy. "I understand your sentiment, my lady, but see, Lady Upchurch is giving a party next week to celebrate the end of the renovation of her manor. Her husband is friends with my father, and I was invited. Lady Upchurch was kind enough to allow me to extend the invitations to some friends, and I thought of Edith. Likely, you, Lady Lancaster, will receive an invitation soon."

No, Edith was done with the balls and parties suggested by Daphne. "Thank you, Daphne, but I'm not interested."

"Wait." Marianne took her arm. "Please excuse us, Miss Ferguson. I need to have a private word with my sister."

"Of course," Daphne said.

Marianne led Edith out of earshot, close to a tree. "I think you should go."

"But we just agreed that Daphne was trouble."

"Yes, but Lady Upchurch is very well known and loved in society. Her parties are always the event of the year with extraordinary performances of acrobats, famous opera singers, and the most famous Drury Lane actors. The renovation of her mansion took five years. This is the first big event she's given in a long time. Showing yourself at her party will greatly increase your popularity. Besides, what could Daphne ever do at that party? It's not one of the seedy gatherings she lured you into. It's a more than valid social event usually with high-ranking peers and foreign dignitaries." She whispered, "Even the princesses attend Lady Upchurch's parties, most of the time incognito, but still, it's an opportunity you can't miss. I'm sure Lord Ravenscroft will be invited as well."

"If you think it's a good idea, then I'll go."

As they walked back to Daphne, the usual nagging voice warned her not to go, but she didn't listen.

A WEEK after the carriage incident, Perry could finally breathe in relief.

Edith's health had improved, and he'd found a promising private detective who was following with discretion the case of the saboteur. He had only one complaint.

"Not another bloody party!"

The invitation to Lady Upchurch's event had arrived at his desk a few minutes before Edith. The invitation was printed on a fancy blue card with golden letters that changed colours whenever he tilted the piece of paper—one of the many unnecessary extravagances of Lady Upchurch.

"Back in the days before the incident, I attended a few of Lady Upchurch's parties," he said. "They're as grandiose as ridiculous."

"Like what?" Edith sat on the chair next to him.

"Once, she gave an ancient Egyptian-themed party. Sarcophaguses everywhere with real corpses inside, bandaged like mummies. I didn't ask where they came from and didn't care. You would've loved it." He huffed. "Another time, an argument started between a French aristocrat and a lord, threatening to start another Hundred Years' War. She usually invites no less than two hundred guests. Ridiculous. But I agree with your sister. An appearance at Lady Upchurch's party will benefit your reputation."

"Which will benefit yours." She snuggled closer to him and rested her head on his chest.

Since the carriage accident, she'd done that a lot.

Holding her, he moved her to his lap. They'd spent the past

afternoons like that, holding each other and whispering words of comfort.

"You're very quiet," he said. "I thought the invitation would cheer you up."

"I'm just worried about the fact someone tried to kill us."

"Only me." He kissed her forehead. The bruise had faded from her cheek, but her pallor remained. "Not us."

"Neville... do you think it was him?"

"Who else?" He caressed her breasts through the fabric of her shirt, smiling as she breathed faster. "He sent me a message to tell me how sorry he was about the incident. Liar. Meanwhile, the police didn't catch the stable hand, but they said they're optimistic, whatever it means."

"Aren't you worried?" She kissed a bruise on his neck.

"For me, no. For you, yes. Tell me the truth. You must be very disappointed about missing your chance to enrol in school, especially after doing so well on the test. I didn't want to upset you by asking."

"I am disappointed and frustrated." She coiled an arm around his waist. "I was so close. But then again, I passed the test. I can do it again."

"I'm sure you can." He scattered kisses on her face until she giggled.

She slipped a hand under his shirt. He sucked in a breath as her soft fingers stroked his chest.

"I missed being with you, Perry. I missed your touch, your lips, and all the wicked things you do to me."

"You destroy me when you say that." He captured her mouth in a savage kiss, or as savage as their still tender skin would allow. "Besides, you lost a bet."

"Happily so." She unfastened his waistcoat and shirt with deft movements until her soft hand touched his naked skin.

"I don't think I ever asked you properly," he whispered, scattering kisses on her lovely face.

"What?"

He stopped her hands. "Edith, I'd consider myself honoured if you'd become my countess, my wife, and my only one."

"Yes." She hugged him. "But only if you take me right now."

"Say no more." He opened the door and checked the corridor for wandering servants.

Empty.

He hauled her up and carried her to his bedroom. Under no circumstances would he take her in his parlour. After locking the door, he laid her on the bed and smiled when she laughed.

"My countess."

He took his time removing her clothes and unbuttoning the shirt to reveal the swells of her breasts, one inch at a time. Once the corset was gone, her nipples pressed against the thin fabric of her chemise. The skirts pooled at her feet when he unfastened them. Her drawers slid off her legs with a soft swish, and then she was all for him.

He kissed her collarbone and breasts before rolling down the stockings. He paused only to caress a few offending bruises on her thighs.

"If my uncle is responsible for these bruises, I'll see him punished." He kissed each bruise until her breathing sped up.

He took care of the bruises on her arms as well, hating that she'd risked her life only because she'd been with him at the wrong time. She ran her fingers through his hair; it was a slow gesture that seduced him more than a kiss.

He closed his eyes, savouring the feeling of her delicate fingers on his scalp. The only good thing about the carriage accident was that it reinforced his determination to marry her.

He caressed the length of her legs, pausing on her inner thighs. Just brushing her delicate skin caused her to inhale deeply.

The candlelight agreed with her. It kissed her creamy skin, giving it a beautiful golden hue. He took his time stroking her breasts and teasing her pretty nipples. She arched her back as he ran his hand over her belly and thighs.

He lowered his head to let his lips follow the path of his fingers. Every inch of her was deliciously smooth skin, scented with jasmine. His body hardened to the point of aching for her. But he wouldn't rush. This moment was meant to be savoured.

She moaned when he drew her nipple into his mouth and sucked hard while rolling the other between his fingers. Crimson flooded her cheeks and lips. Her nipples darkened, too. He went lower, brushing his lips over her belly.

"Oh, Perry!" She lurched when he kissed her intimately.

He was addicted to her sweetness, beauty, and fierce spirit. Her scent dampened the air, intoxicating him.

"I love you," he said before kissing her again.

Her moans grew louder, but he didn't speed up. He wanted to enjoy each little noise she made with the slow lashes of his tongue and tiny kisses.

When she panted and writhed under his lips, he propped himself on his elbows and kept rubbing her, watching her. She was a sight to behold, all flushed, lips and nipples glistening, and half-hooded eyes. Little pulses heralded her release. She muffled her scream with the pillow, but the sound reached his heart anyway.

He kept touching her just because he enjoyed it.

She widened her legs and gripped his buttocks, inviting him. "Take me."

Her voice was deliciously husky, enchanting like a siren's song. "Wait."

He left her side only to slide on a fresh sheath and kiss her again. She hooked her legs around him, pressing her heels against the small of his back.

"Please," she begged.

He buried himself with one push and groaned deep in his throat. She gripped his shoulders and lifted her hips, taking him more deeply. It was a perfect moment with her wrapped like a vine around him and him sensing only her—her softness, her scent, her strength.

They remained still, staring into each other's eyes and sharing their breaths. He traced the lovely curve of her cheek with his fingertip, thanking heaven for having sent an angel to him.

Then he began to move back and forth. When he moved, she moved with him, finding a slow rhythm both because he didn't want to hurt her and because she had to be still sore.

When she sank her pearly teeth into her bottom lip, he shuddered, feeling that bite on his skin. His need for her bordered on physical pain. The slow pace allowed him to stroke her breasts, shoulders, and face, and he loved that she didn't close her eyes but stared at him without an ounce of embarrassment. There was no room for that.

He sped up, and she matched his speed, following him. Their bodies moved together in the most ancient of the dances. He managed to steal a kiss before thrusting deeper.

Their heat and breath mingled, their chests touched, and they shouted at the same time. She sagged in the bed, wrapping her arms and legs around him, and he rested his head on her chest, panting.

Every moment in his life, even the darkest one, was worth it because it'd led him to the embrace of the most amazing woman he'd ever met.

twenty-seven

EDITH WAS GLAD to have agreed to come to Lady Upchurch's party. It lived up to its extravagant reputation. The fountain with mermaids and Neptune in the middle of the ballroom disturbed her, and the water sent shivers crawling down her neck, but she had to admit the whole structure was remarkable. Glass dolphins hung from the ceiling, held by invisible threads, and the maids were all dressed like mermaids. Their glittering emerald costumes ended with upturned hems, resembling a mermaid's tail. Likely not the most comfortable clothes. The footmen were dressed like pirates, and acrobats jumped and twirled in the air without warning.

"Lady Upchurch's obsession with the sea is quite upsetting and for me has gone too far," she said to Perry.

Sea algae filled several bowls scattered around the ballroom to spread the pungent scent of the sea, and she couldn't say she was impressed.

"I told you. Ridiculous," he said, observing the ballroom from a corner with her.

"Honestly, if I'd known the party's theme was the 'enchanting sea,' I wouldn't have come."

"I think the smell is the most awful thing." He smiled and nodded at a passing couple. "Whoever thought that would be a great idea should be sacked."

"How are you doing?"

He lifted a shoulder. "If the trigger of my seizures is fear, I don't see how I might get one here. Although…" He tilted his head back to stare at the floating dolphins. "I'm worried one of those large fish will crush me."

"Actually, dolphins are mammals, not fish."

He burst out laughing but turned serious when Daphne walked over to them.

"Lord Ravenscroft, Edith. I'm so happy to see you here." She bobbed a curtsy.

"Good evening," Edith said.

"I didn't know about the nautical theme. I'm sorry." She touched Edith's hand.

Edith wasn't surprised. It seemed that Daphne never knew anything.

"Your concern for your friend's welfare is admirable," Perry said in a gelid tone. "It really shows your qualities."

Daphne opened and closed her mouth a couple of times before curtsying again. "If you'll excuse me, my lord. Have a lovely evening." She left as quickly as her brocade gown allowed her.

Perry narrowed his gaze at her. "I don't trust her."

"Neither do I, but as Marianne said, with so many guests, what could ever happen here?"

"May I have your attention, please?" Lady Upchurch raised her arms draped in emerald muslin and seashells. They clinked every time she moved.

The orchestra ceased playing, and the constant coming and going of the mermaids and pirates stopped. Only the ominous sound of the water dropping in the fountain could be heard.

"Thank you everyone for being here at my enchanting sea

party," she said, beaming around. "I'm glad you can all enjoy the results of five years of hard work."

Edith and Perry exchanged a glance. Five years for a fountain and some mermaid costumes seemed unjustified.

"I have more surprises in store for you." Lady Upchurch pointed at the sets of double doors overlooking the garden. "Please follow me for the *pièce de résistance* of tonight's party."

Excited squeals and a round of applause swept the room. The pirates held the doors open for the guests, who poured out of the ballroom faster than Edith could say 'splash.'

"Do you want to take a walk in the garden with the others?" Perry asked.

Firm land, or the enchanting sea? Easy choice. "Yes, please." She took Perry's arm.

Torches and braziers lit the garden, giving it a warm atmosphere and, above all, a solid, earth-like quality she needed. All the guests gathered at the edge of the manicured flowerbed and trimmed hedges.

Lady Upchurch stood in front of them. "I have a magical surprise for all of you, the renovation of my gardens that took so long. Please walk only on the paths marked by the lanterns. Do not stray away from them, or you'll have a not-so-pleasant surprise." She laughed. "Please choose a lane and walk along it."

The walk was indeed magical. Holding Perry's arm, Edith strolled with him along a tidy, smooth trail that ran slanted to the others, following the pattern of the spokes of a wheel.

Instead of gravel, as in the rest of the garden, the path was paved with glossy stone tiles. Also, it was a few inches above the ground. Perhaps that was why Lady Upchurch had recommended staying in the chosen passageway. One might twist an ankle, falling off the short step in the dim light.

Small lanterns hanging from the hooks of their stands gave the illusion the lights floated midair, but she couldn't see what was on either side of her. Grass? Cobbles? It seemed a combination of the two.

"It's so beautiful," she whispered, not wanting to disturb the atmosphere.

Perry was tense though. "I reserve my judgement until I understand what this is. I wonder what the surprise might be. After the corpses, I expect the worst."

"Please stop where you are." Lady Upchurch stopped in the middle of the pattern where all the paths ended. "More lights, please."

At her command, several lamps were lit, and a bright yellow glow spread over the paths. The pattern of the paths was exactly like a giant wheel, and Lady Upchurch was standing in the centre. Edith's smile faltered when a noise like that of stone grinding against stone came. Excited mutters came from around her.

"What's happening?" she asked.

"The ground is moving." He held her more tightly. "There are panels on both sides of the path. They're opening."

The panels slid, revealing channels filled with water. Lots of water. A big dark expanse of water.

The paths formed a grid over the largest swimming pool Edith had ever seen, and no, she wasn't impressed. Everywhere she turned, water haunted her.

"Welcome to my Venetian garden," Lady Upchurch said, raising her arms.

Everyone cheered and clapped as fear coiled around Edith like a snake. She drew in a breath that didn't bring any relief. No matter how deeply she inhaled, her lungs didn't work.

"Close your eyes, Edith." Perry's voice seemed to come from a distance.

But closing her eyes did nothing to calm her. The thought of being surrounded by dark water and the guests' shouts triggered her memories. It didn't matter that the people around her didn't shout in fear. In her mind, their loud voices turned into calls for help and screams of pain. She gripped Perry's arm tightly, flinging her eyes open again. Wherever she looked, there was water.

"Close your eyes and trust me. I'll take you out of here." His commanding tone was hard to ignore. "Breathe deeply."

She did as told. He guided her along the path with measured steps while Lady Upchurch talked about something.

"You're doing great. Keep your eyes shut and lean into me." He stopped. "Please step aside. I need to pass."

"What is it?" That was Daphne. "Oh, right. Dear Edith." The way she said the last two words sent a chill to Edith's chest.

"Step aside, Miss Ferguson," Perry gritted out.

"Of course. We don't want a repeat of the scene in the Scarlet Room, do we?"

Edith opened her eyes. Daphne was grinning.

"So tell me, Lord Ravenscroft," she said, stepping aside, "is it water that causes your fits? I think it is. I think the fear of water is what Edith and you have in common. Speak. Don't be shy."

"I'm not shy, Miss Ferguson. I really don't like you. Now move!" Perry held Edith closer.

"I know your secret, my lord," Daphne said. "And I know how to use it against you. Also, watching you twitching on the floor was the most disgusting thing Neville and I have ever seen."

He cupped Edith's cheek. "Close your eyes and don't listen to the harpy."

Shivering, Edith nodded.

There was the shuffle of feet and the swish of fabric, and a few mutters from Daphne, which Edith ignored. Perry resumed walking, but someone bumped into her from behind. She lost her balance, and his arm slipped out of her grip.

"Perry," she screamed, hitting the water.

He cursed but couldn't grab her.

She sank, frozen with fear. Her body seemed to become a slab of marble, cold and stiff. She couldn't even scream. She touched the bottom of the pool, and the water reached her mouth and nostrils. Her skirts turned heavy. The air was punched out of her lungs in large bubbles, and her vision darkened at the edges. Just like that night.

But another scream reached her ears. It was Lady Upchurch. Everyone screamed as if they were all drowning...except that people started saying something that forced her to calm down and focus on the voices.

"The earl is sick!"

"Lord Ravenscroft is mad."

"... should be locked up."

A seizure. Because he was afraid she might get hurt.

She could swear she heard Daphne laughing, but it could be her imagination.

A combination of anger and worry sent a shock through her. It was as if an electric current rushed through her body, energising her. She forced herself to breathe deeply until her vision sharpened. Blinking, she made out the edge of the pool and the path a few inches above it, but she couldn't see Perry. Too many people were around him.

Shaking with fear and shock, she grabbed the edge and pulled herself up. Or tried to. Her wet dress dragged her down, and a groan of frustration came out of her. Frustration was better than fear.

She tried again, her feet slipping on the wet stones. No one was paying her the slightest bit of attention, but she found a step underwater and climbed out of the pool with trembling limbs. Perry lay on the path, convulsing. None of the horrified, shocked people did anything to help. Awful.

"He has a seizure. Help me." Dripping water, she squeezed herself through the crowd and held his head up. "Please help."

"He's possessed," a man said.

"That's the stupidest thing I've ever heard." Her angry tone surprised even herself.

The man glared at her, and she glared back.

"What can I do?" Lady Upchurch asked, quivering.

"Hold his legs still."

The lady shivered, and her voluminous dress hindered her movements, but to her credit, she did her best to keep Perry's legs still until the seizure passed.

"Lord Ravenscroft isn't mad or possessed." Edith raised her voice, so every person in the crowd heard her. "He simply had a convulsion—"

"He should be in an asylum."

"He's dangerous," another lady said. "Men with fits are violent."

Edith caressed Perry's forehead as he blinked slowly. "Not true." Wasted breath.

People shook their heads and muttered. Ladies whispered behind their gloved hands.

Only Lady Upchurch showed compassion. "I believe you, Miss Winkworth. Poor Lord Ravenscroft." She remained crouched next to Perry until he breathed normally.

"It's all right, Perry," Edith said, untying his bow tie. "The seizure has passed. You're safe."

He propped himself up on his elbows. "Edith, are you all right?" he stammered, his lips quivering.

"Don't worry about me."

The guests filed out of the Venetian garden among whispers and sideways glances thrown at Perry.

"What do you need?" Lady Upchurch asked. "A physician?"

"I think the earl needs to go home."

The lady nodded. "I'll have your carriage ready for you."

twenty-eight

PERRY WAS SORE and tired all over. He'd suffered from more seizures in the past few weeks than in the past few years.

When Edith had been shoved into the water, panic had seized him. He'd tried to help her, but the seizure had been faster. If she hadn't found the courage to overcome her own moment of panic, she might have got hurt. And last but not least, he'd revealed his condition to everyone. Dukes, earls, and members of Parliament had witnessed his malady. He'd not been conscious during the seizure, but he could guess what comments they'd made.

After the disastrous party, he'd hidden from society in his parlour with Edith for the whole day. He didn't even want to see his servants around.

"Perry, you must react." She took his hand and stroked it. "We must do something."

"The party was a trap, and we fell for it." He rubbed his aching forehead. "Miss Ferguson and my uncle witnessed my seizure in the Scarlet Room and mistakenly thought that water triggered it, but as it turned out, their mistake didn't matter. They got what they wanted."

She laced her fingers through his. "I have no evidence, but if Neville manages to steal the title from you, I'm sure Daphne will be his countess. The good thing is that I'm not as scared of the water as I was before." She chuckled. "Well, I'm still scared, but I jumped out of the pool on my own."

He kissed her knuckles. "You're a strong, brilliant woman." A horrible thought made its way through his mind. "If the worst happens and I'm declared insane and locked up in an asylum, we won't be able to get married."

Her beautiful eyes shone with a fierce light. "We'll get married. No matter what happens, we'll find a way. I promise you."

He put a hand on her nape and pulled her for a kiss. Her sweet, soft lips parted, and the tip of her tongue darted over his.

The knock on the door interrupted them.

He released her reluctantly. "Come in."

"I'm sorry, Perry." Oliver slid inside the parlour tentatively. "Two letters have just arrived. One contains great news, the other bad news. Which one do you want first?"

"Good news."

Oliver flashed a smile that didn't reach his eyes. "Mr. Lochard, the private detective, caught the infamous stable hand, a John Clarke."

"Yes!" Edith squeezed Perry's hand.

"Lochard is currently interrogating him," Oliver said. "The police are involved as well."

Perry sagged in the armchair. "Great. The bad news?"

He handed him a long letter, his smile vanishing. "I took the liberty of reading it in case it was something unimportant, so that I wouldn't trouble you, but that's not the case."

Perry forced down the wave of worry rising up. "*Under a request filed by Lord Neville St. George, Master of Tallbridge, an official medical report will be issued by a member of the Royal Medical Society to ascertain if Lord Ravenscroft possesses the mental capability and ability to hold his title. Lord Ravenscroft might request to be examined by a physician of his choice, as long as the said physician has been a member of the Royal Medical Society for no less than ten years.* As if that changes anything. *Given the particular circumstances, Dr. Bernard Winkworth is not eligible to be the medical inspector... yours respectfully... etc....*" Perry lowered the letter. "Why am I not surprised?"

"Could your brother be reinstated?" Edith asked.

"Once renounced, the title would be difficult to reinstate without a long legal battle and most likely some scandal. I certainly don't want that." He folded the letter and set it aside. "Besides, my brother is happy where he is. I don't want to draw him into this."

"Not all is lost," Oliver said. "The medical inspector must catch you in the middle of a seizure. Right? He has no means to verify that you suffer from seizures unless he witnesses one."

"Too many people saw what happened," Perry said. "Plenty of witnesses. The visit is a formality."

"We have an ace to play though." She glanced at the curtains covering Astrea. "We can request Sir James as the inspector. He's very much interested in the Star Maiden. We might offer it to him in exchange for a favourable report."

"A bribe?" Oliver sounded both hopeful and shocked.

"Why not?" she said. "Neville and Daphne are playing a dirty game. So can we."

Perry glanced in the direction of the painting. He was fond of the Star Maiden. He wasn't fond of the idea of another man ogling over Edith's nude painting, maybe showing it to his friends. "I'm sure we can find something else to bribe him with."

"Would it be so difficult for you to give the Star Maiden away?" Edith asked.

Perry scratched his chin. "Sir James feels guilty about the carriage accident. He won't refuse to be my examiner. We don't need to use the painting."

"I disagree," Edith said. "He might accept to be your examiner, but if we give him the Star Maiden, he'll undoubtedly produce a favourable report."

"Please listen." Oliver hooked his thumbs into his waistcoat. "How lucky are you to have me?"

"Do you really want an answer?" Perry asked.

"You know I'm always full of wonderful ideas." Oliver beamed.

Perry and Edith stared at him.

Oliver looked affronted. "I saved the day more than once."

"The last time you had a wonderful idea, your medical licence was revoked," Perry said.

"And you'll have to face a hearing," Edith added.

"Yes, but this is a really good idea." Oliver waved dismissively. "Sir James has never seen the painting, correct?"

"He isn't even sure it exists," Edith said.

Oliver grinned. "Have you ever heard of Francisco Goya?"

Perry exhaled. "I hope you aren't referring to the painter but to an assassin for hire we can employ to get rid of my uncle."

"I would never suggest such a thing." Oliver put a hand on his chest. "I'm a doctor. I took the Hippocratic oath. *Do no harm*. Yes, I'm talking about the Spanish painter."

"What does he have to do with our situation?" Edith asked.

"Well, Goya painted a rather scandalous painting of a lady, *La Maja Desnuda*, the naked Maja. The painting caused such a stir in society that he made a more appropriate second one, called *La Maja Vestida*, or the clothed Maja." He spread his arms. "Ask Mr. Carter to paint a second painting, the clothed Star Maiden, and there you have it. Sir James will have his more respectable painting, and Perry will keep his title and the original painting."

"That's actually a good idea," Perry said.

"I don't think Valentine will agree to paint me again," Edith said. "My last encounter with him didn't end well."

"He's a gambler." Perry grinned. "I'm sure I can find a persuasive argument."

EDITH COULD NEVER HAVE IMAGINED she would ever ask Valentine to pose for him again. Never say never. So here she was, once again in Valentine's atelier, with a brooding Perry and a perplexed Valentine.

"... so this second Star Maiden would be more clothed," she said, finishing explaining the situation to Valentine.

He cradled his chin, shifting his gaze from Perry to her. The stain of blue paint on the tip of his nose ruined his serious expression.

"No," he said firmly. "First, my goddesses aren't *clothed*. The whole point of painting them is to show how beautiful the human body is. And second, I don't want a repeat of our last conversation. Thank you."

"If anything," Edith said, matching his annoyed tone, "you'll have the opportunity to create another masterpiece that will be adored."

He folded his arms over his chest. "I'm an artist. I have principles and morals. Inspiration can't be commanded at will. The muse comes and goes as she pleases, and I—"

"I'll give you ten thousand pounds," Perry said in a bored tone.

Edith gasped as Valentine couldn't grab his paintbrushes fast enough.

Her second time posing was very different. For starters, she was dressed in a beautiful silver tunic in an ancient Greek style that covered her from chin to ankle, and secondly, Perry was present, sitting in a corner of the atelier and watching Valentine's every move like a bloodhound.

Valentine smiled at her, holding his paintbrush. She suspected the ten thousand pounds had something to do with his sudden happiness.

"My beautiful Edith—"

"She isn't yours," Perry grumbled from his corner.

"Perry, please." She swept a curl of hair from her face.

He arched a dark eyebrow. "I've just corrected the artist's grammar."

"It's fine." Valentine nodded and smiled. "And His Lordship is right. Please spread your arms and lift your chin."

He worked in silence, fully focused on her. When he concentrated, he lost his debonair look and became more ruthless and serious.

He paused to study her, head tilted. "I think the top of the tunic should be lower. Let's show a few inches of your beautiful breasts." He went to touch her, but Perry shot him a cold glare that stopped him in his tracks.

Valentine shrugged. "Or maybe not."

Edith shot her gaze up. "Please, we need to be quick."

Despite Valentine's efforts, it took hours to finish the painting and an entire day for it to dry and be recoated and dried again, barely in time for Sir James's visit.

When the painting was carefully packed and ready to be transported to Perry's house and his bank account was lighter, Perry shook Valentine's hand. "Carter, I admire your work. You're a true artist, but—"

"Let's end it there." Edith tugged at Perry's hand.

Valentine shrugged. "For ten thousand pounds, I'll accept any criticism from the earl."

twenty-nine

PERRY WAS GOING to growl if Sir James didn't stop ogling Edith.

Oliver had arranged the visit, mentioning the opportunity to take a look at the Star Maiden, and lured by the possibility of seeing the legendary painting, Sir James hadn't wasted time.

"Miss Winkworth, what a pleasure to see you here." He kissed her hand with a slobbering sound that upset Perry. "Lord Ravenscroft, I'm deeply sorry for the carriage accident." He lost his buoyancy. "It was a shock to learn one of my stable hands tampered with your carriage. Shameful. Inexcusable. I fully cooperated with both the police and your private detective."

"Thank you." Perry gave him a nod. "I don't consider you responsible, and your being here is very appreciated."

Edith smiled. "Dear Sir James, I was so relieved to know you would be the doctor to examine Lord Ravenscroft because I know your integrity and professional behaviour."

"Of course." Sir James's beady eyes brightened behind the glasses. "And I'll admit your friend's hint about *that* painting won me over."

"Remember when you asked me if I posed for it?" Edith whispered.

The physician flushed. "That conversation tormented me for weeks on end."

"Well, you were right. I wasn't honest with you. I was worried about what you might have thought of me." She batted her eyelashes, looking adorable.

Perry would fall to her feet immediately if he were the physician.

Sir James giggled. Giggled! "The painting exists."

"Would you like to see it?"

"Absolutely." Sir James shook with excitement as Edith led him upstairs. He also stared at her behind as she went up.

"Sir James," Perry hissed. "I trust you to be a gentleman."

"I am." Sir James shot him an outraged glare.

"There it is." Edith pushed the door to the parlour open with a dramatic gesture.

The light hit the clothed Star Maiden, making her shine with a dozen colours, and Perry had to admit it was a stunning painting.

Despite the fact Edith was dressed, the shadows and colours played a game with the light, giving the illusion that her silver tunic revealed more than it did. Whenever Perry moved and looked at the painting from a different angle, he could glimpse at her nipples, or so it seemed. If he shifted to the right and focused on her smile, she'd appear dressed in a flimsy tunic, but if he stared at her chest, she lost the smile and was fully clothed. A magic trick.

"By Jove." Sir James remained motionless, staring at the painting as if he were in front of a saint. "It's perfect." He walked around the painting slowly, muttering under his breath. "Oh, Miss Winkworth, you have been naughty because I can see..."

"Careful," Perry said. "Shall I remind you that you're a gentleman and talking with my future countess?"

Sir James looked affronted again. "I mean no offence, my lord, quite the opposite. This is pure art. Pure beauty. I'm a surgeon, and let me tell you, the human body looks more beautiful on the outside than the inside." He laughed.

Perry didn't even crack a smile.

"Society wouldn't agree," Sir James continued. "People think that just because a lady poses naked—"

"She's not naked," Perry said.

"Shush," Edith chided him.

Sir James ignored them. "—that she's ruined. I disagree whole-heartedly. Look at this masterpiece." His face was so red and bright that Perry worried he might have a seizure. "Do you think there might be a chance that I can acquire this painting?"

"Alas, it's not for sale." Edith covered the painting with a blanket. "It's for Lord Ravenscroft's eyes only."

"But...but..." Sir James shifted his weight from one foot to the other.

"Sir James, we should proceed with the examination," Perry said. "Let's go."

"But..." Sir James seemed like a child about to throw a tantrum. "I have an idea," he almost shouted.

"Yes?" Edith sounded sweet and innocent.

"Well." Sir James patted his forehead with his handkerchief. "I'm sure Lord Ravenscroft is perfectly fine, and a medical examination is a long and complicated affair with dozens of forms to fill out and signatures. Perhaps I could forgo the examination and simply write the final medical report so as not to trouble you any further. You've been troubled enough."

"That would be lovely," Edith said. "In exchange for your kindness, I'm sure Perry will be more than happy to give you the painting as a gift."

More than happy was an exaggeration. "Absolutely." Perry gave a curt nod.

Sir James brightened. "It's decided then." He stretched out his arm to shake Perry's hand. "Lord Ravenscroft, no one is going to touch your title. Ever."

"And no one aside from you is going to look at my bride-to-be painting."

Sir James bowed. "I give you my word."

SIR JAMES'S report was written, filed, and archived in a matter of days.

With his title secured, Perry had to deal with one last annoying detail before he could focus on what mattered the most—his engagement with Edith.

He checked his pocket watch, pacing in his study. "They should be here already."

"Perhaps Neville had a change of heart," Edith said, reading one of her anatomy books.

"One needs to have a heart to change it."

"He could drag you to court," Oliver said.

Perry shook his head. "Lochard gathered enough evidence to push him to a tight corner."

"My lord." Mason bowed from the door. "Lord Neville, Miss Ferguson, and Mr. Simmons are here."

"Excellent." Perry stood behind the desk between Edith and Oliver, ready for a battle.

Despite his confidence, uneasiness chilled him when Uncle Neville, Miss Ferguson, and Simmons entered the study. Uncle Neville's face was a mask of wrath, and Miss Ferguson was so pale she seemed aged ten years.

The solicitor was the first to bow and speak. "My Lord, Miss Winkworth, Mr. York." He made a point to remind everyone that Oliver's licence hadn't been reinstated yet.

"Thank you for being here." Perry stretched out an arm towards the chairs in front of him. "Not that you had a choice. Let's begin. I have more pressing matters to attend to."

Uncle Neville scoffed, sitting down. "So have I. I have previous engagements and responsibilities." He glared at Edith. "Unlike others, I keep my word."

Oliver laughed before coughing into his fist. "Apologies. I'm allergic to lies."

"Leave Edith out of this," Perry said.

"Shall we begin?" Simmons didn't seem disturbed by the thick atmosphere. He selected a few documents from his leather bag and spread them on the desk. "Mr. Lochard deposited the evidence he'd found against my clients to the police. Mr. Clarke, the stable hand who worked for Sir James, confessed he'd received the sum of five hundred pounds from Lord Neville."

"Cheapskate," Oliver muttered.

Simmons glowered at him. "Mr. Clarke received the money to tamper with His Lordship's carriage in the attempt to cause serious bodily harm and prevent His Lordship from keeping his title. Mr. Clarke also disclosed the involvement of Miss Ferguson as, quote, 'Lord Neville's accomplice.'"

"Shame on you," Edith said.

Miss Ferguson had the decency to lower her gaze.

"Please." Simmons frowned. "If you keep interrupting me with your comments, this affair isn't going to be quick at all." He waited for the silence to return. "Mr. Lochard also provided witnesses to a meeting among Mr. Clarke, Lord Neville, and Miss Ferguson, in which they discussed the details of the tampering, and these are facts. Now, with that established, my clients propose a deal convenient for everyone."

"I doubt that," Perry said.

"Lord Neville will renounce any claims on the title—"

"Because Perry cheated," Uncle Neville said. "Sir James is a bumbling idiot, and you bribed him."

"Why don't you intervene when Lord Neville talks, Simmons?" Oliver asked.

Simmons exhaled. "As I was saying, Lord Neville will renounce his claims, and Lord Ravenscroft will withdraw the charges of attempted murder."

Not good enough. "What about my other requests?" Perry asked.

Simmons exchanged a glance with Uncle Neville. "My client will leave London permanently and live with his allowance. Although Lord Neville asks for a small raise to marry Miss Ferguson."

Perry chuckled. "No raise. Uncle Neville and Miss Ferguson will learn to live modestly. The allowance is substantial as it is."

"Cheapskate," Uncle Neville said.

Perry leant forwards. "Forgive me, Uncle, but I tend not to be generous towards someone who tried to kill me."

He gave a little shrug. "Don't be ridiculous. I never wanted to kill you, just spare you from the humiliation of showing everyone your madness."

"He's a better man than you'd ever be," Edith said.

"He's insane," Miss Ferguson said, regaining some colour. "Just like you. Your fear of water and his convulsions make a good pair out of you."

Enough. Perry wouldn't sit there and listen to two criminals insult his bride-to-be. He stood up. "It's settled then. Uncle, leave London immediately and never come back. Marry whomever you want and leave my countess and me alone."

Oliver rose as well. "And if we see you here, we'll warn the police."

Miss Ferguson tilted her chin up. "Edith, I'm sorry we part this way—"

"No, you aren't," Edith said. "Now leave."

Simmons collected his documents, leaving copies for Perry. "Lord Ravenscroft, it's been a pleasure to deal with you." He paused. "If Mr. York needs legal advice on his situation, I'll be happy to provide it."

"Thank you. How kind," Oliver said.

Perry and Edith turned towards him with matching frowns.

The moment the solicitor and his clients left the room, Perry cheered, Edith hugged him, and Oliver smiled widely.

"I'm the physician of an earl," he said. "Well, after I have my hearing with the Royal Medical Society, my name is cleared, my licence reinstated, and the scandal is behind me." He sighed. "Oh, dear."

Edith patted his shoulder. "My father will do his best, and even Sir James promised to help."

Oliver exhaled dramatically. "I fully trust your father, and I'm sure everything will be fine, but I'm a little disappointed."

"Disappointed," Perry said at the same time as Edith said, "Why?"

Oliver shrugged. "The thrill, the tension, the excitement of the unknown. The experience brought me a sense of danger I didn't know I needed, and now it's almost over. It's somewhat sad."

Edith stared at him. "I don't fully follow you, Dr. York."

"Welcome into my world, darling," Perry said.

epilogue
Five years later

"SAND EVERYWHERE." EDITH brushed grains of sand from her skirt before stepping into the entry hall of her house. "I'm sorry, Mason. I'm leaving pyramids of sand everywhere."

The butler bowed, holding the door open. "Do not worry, my lady."

But she did worry. Being a countess was nothing short of complicated, especially since she combined her social duties with helping her husband in his work and volunteering at the women's hospital—she loved all that.

The years she'd spent reading and practising with her father bore fruit. She'd already known half of the things the teachers taught in class, speeding up the process of her becoming a doctor.

Perry handed his coat to the footman. "Nothing is more invigorating than a day at the beach." He held her hand and went up the stairs. "Tea, please, Mason."

"My lord."

"I don't understand the appeal of the sea," Edith said, slouching against Perry on the sofa.

"Therapy." He kissed the top of her head and wrapped an arm around her shoulders.

They'd spent the day at the beach as part of the treatment Oliver had devised for her hydrophobia. She was a far cry from taking a swim across the Channel, but she didn't have attacks of panic anymore.

"You must admit the beach was beautiful," he said.

"Yes, but I wouldn't spend the whole day swimming." She snuggled closer to him. "But I agree with Dr. York. Besides, since I'm a doctor, I'm supposed to lead by example." Especially since she volunteered not only in Elizabeth Garrett Anderson's women's hospital, but also in one of the poorest hospitals in town, although with all the donations she and Perry were pouring into it, it'd soon become a more than decent place.

"Tired?" He unlaced her boots and put her feet on his lap.

More sand rained on the carpet.

"The train was great, but facing the blue expanse of water was unnerving." She reclined her head as he massaged her feet.

"You're doing great."

"Marianne was quicker than me to overcome her fear."

"Your sister is different. Your sister wouldn't have posed for the Star Maiden." He glanced in the direction of the covered painting.

"She's wiser than I am."

"Actually, I'm very happy you posed for the Star Maiden. So is Sir James."

The physician-in-ordinary to the queen had kept his word and never mentioned the painting to anyone. The legend of the Star Maiden still lingered with rumours about its existence and the model who had posed for it. Valentine was enjoying a moment of unprecedented fame and money while Neville and Daphne had moved to France. Perry's seizures hadn't tormented him in three years, which was promising.

"Also, the sand nearly ruined the beautiful gown Mrs.

Richards made for me." She brushed more sand from the embroidered hem of her skirt.

"I'm happy Mrs. Richards made a full recovery," Perry said.

"Between our help and my father, she's one of the most requested seamstresses in London."

Life couldn't be better.

"Are you dressed?" Oliver asked from the other side of the door.

"Of course," she and Perry said together.

"This is so difficult. So difficult." Oliver sat on an armchair, a hand on his forehead. "Had I known that being the physician of an earl would require so much work, I would have refused and become a gardener."

"No, you wouldn't have," Perry said, rubbing her toes. "What is it now?"

Oliver's licence had successfully been reinstated, but it had taken over a year. Then he'd finished his studies in alienism. Since then, he'd found one drama after the other to keep him busy.

"You can't find a leather bag that matches your Italian leather shoes?" she asked.

"Your stethoscope is out of fashion?" Perry asked.

Oliver lowered his hand. "Very funny. Shall I remind you that, if you're conquering your personal fears, it's thanks to me? *Fears must be mastered*, that's my motto." He fished out a few pieces of paper from his pocket. "Here's the problem. How can I choose?" He put the cards on the low table.

Edith leant over. Each calling card had a different style and colour, and the writings 'Dr. Oliver York Physician and Alienist' shone with distinctive types of characters and colours. On the back, the motto '*fears must be mastered*' was embossed.

"If I choose the wrong one," Oliver said, "no one will take me seriously."

"I don't think the card is the problem," Perry said.

Edith poked him with her elbow. "Be nice." She picked up the blue card with the characters in gold. "I like this one."

Oliver took it. "Yes, I—" As he turned it around, the sharp edge cut his fingertip, and a ruby drop of blood trickled down his finger. He paled. "Blood..."

"It's just a paper cut—Oliver!" Edith wasn't fast enough to catch him before he fainted and slumped out of the armchair.

"I can't believe it." Perry held him up and slapped his cheek. "Oliver."

"He's scared of blood. He's a doctor."

"So much for his motto." Perry laid his friend on the sofa.

"But he's right. He helped us." She checked his pulse.

Perry kissed her lightly on the lips. "He did, but it was you who conquered all my fears."

about the author

Love stories have always captured my imagination. What's better than two people falling in love with each other? I write steamy romance, usually with a paranormal twist in an historical setting. Add a touch of suspense and mystery and a pinch of darkness. I love stories with strong, sexy heroes and mischievous heroines who pull no punches.

I live in the City of Sails, New Zealand, drinking tea (coffee gives me anxiety) and devouring books.

Join my newsletter for exclusive content and the chance to receive an ARC copy of my books. Just copy and paste this link into your browser:

Barbara's Newsletter

also by barbara russell

Check out the rest of the series:

Victorian Outcasts

If you love steamy paranormal romance set in Victorian London, my Royal Occult Bureau series is for you:

The Royal Occult Bureau Series

Are you into shape-shifter romance? Check out my da Vinci's Beasts series, set in WW2:

da Vinci's Beasts Series

For more Victorian paranormal romance with witches and sexy warriors, see the Knights of the White Blade series:

The White Order Series

Love steampunk? Check out my Auckland Steampunk series:

Auckland Steampunk Series

www.ingramcontent.com/pod-product-compliance
Lightning Source LLC
Chambersburg PA
CBHW020419110726
47899CB00006B/2050

*9 7 8 1 6 4 8 3 9 7 7 8 3 *